"Will you keep my secret?" He stood close to her in the darkness, the warmth of his body making her shiver.

"Secrets are dangerous," she warned him, wishing she had listened to that counsel when her old nursemaid had bestowed it upon her long ago.

"Aye. All my life is a secret to me and it puts me in danger every day." The heat behind his words presented an illusion of truth. He spoke like a man tormented by demons of his own.

"I owe you for helping me rejoin the world today, if only for a few hours." She had enjoyed the intense interest he seemed to take in her. "I will keep your secret until we meet again."

"When will that be?" he prodded, seeking answers she did not have.

"You may return to the cottage in daylight, but let us not meet under the cover of night anymore."

There was an intimacy about it. A sense that they shared more than secrets in the darkness....

* * *

The Knight's Return
Harlequin® Historical #942—April 2009

Joanne Rock

The KNIGHT'S Return

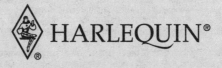

HARLEQUIN®

TORONTO • NEW YORK • LONDON
AMSTERDAM • PARIS • SYDNEY • HAMBURG
STOCKHOLM • ATHENS • TOKYO • MILAN • MADRID
PRAGUE • WARSAW • BUDAPEST • AUCKLAND

Recycling programs for this product may not exist in your area.

ISBN-13: 978-0-373-29542-5
ISBN-10:   0-373-29542-1

THE KNIGHT'S RETURN

Copyright © 2009 by Joanne Rock

For Dean, who ensures there is never a dull moment…

Chapter One

North of London, 1169

Waking proved difficult when one's eyes were stuck shut.

The dizzy-headed man stretched the muscles in his face from his position on the hard pallet. He willed his lids to open so that he might see the world about him. The scents that assailed him were at once familiar and strange. Sheep dung. Hay. The burnt remains of some poorly cooked meal. Likewise, the sounds did not provide any clues. He heard children shouting and laughing. A woman's voice yelling. Animals braying, naying and snorting.

The effect was unpleasant and not what he was accustomed to. Or was it?

Worry crawled along his forehead as he struggled to envision a normal morning. A normal day? He was not sure of the time let alone the place.

"The border leaves this morn, Meg," a man's deep voice barked nearby. "His illness is a burden on this family that robs our own children of food."

"Have you no Christian charity, husband?" The softly sweet feminine tones sounded almost musical in the cool room.

Was he the topic of discussion? It was no leap to guess his health was poor since he could not open his eyes. His body ached with weakness, his limbs too heavy to lift.

"You are not a lord's wife, Meg. If you want this unconscious lump of humanity to have his fill of food and broth, take him to a family who can afford him. You ken? He leaves today or I bring him to the village square to be with the other half-wits unfit to feed themselves."

Something stung inside him. His pride, he realized. He was not a half-wit. Just a suffering man.

"But John, what if he is someone of consequence? Young Harold says he brought in a horse and he hardly looks like a stable boy..." The woman continued pleading with her husband but their conversation became muted as another voice sounded closer to his ear.

"You must leave if you do not want to become fodder for the village pigs next week," a boy's voice—close to his bedside—whispered.

With a last great effort, the man dragged open one eye and then the other.

He was in a small wooden cottage with a dirt floor and one large chamber. Animals walked as freely as the four humans in residence. Well, four discounting him. The man was not sure he felt quite human and the consensus seemed to put him well below both people and animals in importance.

A lad peered up at him in a small wooden cottage, his face covered in dust, his filthy hair matted against his cheeks. The eyes were lit with interest, however. As if pig fodder proved fascinating.

"My brother says that is what they do with half-wits if they provide no service," the boy continued.

The man touched his temple and winced. The hair had been trimmed, his forehead sutured with neat stitches. He knew at once the sewing had been the work of the sweet-voiced woman. No doubt he owed his life to these strangers.

"What is your name?" the boy prodded, poking him in the shoulder.

His eyes fell shut again and he scarcely heard the conversation growing heated across the room. By the rood, he would get up and leave if he could.

"Don't you even know your own name?" The boy sounded exasperated, his speech mirroring his father's in cadence.

"Hugh." The man answered without thought, but that lone name was all he managed. Now that it hung in the air between them, he wished to add something to it—to claim his family and legacy with some other title.

Hugh son of someone. Hugh of York. Hugh of the Black Garter. But he could not find any hint of a second name in the chaos of his foggy thoughts. His head felt scrubbed clean of the past, as if it had retained nothing prior to this moment.

Panicking, Hugh slapped the thighs of his hose and waist of his tunic, searching for personal belongings. There was no sword. No eating knife with a family crest that might help identify him. No leather pouch of belongings or some lady's favor.

And why would a man wearing rough woolen hose and a worn cotton tunic be possessed of some lady's token? The idea seemed incongruous and yet…

Who in Hades was he?

"I don't mind you eating my gruel, Hugh." The boy sniffed back a wet inhalation and scraped his sleeve across his face for good measure. "But me da says you must go because, even though you came into my master's stables leading a horse, you might not be more than a common thief."

"A horse?" Hugh wondered if he might have belongings stored with the beast's saddle and bags, though he suspected not since the cottage's inhabitants were ready to toss him into the streets. Surely if he had possessions to speak of, his hosts would have taken them in recompense for their trouble.

"Aye."

"How long have I been here? Where did you find me?"

"You came into town on Monday and left your horse in the care of my da's stable. Later that afternoon, we discovered you in a ditch beside the alehouse, your head split wide and bleeding like soup from an overturned pot."

Hugh searched his memory for some recollection of the event. Was he a drunkard then?

"And what day is it now?"

"'Tis Wednesday."

"Can you take me to the mount?"

The lad nodded. Across the cottage, the other family members seemed to have noticed he was awake and speaking. The woman hastened to his bedside while the man hung back.

"I will leave immediately," Hugh called to the crofter, determined to figure out why his head ached like the bloody devil and his brain seemed blank as a newborn babe's.

Both the man's and the woman's raised eyebrows demonstrated mutual surprise.

"You must not go—" the woman began.

"You owe my boy for the care of the horse. Perhaps you could trade those shoes," the husband suggested.

Sweet Jesu. Was this what his life had come down to? Selling his shoes to stable his mount?

Hugh had the feeling he had not been raised in this kind of struggling world, though perhaps he just wanted to cling to a pleasing vision on a hellish day. But Christ above. His leather boots were not the frayed scraps of cloth his host wore to protect his feet from random sheep dung lying about the cottage. Perhaps his gut instincts were not pure fancy after all.

"I am beholden to you and your whole family." Hugh attempted an inclination of his head to show respect to these people living with their pigs, and immediately regretted it. "I will give the lad the shoes upon retrieving my mount."

A scant while later, his body aching after following the boy through a narrow street past women doing their washing, Hugh realized suspicious eyes turned toward him from every direction. No doubt the inhabitants of this area had heard of his condition from their neighbor. He would invent a full name for himself to ensure his wits were not in question. He could pretend a sanity he did not feel. But he would not allow himself to be taken for a victim of mania. Or drunkenness, for that matter.

"Here," the lad said finally, pointing the way to a stall hardly worthy to be called a stable.

Yet the mount was a warhorse of great breadth and strength. The saddle that hung from a nearby post bore no unusual markings, and there were no bags or bundles through which to search for clues to his name.

"Thank you," Hugh said carefully, leaning forward to remove his shoes while the boy saddled the horse. Hugh's head pounded with the small effort to unfasten the boots, but he struggled to hide his weakness in front of the villagers' peering eyes. "I am grateful to you, son."

"Thank you," the boy returned, eyes shining with pleasure as he took the offering. "Good luck to you in Connacht, sir."

The farewell made Hugh straighten. The sound of the name rang with the familiarity of an old friend's face.

"Pardon?"

"That day you dropped off the mount, you said you were riding to Connacht on the morrow, but that was some days ago. Me da says that's a town in Wales, but the blacksmith who lives yonder claims it's a kingdom across the Irish Channel."

Hugh knew with a certainty he could not explain that he had planned to attend to some affairs in the Irish petty kingdom. Though for what purpose, he had no memory. But it was more of a clue than he'd had so far about his purpose. His place in life. He would go to Ireland to retrieve his sanity.

"I make my way to the Ireland. Fare thee well, boy." Hugh stepped lightly to his horse, avoiding the filth in the road before he raised himself up on the mount's back.

He did not know his own name, but he knew with a bone-deep certainty he could make his way to Ireland by his wits if nothing else. A fierceness roared within him.

He would discover his name. His legacy.

But first he needed to discover why the mention of a far-flung Irish kingdom sent the first tremor of recognition through his addled brain. He knew absolutely that some great task awaited him in Connacht. A matter that needed tending to with all haste.

A mission he might already be too late to accomplish.

Connacht, Ireland
Two months later

Sorcha ingen Con Connacht felt the presence of a stranger before she heard his footsteps in nearby woods.

Stilling herself, she reached for her dagger with one hand and hugged her young son closer with the other. No one walked the paths near Sorcha's home. All of Connacht knew her shame.

Being banished from her father's small Irish kingdom had put her into exile for over a year now, and the isolation in a remote stretch of forest made her senses keen to the presence of another soul. She could feel a change in the air when anyone neared—even when a maid from the keep delivered food stores or a villager traded meat for clothing from Sorcha's loom. But when an approaching stranger was male, her senses sharpened all the more acutely.

Sharpened with the undeniably primal instincts of a mother protecting her babe.

Every day she half expected her father's guard to arrive to take her son away and deposit her in a convent. Her father had threatened as much by summer's end. But surely her father's knights would not arrive quietly. They would storm through the forest with a full contingent to seize her.

"Who goes there?" she shouted into the trees in a harsh voice, determined her son would come to no harm even though they were vulnerable here—far removed from her father's lofty keep on the coast. "My sire is lord of these lands and will allow no harm done to his heir."

Her boy, Conn, squealed in response to her raised voice from his seat upon her hip. She hushed him softly while concealing her dagger up her sleeve. Should she run? Or did that invite some thief to give chase?

She cradled Conn tighter, squeezing the weight of his year-old body closer. He squirmed now, his hand gripping a hank of her hair and pulling hard.

"I seek the lord of these lands, lady, and I mean you no harm." A masculine voice preceded the trespasser from the other side of a small clearing at the base of the mountains that protected the headlands of Connacht.

Sorcha roamed the mountainside daily since she'd been confined to an outpost at the edge of her father's lands, the hills and valleys her refuge from the world's disdain.

She'd always felt safe here, even if she was scorned. Now she couldn't help but recall the warnings she'd received from her father's keep that war might come to Connacht at any time. She walked steadily backward as she watched the man emerge from the trees.

And if the resonant thrum of masculine tones had been impressive, his size was twice as daunting.

The stranger was easily the largest man she'd ever seen. Thick-chested and girded by muscles that could only be honed for sword fighting, the traveler had to be a warrior even if he rode no horse and brandished no sword. Squinting through the late-afternoon sunlight, Sorcha struggled for a better look, only to feel faint as his features came into clearer view.

"For the love of Our Blessed Lady." Her grip on her child slipped, the boy's chubby fists shoving her mercilessly in an effort to walk on his own. She had no choice but to put him down if she wanted to maintain her grip on her weapon, so she tucked him behind her skirts.

She straightened, not believing her eyes. Did the dead return to walk among the living? She tucked the knife closer to her body, wishing the point did not scrape open her finger as she held it in place. Still, if the stranger stalked any closer, she would be glad to have the blade within easy reach.

"My lady?" The man paused, as if attempting to prove his claim he meant no harm.

Did he realize how much harm he caused with no more than his starkly featured countenance?

Dark hair streamed down his back, glistening in the sunlight as if he had just rinsed it clean in some fast-running spring brook. His gaze took on a curious gleam, although she could envision those dark, gold-flecked eyes turned to her in anger.

Or in passion…

Heaven help her, but did she have to be reminded of her sins at every turn?

"What business do you have with the lord of this place, sir?" Her words were raw in her throat, stripped of any soft courtesy.

A tremble tripped through her skin, followed by a tangle of emotions in her belly that seemed too convoluted to sort through now.

"Your expression makes me wonder if we have met, my lady." The stranger did not incline his head like a courtier. He only continued to stare at her with an attention all the more rapt since she began her careful perusal.

And yet, this was not her former lover. She could see the differences in this man's face now that he'd moved closer and the sunlight no longer played tricks with her vision.

Still…the trespasser's resemblance to the father of her son was remarkable. Suspect.

"We are unknown to each other, sir. Pray excuse my surprise at seeing you here when I am accustomed to privacy upon this side of the mountain." Wanting to escape him and flee the quiet glade where no one would hear her if she cried out, Sorcha bent to retrieve the blanket she'd brought along with the basket she'd used to gather flowers. "Conn, we must go, my love."

While smiling reassuringly at her son, she never took her eyes off the man, watching his hands for any sign of movement toward his weapon. Cursing her father for consigning her to this godforsaken borderland, Sorcha would never feel safe in these woods again—not when Conn's life depended on her. Keeping her boy secure was the only benefit of allowing her father to dispatch her to the convent. The king would protect his grandson. She would merely have to relinquish all contact with her child and trade the rest of her days to give Conn a future.

For now, she tried to keep her movements unhurried despite the maelstrom of memories, emotions and questions that attacked her from all sides. Not even the scent of spring flowers all around her could cover up the stench of her fear.

"Pray do not let me disturb you." The man held up a hand in a show of surrender, keeping his distance from her and Conn. "I have journeyed far to see your sire and I would not let anything delay me from the task."

"You would make better time on a horse, warrior." Could he be a spy for the invading armies, surveying the lands before others arrived? She could not understand his alliance or his possible purpose here.

The man lacked the accoutrements she associated with a knight. He wore no sword, although a dagger gleamed from its sheathe at his waist. His garb bore no hint of family or heraldry, which she supposed was not strange for a mercenary, and yet his clothes had almost too humble an air for a man of such imposing stature and breadth. Still, given his resemblance to her onetime lover, she half expected to see the du Bois crest upon his person—the white stag rampant upon a blue field.

"I was set upon by thieves some leagues hence," he explained, locking his hands behind his back as if to reinforce his message that he meant no harm. Unfortunately, Sorcha was well acquainted with men who were not at all what they seemed. "Their numbers were too many to defeat for a lone knight."

"Thieves?"

He shrugged as if the loss of his horse and weaponry were no great offense, when she knew some knights owned nothing in the world save their armor and their mount. Had he made up the story about the thieves to explain away his presence here? Had his family sent him to find her? Curiosity grew, but she tempered it with wariness.

"I thought to offer your father my services in cleaning out the lot of them if he can provide me with a horse. Nothing would please me more than to rescue my own mount with the blood of his captors." He inclined his head again, strangely polite for a mercenary, especially one with Norman forebears. "Begging your pardon for the threat, my lady."

Something tugged at her hand and she nearly lost her grip on the knife up her sleeve as Conn tried to get her attention. Heart squeezing with a trickle of fear that the stranger might perceive the flash of a blade as a threat, Sorcha gave herself another cut as she shoved the blade back in place.

"My father is wily with horseflesh, sir." She spoke quickly to deflect the man's attention from the way she hitched at her sleeve. "So be careful to look upon the mount he provides. But I have no doubt he will gladly make such an exchange." The lord of Tir'a Brahui had ascended to the throne with as much cunning as might, and while Sorcha did not appreciate his treatment of her, she could not deny her father the respect that was his due.

She could, however, torment him gently through this unseated warrior by encouraging the man to barter. The thought made her smile right through the strain of this odd conversation with a total stranger.

The sun slipped lower on the horizon, causing the man to shield his eyes.

"Might I know your name so that when I speak to your father I may tell him we have met?" He stood bathed in sunlight, his rough-hewn garments taking on a golden sheen as he studied her.

And once again there loomed a flash of recognition, a sense that she had once known him… Perhaps it was a good thing her knife was not more accessible.

"I am Sorcha." She owned her identity with pride despite her father's desire to make her regret all that she was. "And I assure you that your bargaining will prove more favorable if you do not mention my name to my sire. Fare thee well, sir."

Turning, she kept the knife tucked up her sleeve. She wanted to put distance between her and the source of her muddled feelings—fear and resentment at his intrusion on her privacy, worry that he was some relative of her former lover. She recoiled at the thought. Her exile gave her far too much time to mull over past mistakes and fret for her son's future. She didn't need any more worries. There was no choice but to forget she'd ever met this dark-eyed stranger.

"You do not wish to know my name in return?" the stranger called to her.

"We will not meet again," she returned without looking back, holding Conn's hand with her free palm.

"Sorcha?"

Sighing, she paused. Turned.

"Aye?"

"You must hold the blade at your side. Within the folds of your skirts."

"I beg your—"

She stopped when his gaze slid unerringly down her body toward the hand concealing her weapon.

"Your hold is too awkward to be unnoticeable. Whereas if you grip the handle in your palm, you are more comfortable and in more of a position to use it quickly. For instance, if I came at you now—"

He stepped forward.

"Do not." She pulled Conn behind her again. Shaking her arm, she slid the blade free of her sleeve so she could use it if necessary.

By God, she would let no man touch her son. Not even one who looked strangely like the boy's father.

"I only meant to suggest you could not react quickly enough with a dagger inside your sleeve." He halted his progress, although she guessed he felt little threat from her blade. "I will pray you never have need of your weapon, but if you are inclined to use it, you would do well to draw blood from the enemy and not from your forearm. God-speed, Sorcha."

The mercenary spun on his heel, a crude excuse for a shoe covering his foot in straw and linen as he walked away. Was he a desperately poor knight? A common thief playing games with her? She could not imagine how a commoner could have taught himself such a pretty accent, but perhaps that was no more strange than a horseless English knight strolling through her father's kingdom on shoes of straw.

Either way, she was well rid of his company and she would be more careful in the future. Hadn't she heard the foreign wars would find their way to Connacht before long? And how sad that she feared the idea of foreign invaders less than another, more personal threat against her.

Her son.

Plucking up Conn in her arms, she ran home with all haste, grateful for another day of freedom from the convent to be with her child.

Chapter Two

She knew him or she knew *of* him. Of that much Hugh was certain.

He paced an empty antechamber within the walls of Tir'a Brahui, the coastal keep belonging to Tiernan Con Connacht. Hugh had reached the holding the night before but did not wish to intrude in the dark and appear a threat. He truly had lost his horse and his sword, but not to thieves as he'd told Sorcha. He'd needed to trade them for various supplies on the long journey since he'd had no funds to speak of. Last night, he'd foraged for food, stamping down the desire to build a fire, and spent the night anonymously in the king's forest, the same way he'd spent so many nights these last two moons on the road.

Now, at midmorn, he paced the sparse room adorned in naught but colorful tapestries that were surely aged and tattered a hundred years ago. The petty kingdom ruled over by Sorcha's father was subject to a higher king of Connacht, but Hugh's understanding of the country's leadership stopped there. He'd been too focused on figuring out who he was and how to survive the long journey to pay attention to politics and the incessant warmongering that seemed to take place among the smaller kingdoms.

Now that he'd come to Ireland, he hoped to see something or someone that would nudge a memory. His impression of Tiernan Con Connacht was not favorable thus far and Hugh rather hoped they were not related. What king allowed his daughter to live unprotected on the fringes of his kingdom? Hugh could not envision the woman and her son surviving for long with Norman invaders at Hugh's heels.

The idea of harm befalling her did not settle well. In fact, he'd felt pulled to her so strongly he guessed they must have met. And yet she'd denied any knowledge of him. Still, even without a connection between them, he'd been compelled to protect her. The memory of her gripping a knife so fiercely her fingers bled stayed with him long after night had fallen yester eve. The warrior in him recognized her absolute commitment to protecting her son at any cost, and he had no doubt she would have wielded the blade fiercely if Hugh posed a threat.

Had he left behind a woman so devoted to family? Stopping in front of a faded yellow tapestry depicting a man and a woman releasing their falcon, Hugh smoothed his hand over the lady's face. He'd given little thought to the possibility of being married, but the stirring in his blood at the sight of Sorcha made him consider the likelihood.

Could he have forgotten a wife? A child?

"You may see His Highness now," a man announced as Hugh spun to see him. A servant was dressed in red and blue, his clothes as vibrant as everyone else's in this strange land.

"Thank you." Hugh released a pent-up breath, more than ready to get answers about his identity.

He'd offered up a false name at the gate to Tir'a Brahui, calling himself Hugh Fitz Henry. The surname was common enough, the kind of moniker bastards received all the time when their mothers wished to point fingers at a father. Other times, the name was chosen in homage to a king since there had been a Henry on the English throne for nigh on seventy years.

How sorry was it that Hugh remembered more about the king's seat than his own place in the world?

"Follow me," the servant said, disappearing into the corridor lit by a torch despite the daylight hours. The keep allowed in precious little sun, and the interior corridors remained shadowy.

Squinting to adjust to the dimness, Hugh planned his strategy for this meeting. He needed to pinpoint the king immediately—to gauge the lord's reaction before he could mask his response to Hugh's presence.

Perhaps the king was a friend. But what if he was somehow behind Hugh's predicament? The stitches healing in his head told him someone had brutalized him. Was his lack of memory due to the beating? He knew he was no half-wit since his skills with a weapon and his instincts for survival had proven well honed on the journey here.

"This way, sir." The servant paused beside a door but did not enter it, standing aside to let Hugh pass.

Hugh nodded and surveyed the portal. Light streamed from the chamber. The one wall within his view contained a rack of swords polished and ready for use. Steeling himself for the meeting, Hugh walked through the door.

Any expectations for a crown-wearing lord in a high throne were dashed by the sight of twelve men seated at a table, none higher than the other. He scanned the faces quickly, his eyes starting at one end of the table and working down, only to be struck by the sense that the king was the largest man seated in the center.

That noble wore a jeweled brooch at his collar and the ruby at the center was the kind of stone few lords would possess. In a land where the number of colors a person wore seemed significant, this person's garb contained the most. Purple and yellow vied with green and blue. Checkers on his tunic were not enough ornamentation. Stripes on his crimson cloak made him a target for the eye. Every other knight at the table wore bright silks and satins.

But for a court that adhered to a hierarchy of dress, giving slaves but one color to wear and the king as many as imaginable, Hugh was surprised the king did not take a seat at a higher table or even at the head.

If Tiernan Con Connacht was a man of traditional custom, Hugh had yet to see a sign of it.

He also had yet to see any hint of recognition in the sovereign's face. While it was disappointing not to discover an answer to the matter of his identity, it also meant he was able to relax without having to pretend to know someone he did not recollect.

"Your Highness." Hugh swept a low bow. "Thank you for seeing me."

Bowing did not feel natural to him. Another hint he spent more time battling enemies than licking royal boot soles.

"If you are here to talk peace between our lands, you are the strangest courtier I've ever seen." The older man spoke between sips of ale, the knights around him going quiet. "Ye look more like a warrior than a peacemaker."

The knights clustered around the king appeared ready to lunge for their knives at any moment.

"Peace is no business of mine. I come to offer you my sword if you have need of a mercenary."

He had no sword, of course. He'd bargained with lords and thieves, merchants and even a child who had taken the bribe of a cake in exchange for help unlocking an armory on his way to their seaside kingdom. He'd not stolen any weapon from that armory, but he'd needed a blade to obtain a meal, after which he'd replaced the knife. In that way, his journey had been unbearably slow, but he'd arrived in Connacht at last.

He would talk his way into a place among the king's court until he had time to know these people. To understand what connection bound him to them.

"I find it hard to believe you would offer that which you do not possess." The king's keen eye assessed Hugh's lowly garments. "I spoke with my man at the gate and was told you carried no weapon save a dagger, and I would be more than surprised if you could inflict much damage on a sword-wielding enemy with such a knife."

"You might be surprised what cunning will accomplish when it allies with such a knife."

Someone at the king's table snorted.

"And think you I will take your word on this skill?" One sandy eyebrow arched and Hugh knew he was a moment away from being dismissed.

His lack of checkered clothes and leather shoes put him at a disadvantage.

"I am content to prove the claim."

For a moment, no one at the table spoke, and then the king barked with laughter.

"Do you hope to cut down my men from inside my walls, English? Are you my enemies' latest weapon?"

One of the king's men stood, his hand still on his sword, although he did not draw it.

"I would lay waste to any enemy first, my liege," the younger man swore, his cheeks flushed with impassioned feeling.

"No need, Donngal." The king waved him down, still studying Hugh. By now, Hugh thought he spied a hint of interest or—possibly—respect in the other man's eyes. "I would ask that Fergus do the honors."

With a nod to the man seated at his right, Tiernan Con Connacht as good as gave the battle order.

"You must know your gatekeeper relieved me of my knife." Hugh gauged the other man's height. His breadth.

"Donngal, give him yours." The king took another sip of ale and leaned back in his chair at the table. He seemed ready for a show.

Hugh would strive not to disappoint. Being taken in as a mercenary meant earning the right to remain in the court, where there must be a clue to his past. The right to remain in Connacht long enough to discover why Lady Sorcha's eyes lit up when she first spied him.

The boy who'd risen to threaten Hugh now flushed even deeper to hand over his dagger to an English knight.

"Thank you." He accepted the blade as Fergus stalked around to Hugh's side of the table.

Before the knight stepped within sword's reach of him, Hugh reacted. He arced back the blade and let it fly, seeing the knife launched from his hand before he had time to wonder if he possessed the necessary skill for such a trick. The knife traveled end over end, spinning through the air until it found its mark under Fergus's arm, pinning the fabric of his tunic and cloak to the wall behind him.

The captive cloth pulled the knight back in midstride. Steel clanked and reverberated as ten men drew their swords in response. Hugh marveled at this newly discovered talent even as he thanked the saints he did not kill the warrior. Every day he learned more of his skills and he had to think he'd once been a powerful knight. A leader of men, perhaps. Or a battle tactician.

"Hold." The king lifted one arm, a heavy gold nasc thick with engraving about his wrist. "Donngal, free Fergus and sheathe your knife. Men, you may put away your swords around our unarmed friend."

When Donngal looked as though he would argue, Fergus growled low at him and that was all it took to quiet the younger man.

"Leave us, my friends," the king continued, motioning to his knights.

Hugh watched as ten men filed out, some glaring at him, others paying him little heed. Only Fergus and the king remained. He sensed that boded well. If Hugh had been destined for death, he suspected the king would have accomplished the deed in front of all his men.

"Well done, sir." The king's whole aspect changed as he waved Hugh closer. "I have need of a man with your skills in the matter of my daughter."

Warning hummed over Hugh's skin. Did the king despise his exiled offspring so much that he would hire a mercenary to… He could not complete the thought. And he would not hurt a woman no matter what the prize.

"I hoped to fight at your side, Your Highness." He inclined his head to show respect in an effort to balance his words of disagreement.

"You have already met my daughter."

His head snapped up.

"She may be in exile, but that does not mean I do not watch over her."

"It is true we exchanged words," Hugh acknowledged.

"You could have killed her. Or worse."

"I would harm no woman."

"Precisely why you show potential as a protector for her."

Who entrusted a princess to a foreigner, and a stranger at that? Tiernan would be at war with the Normans before the year was out. The king had no reason to trust Hugh.

"Why not a man of your house?" Why not Fergus?

"She is protected from afar, but not from up close, and she has always been too willful to allow my guards near her, even when she lived within my walls." He scowled. "She once sneaked from the keep to ride with my men on a campaign against the Norsemen. She journeyed halfway across our lands in the guise of a man's garb before she revealed herself, informing Fergus she was bored and wished to return home."

Fergus grunted, shaking his head at the memory.

"Do you know she refused to allow him to escort her and made it a point to escape him at every turn until he had to tie my daughter to him like a captive?"

"A bold and unwise scheme on her part, Your Highness, but now that she is a mother—"

"She came to be a mother through deceiving me shamefully and cavorting with a man I've never had the chance to lay eyes on, lest he would be in his grave in many small pieces." The king shouted for more ale as he clamped a gloved hand to his forehead. "The lass is a danger to herself and possibly a danger to her son, who is innocent of her crimes. I will send her to the convent by summer's end, but until then, her son is too young to be taken from her. I would reward you generously if you would consider watching over her these next two moons without letting her know you are her protector."

"And how do you suggest I would succeed where your men have failed?" Hugh was more than ready to take on a task concerning the princess after the leap of recognition in her eyes upon their first meeting.

"Ye boasted enough of your skills with or without a sword. Have you no answer for the chance to serve a wealthy king?" Tiernan Con Connacht held out his flagon as a flame-haired maid approached with a pitcher. "And have you no idea how to win a lady's favor?"

"I am a knight, not some court poet to sing praises to a lady's elbow."

"You will court her." The king took a long drink. "Offer to escort her about."

"Surely you cannot propose a union when—"

"Of course not." The fire in the king's green eyes suggested he did not wish to imagine any man touching this spoiled daughter of his no matter how much he bemoaned her headstrong ways. "You may leave here a wealthy man come harvesttime when a convent is willing to take her in. As long as she is untouched and you have not revealed your true purpose to her by then, you may have your choice of rewards from the royal treasure stores."

Guard a willful princess through the summer months until he could discover who he was? He guessed there must be drawbacks to this task that the king could not find a man of his own to manage the chore. But then, Sorcha would recognize all but the newest of her father's knights.

Regardless, he would walk away from this a richer man,

even if he did not regain his memory. He could not afford to say nay.

"What makes you think she will agree to this courtship?" Hugh did not deceive himself that he would hold any great appeal for a woman raised in the lavish setting of Tir'a Brahui. And his pride would not allow him to beg for any woman's favor.

The king smiled. "I have banished her for over a year, son. The lass has had nowhere to go save a few quiet hills in the forest. She rejected the courtship of other noblemen at first, but I think she might be more amenable now if only the offers for her hand had not ceased long ago." His eyes brightened. "By now, I suspect she would allow the devil himself to woo her if it meant being allowed to leave her domain."

Sorcha unfurled the scroll from her father onto a worn table, the first missive he had sent in many moons.

In the early months of her exile she had burned his letters, refusing to hear anything he had to say after he cast her out. He had not listened to the explanation behind her growing belly. Had not cared that she was grievously deceived into thinking she was married after a false priest had said all the proper words to bind her to a man she thought would be her husband for eternity.

But time and motherhood made her less rash. While she would still not allow her father or any of his men near her, she had read his last three missives. They no longer contained recrimination and accusation. He had written her of how his sheep fared. Of negotiations with his allies as he prepared to fend off the oncoming Normans. She missed knowing the workings of the kingdom.

She used to read to her father once his eyesight began to

fail and she'd taken pride in the education he'd granted her when most women had no such privilege. Her father had given her much, but had expected unswerving loyalty in return. A loyalty he considered betrayed.

Sweet heaven, she could not live in the past any longer. Staring down at the page, she read:

Daughter,
I have shielded you from suitors while you were in confinement and for many moons afterward, but by your leave, I will forward all future entreaties to you. As you do not wish my counsel, I will not offer it. Hugh Fitz Henry, a mercenary who wandered into our lands recently, will arrive at your cottage this day.
Yours,

The bottom was signed with all her father's assorted titles in the way he might sign an official document. Lord of this, baron of that, and so on. Sorcha stared at the missive in vague horror. Her father did not bother to soothe her with any niceties.

A stranger wished to court her? A wandering mercenary, no less? Clearly her father did not think she was worthy of a noble union anymore. And didn't it surprise her how much that could still sting her heart after all this time?

She blinked furiously at the burning in her eyes, determined to live with the choices she'd made. Choices she could not regret when they had given her the precious blessing sleeping two rooms away with his nurse. How quickly a woman's life and all her illusions could be torn asunder.

She did not know how long she stood in the middle of the

cottage's small hall, numb to the core. Should she send this suitor away the way she had rejected her father's other overtures? Sorcha had to admit this one did not seem so much like an offering, however. Her father's note had implied he was giving up on her.

Could this be one of his tricks? Some overgrown nurse in disguise sent to spy on her? Or was he truly giving her one last chance before he made good on his threat to send her to the convent?

The knock at her door reminded her she'd been thinking for too long. What had happened to the days when she had followed her heart and trusted her instincts?

Glancing out a narrow window, she scanned the tree line for signs of her father's men but found no one save the imposing warrior on the other side of her threshold.

Or, from what she could see, he appeared to be a warrior. The only visual her tiny window allowed was the sight of the man's bulging bicep fitted with a golden *torc*.

A soft gasp leaped from her mouth before she caught it with her hand and stepped back from the wall. By the mantle of Our Blessed Lady, she had not even seen the man's face and already her heart quickened. This Hugh Fitz Henry did not lack for virility. Slipping over to the window once more, she eyed the man's strong arm again, his bronzed skin setting off the brighter gold of the *torc*. The ends of the ornament were fashioned into the heads of two bulls, which were surely a fitting device for a man whose arms were easily the size of her thighs.

When he knocked again, Sorcha stuffed her father's parchment in a leather pouch that hung from her girdle and opened the door.

A towering man awaited her. Easily reaching the top of

the door frame, he would have to duck to enter her home. A white linen *liente* gleamed with bright newness in the spring sun, the short sleeves showing the arm she had already admired.

The warrior was far more sleekly handsome than she recalled after their meet in the glade two days prior.

"It's you." She could not contain her surprise.

The warrior bowed, his limbs falling in graceful lines despite the massive bulk of his body. He watched her with eyes that were not deferential in the least.

"Hugh Fitz Henry, at your service."

Muscle rippled in his back and across his shoulders as he moved, his shirt stretched taut from the bow. As he straightened, she found new muscles to study, her eye lingering on the shadows beneath his light tunic.

Powerful.

The sheer size of him separated him from another knight she'd known. The knight whose face resembled his in some ways. But close up, Sorcha found differences she hadn't seen that day in the clearing.

Still, those external dissimilarities did not mean they didn't share the same black heart or the same opinion of women. Why would this man choose her—a fallen woman of the most public sort—to court?

His motives could not be honorable.

"Your service is highly suspect here, warrior. I suggest you find your path back to my father's keep." Backing up a step, Sorcha swung the door closed, unwilling to let any scheming mercenary into her home, no matter how appealing his appearance.

Chapter Three

The warrior caught the door neatly in his hand, his fingers wrapping around the wood at the last second.

The move was quick, silent and unexpected.

He reopened it slowly, his broad arm coming into focus by degrees until she could see the whole impressive length holding open her threshold. And wasn't that just a little bit…dominating?

Sorcha searched for her old grit and fire—the willfulness her father had bemoaned half her life—and found only a maternal fear for the babe sleeping two rooms away. She would not allow any strange male in such proximity to her son, especially not one who would flex his strength in direct opposition to Sorcha's wishes.

"Be careful, sir. I practiced my hold on my knife and I assure you I can wield it more easily thanks to your advice." She kept her hand hidden in her skirt to perpetuate the idea that she might hide a blade from him.

"You closed the entryway with that hand." He smiled as he released the slab of wood, the removal of that strong arm making her feel less intimidated. But then, she remembered that about him from the glade where they'd met. Hugh Fitz Henry was skilled at giving the illusion he would not harm someone. No doubt he'd needed to cultivate that talent from a young age, given his size.

"I reached for it after I closed it." She was no stranger to deceit when a situation warranted.

Her fear had diminished somewhat, but she could not be too careful.

"Lady Sorcha, will you feel more at ease outside?" He gestured to her small plot where a few wildflowers had grown since winter. "I just wish to speak to you and if you are still as unmoved by my suit afterward, I promise to leave and bother you no more."

Ah, they could be so accommodating when it pleased them, couldn't they? She peered past him to the fresh spurts of spring grass and budding trees, an awakening world she'd spent little time noticing until she'd had naught to entertain her but the seasons and her son.

Would it be so dangerous then, to sit in the garden with him, this man who had already proven no threat to her well-being? She had not spoken at length to any noble person— any adult noble person—since she had been banished. Her sister, Onora, had attempted to visit her, but Sorcha had feared Onora would suffer at their father's hands for the efforts and had forbade her younger sibling to visit the cottage anymore.

Surely Sorcha could keep this knight at bay when his intentions were more—corporeal than violent. After her first romantic encounter with a man, she'd learned too late the power of a woman's ability to say no, but she would put that lesson to use well now, if necessary.

"I will join you shortly." She pointed to the left where her garden awaited. "There is a bench nearby. I will bring us some mead."

Hugh's head tipped back and a short bark of laughter sounded.

"And a knife, I'll warrant." Nodding, he stalked out to the garden, reading her far too well.

Had her expression become so transparent in her year away from court that even a knight with such unpolished manners would see through her purpose so quickly? Ach. She was as awkward and unpolished as he after keeping no company for so long.

Perhaps she should not turn away Hugh Fitz Henry without a bit more thought. Conversation might do her good. She could hone her skills and sharpen her mind grown dull from lack of use. If she hoped to talk her father out of locking her away in a convent, she would need a smooth tongue and sharp wit.

Tucking a sheathed blade into her garter, Sorcha hurried around the kitchen to assemble a tray. A pitcher of sweet mead. Freshly baked honey bread. Two flagons. When all was ready, she carried it out into the garden and set it on the bench.

Hugh was nowhere in sight.

Had she scared him off already? Perhaps a woman who threatened him with a blade had not been what he'd hoped for in a courtship. Surprised at the twinge of disappointment that filled her throat, she was about to retrieve the tray when she heard the rustle of tree branches and a crack of wood.

"Sir?" She peered around the garden to the woods nearby and didn't see anything.

Until she looked up.

And spied Hugh Fitz Henry perched in a tree, his big body balanced on a thick limb as one boot dangled from a freshly broken branch. With one hand, he held tight to the oak. With the other, he reached out for a tiny puff of white and black. Her son's six-week-old kitten.

"Oh!" Sorcha raced over to stand beneath the tree, nervous the animal might fall. "The bold little thing. He is not yet weaned and he would scale heights as if he were a bird."

She lined up under the small animal, holding her skirt out from her body like a cradle to catch the poor thing if he should lose his tenuous grip. Conn would be sad and puzzled should any harm befall his wee friend.

But Hugh stretched a hand's span more and snatched the animal up while the kitten mewed piteously. Relief flooded through her. For although the kitten was a small thing and the mother cat had litters of many to safeguard against the loss of one, this particular little beast remained special to her son. And therefore, tremendously special to Sorcha.

"Thank you." She waited impatiently for Hugh to descend, finally taking the kitten from him when he was but a few feet from the ground. "You have averted tragedy, sir, and I appreciate it greatly."

She wrapped the mewling creature in her long sleeve as she crooked her arm, smiling as the feline licked her wrist in joyful obliviousness of his near accident.

Hugh leaped to the ground as nimbly as a squire, though the expression on his face bore little resemblance to a boy's.

"You should have a care with the revelation of your legs, my lady." His voice took on a growling note that surprised her in the middle of her happy reunion with the cat.

And then she recalled lifting her skirt.

"Thankfully a woman's garments allow her to dispense with a layer without revealing—anything." Her cheeks heated nevertheless. And while she would like to pretend that it was her long and lonely exile that had turned her manners so coarse, she suspected she would have been as quick to flash her underskirts even while she lived beneath her father's roof.

"You forget that men require little encouragement to envision the exact shape and texture of a woman's thighs." He stormed past her, boots pounding an angry tempo on the ground as he closed in on the pitcher of mead. Helping himself to a flagon, he downed it quickly, readjusting his tunic.

His braies.

Sweet. Merciful. Heaven.

She needed to remain mindful of being around a man. Heat washed through her like a summer fever even though she had no business imagining anything so—*physical* about this bold and unusual warrior. Quickly, she averted her eyes, although she hadn't *seen* anything untoward. It unsettled her enough to have imagined the discomfort his movements hinted at.

Flustered and frustrated with herself that she only per-petuated the man's probable view of her as having loose morals, Sorcha kept her distance while he took a seat beside the tray of bread and mead. The scowling expression on his visage told her to run back inside the cottage. Yet he held himself firmly to the bench as he poured a second cup full of mead.

The man possessed restraint, if the flexing and tighten-ing of the knot in his jaw proved any indication. That spoke well of him.

Still…how to proceed? She'd had every intention of

sharpening her conversational skills and improving her manners, yet here she stood, speechless and supremely ill at ease.

It did not help matters that her thoughts had turned as warmly intimate and disconcerting as Hugh Fitz Henry's must have. But then, how could a woman's thoughts remain pure when a man insisted of speaking about the shape of her… er… legs?

"Forgive me for my lapse of judgment, sir," she said finally, only half meaning it. She'd hardly flaunted her body in front of him, but if she was going to humble herself enough to ask her father to let her raise Conn, she would need practice in swallowing her pride.

The task had never come easily to her.

"No, it is I who should ask your forgiveness. It is not your fault that a man's thoughts are wayward and inappropriate." He poured the other flagon full of mead. "Here. Come and join me, my lady, and I pray you do not hold my ill-tempered outburst against me. Your mead would soothe the ragged beast in any man."

He lifted the second cup, holding it out to her. Entreating.

Saints protect her, she felt as frightened as the tiny kitten must have, perched on a high branch and teetering against a fall only to be given an alternative that appeared every bit as scary. But she, too, found herself moving inexplicably toward Hugh Fitz Henry.

She came to him.

Hugh thanked all that was holy that he had not scared off the woman who might be his only link to his past. For that matter, even if Sorcha could provide him with no hints of his identity, at least he had been admitted into her father's service. Where else would a man with no past and no true name obtain such a chance? There was a certain safety in that acceptance that he would not risk for the sake of the heat Sorcha stirred within him.

"Thank you." She gripped the cup he offered and brought it to her lips with a hand more steady than her breathing.

He turned his attention back to his own drink lest he lose himself in watching the way her lips cradled the smooth silver vessel.

He knew in that moment she was not like most women. But *how* did he know that? As soon as he formed the thought, he attempted to chase down the root of it. What other women in his past had helped him form the basis for comparison? He possessed a sense that females did not appreciate being reminded of a man's baser nature. Many a noblewoman would have fled his presence at the mere suggestion of what the shape of her legs did to him.

Yet all his struggle for an image of any other woman yielded nothing. No face of a mother or sister, wife or betrothed.

The only woman he could see was the one who sank slowly to the bench beside him, her cup clutched in a tense grip. Had her father been correct in his assessment that she would permit any man to court her—even one as coarse as he—if it meant she might gain freedom from her exile?

"Your gardens are a sight to behold," he observed lightly, needing to divert their attention.

And yet even that topic weighed awkwardly on his tongue. How could he comment on the lushness of her budding fruit or the heavy blossoms on the vine without sounding like he meant something else entirely?

"I have far too much time to tend them," Lady Sorcha returned mildly. "I do not know what you have heard about my situation, but as an exile, I am not allowed in my father's presence and I have no duty to his house. That leaves me with substantial time to tend the flowers."

Settling her empty cup on the tray beside his, she refilled them both from the heavy pitcher before proceeding to slice a squat loaf of sweet bread.

"He gave me the impression you were free to leave your home with a guardian." He extended his palm to receive the bread, but she was careful not to touch him as she handed it to him.

Instantly, he regretted putting her on guard to such an extent.

"Did he suggest I might be endlessly grateful for the chance to escape?" She arched a brow and studied him assessingly, her earlier discomfort fled in the face of her irritation.

He debated the wisdom of a lie and decided such a course would be unwise with this woman. Clearly she knew her father well and, perhaps, was as well versed in manipulative games as her sire.

"Are you so content with your banishment?" he asked instead, tearing into the honey bread with the enthusiasm of a man still recovering from a long journey.

His food on the road had been sparse and dependent upon his hunting, something he indulged only upon dire need with his focus so keen to discover his name. His home. He savored the rich texture and delicate scent of the honeyed bread, so different than any scantly cooked beast on his travels.

"No one would seek such isolation as this, and yet I have

discovered small delights in the silence of a summer night where there are no servants to sneak about the courtyard stealing embraces or reveling knights to sing and jest till sunrise." Sorcha broke off a bit of her repast and nibbled the morsel. "Here, I am not subject to my father's tempers or marched in front of his guests like an exotic animal on display."

"So you do not wish to hasten your release?" He helped himself to more bread, suddenly aware of how long it had been since he had eaten well.

Or perhaps he merely ate to quiet another hunger. His gaze strayed entirely too often to the princess's mouth as she licked a crumb from her lips or tasted her mead.

"On the contrary, I cannot wait for my release." Her green eyes took on a new fierceness. "But I will never be so desperate that I will accept any man my father places in my path in order to secure freedom."

"I would like to think I have placed myself in your path." He studied her with new respect, appreciating her shrewd assessment of the situation. "I was not summoned to Connacht by the king. I arrived at his gate under my own accord."

"If you do not see my father's larger designs, you are not as clever as I suspected." She returned her cup to the tray between them with a thump, startling the wee kitten that had fallen asleep in her lap.

The furry beast lifted its head and blinked bright blue eyes before dropping back into slumber amid Sorcha's skirts.

"I suspect your father wishes you to wed so he does not have to send a cherished daughter to the convent." Hugh stretched his legs and tipped his head back to the warmth of the spring sun, not daring to gaze upon the fiery Irish princess for long lest his thoughts stray again into uncomfortable terrain.

And while Sorcha might not be desperate to accept his suit, he needed her acquiescence with every fiber of his being. If she refused, he would be dismissed from Connacht and separated from the only clue he had to his past.

"I hardly think my position on the far outreaches of his lands makes me cherished, but you have seen his purpose well enough." She shifted on the bench beside him and he straightened to see her rise, the kitten now in her arms.

Her feet followed a stone path through the hedges and flowers, a small nod to order in a garden overflowing with pleasant disarray.

"And you know my purpose as well," she continued, halting to meet his gaze from where she stood. "That leaves me at a disadvantage because I do not comprehend your motives at all."

Her searing gaze told him she would not tolerate lies lightly.

Nor could he tell her the truth.

That left him in uncharted terrain, just like the whole rest of his anonymous life. He settled for shades of the truth instead.

His eyes raked over her, taking in her proud spirit and womanly form. From her straight shoulders and proud tilt to her chin to the way she cradled the young kitten in her arms, Sorcha was a study in contrasts. And underneath his need to know why she recognized him, Hugh simply wanted to know her.

"I couldn't forget you after I saw you in the forest yesterday."

Chapter Four

Onora Con Connacht stifled a gasp of surprise at the strange knight's presence in her sister's garden.

So this was the Norman mercenary who had caused such an uproar in her father's court? She urged her mount closer to the garden wall, determined to obtain a better view. Standing on her palfrey's back, she could just see over the moss-covered enclosure where the kings of old used to install their mistresses or—occasionally—a widowed queen out of favor with the new ruler. Now Sorcha lived here, a prisoner in her own realm for daring to defy their father.

"Be still," she hissed at her horse, her balance unsteady as she stood on the mare's back. "I'm almost there."

Gingerly, she reached past the thorny branches of a yew tree to the smooth trunk of a young pine. As the palfrey stilled beneath her, she bent her knees and leaped, keeping the pine in her grasp as she flung herself to the top of the garden wall.

She must have disturbed a group of birds, because there was an outcry nearby and the flap of wings. Onora held herself steady, waiting to be discovered and hoping against hope she would not be.

This wasn't the first time she'd sneaked into Sorcha's domain, though her older sister forbade the secret trips. Onora missed her sibling dearly and knew if their positions were reversed and Onora had been banished, she would want someone to visit her. As it was, Onora took great pains to escape her father's watch, his vigilance far more formidable with his younger daughter than it had been for Sorcha. A fact that had proven a vast inconvenience, but she took pride in finding new ways to elude her protectors.

Of course, she could never remain away from her father's keep for long and she confined herself to bringing the occasional length of exotic silk or a wildflower cutting. Her presents were small and often attributed to one of Sorcha's attendants. But it pleased Onora to know she'd touched her sister's life anyhow.

When the garden quieted again, Onora felt certain she had not been discovered. Carefully, she seated herself on the stone wall to watch amidst the cover of thick branches. In the distance, her sister conversed with the tall Norman, their talk too low for her ears.

How could her father have permitted this stranger to visit Sorcha with no guard? The Normans would march on Ireland before long now that the exiled king of Leinster had asked the Normans for help regaining his kingdom. The Normans always rejoiced at trouble in Ireland since they lived for the chance to steal power in the greatest land on earth. So why trust a Norman with his own daughter?

Or could the stranger bring an honest offer to Sorcha that might save her from the convent? Onora's romantic nature rejoiced at the possibility.

"Lady Onora?"

From outside the wall, a man's voice startled her.

Her hand flew to her waist and the protection of her dagger as she turned. There, standing at the base of the wall, stood a frowning young groom she recognized as the caretaker for Sorcha's horse.

"Eamon," she whispered, wishing she did not feel a pang of feminine pleasure at the sight of someone so wholly inappropriate to her station. Why couldn't her heart beat with such speed at the sight of a noble who came to court her instead of a man destined to wed a village girl?

He was broad shouldered in a way that made the female servants of the court sigh, his muscular form filling out his tunic admirably. His dark hair and blue eyes marked him as Irish, while the deeper shade of his complexion suggested a hint of the exotic, as if his mother had been wooed by a spice trader at the village fair.

"Come down at once before you are injured." Eamon glared at her with the displeasure one might cast upon a disobedient child. Then he began to scale the wall.

Hand over hand, he climbed quickly, his nimble fingers finding purchase between the mossy rocks. Alarm tingled up her spine.

"You cannot order me about." It was difficult to infuse her voice with the proper authority while striving to whisper, but she did not wish anyone to hear them.

"I am keeping you safe, Princess," he retorted, closing the distance between them rapidly.

"Shh!" she hushed him, fearful now for him as much as her. At least her rank would save her if she was discovered. "Have a care with your voice. My sister is within."

Eamon reached the top of the wall, his long, tanned

fingers splaying along the rock so that the smallest of the digits rested a hairsbreadth from her bottom. She scooched back a bit, the pine tree impeding her movements.

"All the more reason you must descend." He pulled one leg over the wall so that he straddled it like a horse.

He faced her, his thighs bracketing her without touching.

"You, sir, are highly improper." She glared at him to cover her nervousness.

"Unfortunately, sneaking out to your sister's cottage against your father's orders is even more improper." He winked, a wicked smile revealing straight, white teeth. "It's not me who'll have to worry if we get caught. If you'll allow me, I'll help you descend safely."

He extended his hand like a high king shuttling his queen about the great hall with much ceremony. Being the center of a handsome young groom's attention would not have been a hardship, except that Onora had the impression that Eamon thought she was more of a bother than anything. And that wounded her feminine pride far more than a tumble off the wall would injure the rest of her.

"I will allow no groom to command me." She looked down her nose and ignored the girlish urge to accept his hand.

Her heart fluttered oddly in her breast as she kept her eyes trained on the garden. Unfortunately, she had moved too far behind the pine tree to see Sorcha or her knight any longer. She could see only a pitch-covered trunk and, if she looked to her right, a small waterfall in the brook that trickled through the garden. Peering to the right was not an option, given Eamon sat so near.

"You see naught but a groom then?" He lifted a hand to a leafy limb of an overgrown apple tree and followed Onora's gaze. "Are you always so quick to believe what you see?"

"What else would I believe?"

He plucked a white flower tinged with pink and rolled the stem between his fingers.

"We sit among branches that bear naught but decorative flowers today." He stilled the bloom and offered it to her. "Yet the tree has not revealed its true purpose with the fruit that will follow, wouldn't you agree?"

"Do you mean to suggest you are working toward a higher purpose?" She knew some ambitious villagers lifted themselves out of drudgery to become clerks or even clerics.

But as she cast a wary eye upon her strong and virile companion, she could not envision him taking priestly vows.

"I mean you have not discovered my hidden task in dismissing me as a mere groom."

He turned his sea-blue gaze upon her, unsettling her with the frank assessment contained therein. The look he gave her bore none of the subservient ducking or downcast eyes she usually received as the king's daughter. Eamon studied her the way a man might research a keep he wished to conquer. He seemed to seek out her weaknesses and strengths, as if he viewed her for the first time.

Awareness swirled inside her, a warm, tingling sensation that danced through her veins like a sip of well-made wine.

"You overreach to suggest otherwise," she complained, although he certainly gave her pause. Why claim to be something he was not? "I have seen you tend my sister's mare these last many moons."

As soon as she said it, she regretted the implication that she'd noticed him at all. Flirting with grooms—even grooms who aspired to a higher station—was out of the question. If her sister had been exiled for being with a knight, what would the king do to a daughter who dared dally with a servant?

Turning on the wall, she lifted her legs over the other side so she could climb back down. Her visit with Sorcha would have to wait. She didn't wish to have witnesses to the news she brought from the keep.

"Allow me to help you, Lady Onora." The man plucked the apple blossom from her fingers and tucked it behind her ear, using the stem to secure a bit of her hair along with it.

He touched her so quickly that she scarcely had time to protest. Her pulse pounded in her veins, warming her skin all over. Even now, he moved to steady himself on the top of the wall, lying on his belly so that he might guide her down the sheer face of the enclosure.

"Nay." Shaking her head, she refused his help. "I will depart on my own, but it will be the last time you chase me away from my own sister. Whether or not my father approves of my visits, he shall hear of your presence if I see you on the premises again."

"That would only aid my true purpose, and for that I would thank you." He kept his eyes upon her as she made her way carefully down the wall, her toes seeking chinks in the rock more slowly than his had done. "Be sure to mention I tried to keep your pretty neck intact."

She flushed even warmer, confused by the strange encounter. Shoving the thought from her mind, Onora leaped to the ground.

"I will not give any credit to you for saving a neck that was never in danger." She turned on her heel and wondered how she could mention the strange meeting to her father. She was curious now, and wanted to know about this mysterious groom even more than she wanted to know about Sorcha's new Norman.

But she could not risk her father's wrath in admitting this

visit since that might encourage Tiernan Con Connacht to rid himself of his eldest daughter all the sooner. Onora had only come to tell Sorcha her time avoiding the convent was almost over. Their father made plans to send Sorcha away before harvesttime.

And Onora would not lose her sister to the nunnery without saying goodbye.

"I think you'd better take your leave." Anger poured through Sorcha. Did Hugh think her so daft that she would believe such idle flattery?

"Have I offended you by declaring a fascination with you?" He remained seated, a fact she appreciated since his physical size would intimidate her even with a whole slew of her father's knights to protect her.

And, truth be told, his imposing presence made her acutely aware of her femininity. Her petite stature and slender limbs. The sexual element of that contrast was never far from her mind and she could not understand why. How many times had she regretted her passionate decisions? She could not afford any more. Especially not with a man who bore a strange resemblance to Edward.

"Nay. You offend me by not speaking the truth." She knew he had come to Connacht for reasons he did not reveal. Anyone looking upon his fine, strapping form and the sharp intelligence in his eyes would see a knight in his prime. A knight accustomed to command. He must have a reason for being here besides courting an exiled princess far from his homeland.

"Do I not?" He shot to his feet and a few quick strides carried him close enough for her to touch. "I would be more than happy to prove my…interest."

She bit her lip, unsure how to respond. Unsure what exactly he had just offered.

"That will not be necessary." Her voice failed her, emerging from her lips in a cracked sound.

Her first lover might have only visited her bed a handful of times before fate and an enemy's sword had felled him, but their time together had taught her the way of things between a man and woman. And even if the coupling had not fulfilled her every last romantic dream, it had taught her much about the way a man could turn a woman's steely will to molten want. Edward hadn't provided her with that elusive pinnacle of pleasure, but his embrace had taught her she was as passionate in bed as she'd always been outside of it.

She would do well to rein in that fire now before she allowed it to dictate the course of her life again. Except Hugh's sinewy form emanated a heat that warmed her, while the spicy male scent of him tempted her to lean closer and take a deeper sniff.

"You've no right to call me a liar, lady, lest you are willing to let me prove I speak the truth." His amber eyes locked on hers, the whiskey-golden gaze seeming to see past her defenses to the woman beneath.

A foolish notion, and yet those eyes undid her.

She swayed on her feet, perilously close to him. Who knows what folly she might have fallen into if the rustle of birds in a nearby tree hadn't distracted her. Straightening, she shook off the spell he seemed to have cast upon her and took a step back.

"I owe you naught, sir. I risk much by even allowing you within the walls of my home." She had no guards to protect her here, just a wet nurse for her son and a groom who helped keep the horse fed and exercised.

"Then you have all the more reason to trust my ability to restrain myself with you." He reached toward her and for one heart-stopping moment she though he meant to touch her, but instead he merely scruffed the head of the sleeping cat within her arms. "If my intentions had been less than honorable, I could have easily exercised my will here in the privacy of your gardens. Will you not trust me to escort you to the village fair on the morrow where we will be in full view of many watchful eyes?"

Her gaze dipped to his broad hand gently stroking the kitten's fur, his fingers a hairsbreadth from her breast as he did so. Her breasts ached in warm response and she was grateful the tiny beast and her folded arms hid her body's reaction.

"Think about it, Sorcha," he prodded, lifting his hand to tip her chin, forcing her to meet his clear-eyed gaze. "When was the last time you enjoyed the taste of freshly baked meat pies and the scents of a spice trader's cart? I hear there are minstrels from Scotland who are known to perform long into the night."

He dropped his hand, but her skin retained the memory of his touch.

"You do not play fair, sir," she complained, already smelling the smoke of a bonfire heaped with fragrant dried wood. "It has been many moons since I attended a feast day, let alone a full-fledged fair."

"In truth, I cannot remember the last time I had the pleasure of such entertainment myself." His grin beguiled her, calling her to forget her worries and join him in whatever mischief he had planned for the morrow. "We will make a merry pair."

"Too merry, I think. The whole village will think we are

courting." She snuggled the kitten closer to her face, rubbing the fur along her cheek, but not even the animal's warmth could replace the memory of Hugh's gentle fingers. "And while I am pressured to wed, you must know there will be equal expectations heaped upon you."

She worried her lower lip as she replaced Conn's kitten on the ground. She should have already refused Hugh's offer. Joining him at the fair day would only complicate matters. Yet what if his presence soothed her father's haste to send her to the convent and bought her more time with her son before she had to give him up forever?

"Not even an Irish king could force a marriage upon me that I did not wish." He narrowed his gaze for a moment and she shivered to think what kind of enemy Hugh Fitz Henry would make. "I vow no amount of pressure would sway me."

She had spent every day since discovering her "husband" had played her false telling herself to trust no man. And still the fiery truth in Hugh's eyes swayed her as much as her longing to dance a merry round while the minstrels played and the bonfires yawned flames into the night.

"Aye." She could not resist the opportunity to break free of her exile. The chance to make a happy memory before she was confined to a life of toil and prayer. "I will attend the fair day at your side."

"Excellent." His smile brought forth an answering grin from her lips and she thought for a moment she might actually have fun with this mysterious Norman who chided himself for peering at her thighs and devoured her sweet bread like a starving man. "I will call for you at noon."

She would have to leave Conn in the care of his nurse, but by the saints, she would venture out of her narrow domain and into the world again.

"Until then." She dropped her gaze and dipped her head as a polite courtesy even if she had once outranked him.

For a moment, she thought he might attempt to steal a kiss. Oddly, she did not recoil at the notion. No matter that her passions had been used against her so cruelly once, the old flame still leaped to life as she envisioned Hugh's mouth brushing hers.

She licked her lips as heat flowed through her veins.

"Until then." With a quick bow, he spun on his heel and departed, leaving her surprisingly bereft and more than a little indignant.

Did he seek to toy with her affections by granting teasing touches? She was no maid who needed her passions awakened, but an experienced woman with desires long suppressed.

Sorcha might not drag the man into marriage to save herself from the convent, but she would be hard pressed not to give Hugh a taste of his own teasing medicine at the morrow's fair.

Chapter Five

After departing Sorcha's cottage, Hugh waited for the nimble lad to descend her garden enclosure before he accosted him.

As the spy's face came into view, Hugh discerned the man was older than he'd first presumed. Lean and wiry, the stranger moved like a youth with his easy grace. Yet his face revealed the dark growth of a mature beard and there were faint lines about his eyes.

Concealed behind a hemlock tree close to the garden's wall, Hugh began his protective assignment from the king with all haste.

Silently, he slipped from his hiding place and stepped behind the unsuspecting young man. With lightning speed, he wrapped an arm about the man's neck and another his sword arm, preventing the spy from reaching for the short blade at his waist.

Hugh held him immobile for some moments while his quarry attempted to thrash and then finally stilled. Hugh did not, however, release him.

"What business have you here?" He would wait to identify himself in the hope the man recognized him. Someone must know him. But for now, Hugh kept the agile climber turned away from him so the spy could not see his face.

He understood that not knowing what enemy you faced was more unnerving than confronting an obviously powerful foe. At least then, a man could formulate a strategy. He also understood that if he yanked hard to his right with the man's head clamped in his right arm, his opponent would expire instantly.

The knowledge gave him pause. Had he ever harmed someone thus?

"Eamon ap Dermot," the stranger uttered through clenched teeth. "Man-at-arms to Tiernan Con Connacht."

"I serve the king as well," Hugh warned. "I will put your story to the test."

He loosened his hold, but not his guard. Eamon freed himself and spun on his heel to face him. However, Hugh could not discern any recognition upon the man's face.

"As will I," the dark-haired Irishman threatened. "'Tis my duty to guard the princess, as it has been every day since her banishment."

Eamon ap Dermot stepped back and rubbed his throat, a gesture no warrior would make since it revealed a weakness.

"You guard her?" Had the crafty old king omitted this detail on purpose when he asked Hugh to protect Sorcha? If so, he must have known he risked the young man-at-arms's life.

Or was the spy lying?

For a moment, Hugh considered the possibility that Eamon was a consort to Sorcha—a lover taking advantage of a young woman's isolation. The thought burned through him with sudden fury and he tightened his hands into fists on instinct.

"As well as one man might," Eamon answered, oblivious to the dangerous direction of Hugh's thoughts. Ceasing his ministrations to his neck, Eamon straightened to his full height. "I am to act as a lowly groom in order to remain close to her. But my blade is a weapon of the king's house and I protect the princess with his authority."

Eamon reached for the blade and proffered it, but by now, Hugh no longer saw him as a threat. There was truth in the boast, and his speech had the ring of a well-remembered charge that had changed Eamon's life forever. No doubt the king had raised up the youth in station to do his bidding.

And, looking him over more carefully now that he was certain Eamon was not a secret paramour for the princess, Hugh decided the guard was a wise enough choice. Nimble and quick-witted for a common-born laborer, he must have been keeping a watch over the events in the garden this morning.

"If that is true, you will serve me in the future. The princess is now my charge." He gave Eamon a hard look. "If I were to ask you about the princess's activities today, what would you tell me of your observations?"

"My lady received a strange knight who cast a bold eye upon her person though he did not treat her with disrespect." Eamon met his gaze with a narrow look of his own and Hugh saw promise in his intelligent speech and sharp assessment.

"Well enough. You must pretend to be a lowly groom?" Hugh suspected that had been the man's position before he'd been assigned the new task as well, but he could easily see where Eamon would use his duty to pull himself up in station. "You know the Conqueror himself was descended from a tanner on his mother's side."

Another random piece of information he knew not how he possessed, yet if he chased the thought through the channels of his brain, it darted elusively away.

"Some men make their own destinies from naught," Eamon agreed, sheathing the king's blade.

Hugh tensed to think of his own situation. His very survival depended upon seeing this through. He couldn't allow himself to indulge in softer feelings for the fallen princess. Sorcha had the protection of a caring father. Hugh had naught but his own cunning. He didn't even know his own name.

"Aye. Some men more than others."

St. Erasmus was little more than a name to Sorcha, yet the saint who protected sailors received high praise along the Irish coastline where unpredictable winds and waves could whisk a man off to a watery grave with no warning.

It was his feast day the village celebrated, inspired by a devout nobleman whose seafaring son returned safely home one year after a journey to the continent that lasted half the nobleman's lifetime. He'd thought the son dead all that time, and his joy in his offspring's return had called the father to sponsor a small chapel on the coast overlooking the sea.

Mostly, Sorcha was grateful to Erasmus for providing the excuse to leave her cottage for the first time since her father learned she was expecting a child. The realization had come late in her confinement thanks to his frequent trips away from the kingdom for warmongering. Still, upon seeing her swollen figure, he'd wasted no time in sending her away despite her protests that she'd been deceived.

The betrayal from a beloved father still hurt, even more

so close on the heels of discovering the treachery of her first and only lover.

"What say you, Lady Sorcha?" her companion inquired, gesturing to the group of tents and bonfires, peddlers' carts and children at play on the fringes of the festivities. "Are you not glad to see your neighbors and friends?"

"I am most pleased to see the meat-pie maker." She pointed toward a cart at the end of one row where an old man and two of his daughters worked beside a brick fire pit. Her belly growled in anticipation of her favorite treat.

"Then I shall deprive you no more." He ducked beneath a ribbon strung between the trees for some kind of a game a group of children played and led her toward the cart heaped with food.

The scents of roasted capon and venison mingled with heavy spices as they reached the small table beside a temporary hearth erected for the fair. Hugh purchased a pie for each of them along with a cup of wine, then guided her toward a small hill overlooking the gathering.

Happily, she took a seat on the warm grass and bit into the delicacy while absorbing the sights and sounds of the crowd.

"Better?" he asked, watching her while she ate.

His appearance at her door that morning had taken her aback, his appealing looks a surprising enticement to a woman who wanted nothing more to do with men. At least not until she resolved the rift between her and her father.

But Hugh Fitz Henry was no pox-marked and flap-bellied nobleman who staked his manhood on a birthright he'd done no more to earn than emerge from the womb. Nay. Hugh was a warrior in full measure, a man who clearly lived by the sword, if the breadth of his shoulders and the scars upon his person were any indication. The backs of his hands were laced with healed wounds, while a long gouge marred his throat and disappeared in his tunic. She admired the strength of spirit in a man who fought for his lands, the way her father had fought for his kingdom.

And yet, what did Hugh fight for here? Why did a brave knight linger with an exiled Irish princess? The obvious answer was a political marriage. But he did not pursue her the way any other man ever had. He did not boast about the wealth of his lands and stables to sway her, or worse, assume her father would force her to wed no matter if she cared for the suitor or not.

"Aye." She reached for the cup of wine he'd settled between them, mindful of his amber eyes upon her and the fluttering sensation they caused deep in her belly. She'd best mind her wits before she repeated all her old mistakes and ended up with another babe causing the next gentle flutter within her. "But I cannot relax and enjoy the day while I ponder your motives."

She sipped the wine while he finished his meal. The fact that he never needed to rush into speech intrigued her, his manner so at odds with her father's fiery temper and quick tongue. Too often, she and her father had found themselves in a disagreement because neither of them could leash their responses the way this controlled Norman could. If anything, Hugh seemed to savor the time to think before he answered, as if he rolled his thoughts around his brain the way she rolled the spiced wine about her mouth to dissect the complex flavors.

"I thought we clarified the matter of my interest in you yesterday." His voice hit a lower note and the deep tone rumbled through her skin to vibrate along her senses like a drum.

Her flesh heated from her breasts to her neck, the flush crawling more slowly up her cheeks.

"I mean—" She cleared her throat, determined to speak her mind without growing distracted. "What motive have you for your presence in Connacht? Why would a Norman knight approach an enemy king when war between our people seems imminent?"

"You are aware of our politics despite your long exile, lady?" He appeared surprised.

And, she hoped, just a bit impressed with her knowledge.

The saints knew her father had never been overly fond of her interest in the running of a kingdom. He called her political interests "wholly unnatural" for a woman. And while she did not regret her choices to learn all she could about the governance of the kingdom, she rather wished her head-strong sister had not followed her direction. Onora appeared determined to oppose their father's rules wherever possible, from defying his dictate that she not see Sorcha, to dodging prospective husbands by all possible means.

"I know my father is an unpopular choice for High King. As much as he might want the position, the king of Leinster is already drawing Norman support to be High King instead. Connacht will feel the brunt of Norman blades before the matter is settled."

"And you think I come to make war on your father?" He took the cup from her hand, his fingers brushing hers in a fleeting caress that should not have been half as pleasing as it was.

"You are a long way from home."

"I seek only friendly relations with your father, who I might add, was not half so suspicious as you."

He kept his gaze upon her as he finished the wine.

"As a man, my father can test your words by the sword. As a woman, I must seek more subtle reassurances."

The sight of his sculpted mouth glistening with the last of the dark red wine had her turning away to find distraction among the fairgoers. She watched two village girls smile and tease a pair of farm boys selling their young goats. She wondered if the maids knew the dangerous game they played.

But then, perhaps they would not push their play to the limit the way Sorcha had once done with the smooth-tongued young stranger who had wooed her in her father's absence.

She had thought to divert herself with that game again today with Hugh, if only to chide him for his hasty retreat yesterday at her cottage. But Hugh was no Edward du Bois. Hugh had already warned her of her effect upon him. She would not make the same mistakes of her past simply to soothe a wound to her feminine pride.

Besides, exchanging a kiss with Hugh could land her in an unwanted marriage as part of whatever political maneuvering Hugh attempted. She would not be used again.

"Sorcha." His hand was suddenly upon her elbow, a warm entreaty to face him. "I cannot tell you the full extent of my task here, but I vow I mean you and your family no harm. I will protect you at all costs. I swear it on the strength of my sword arm since you have no reason to trust in my honor."

Oh. As pledges went, Sorcha found his moving. His words tempted her to believe him as much as his hand upon her arm tempted her in other ways.

"Sorcha!" A feminine squeal a mere stone's throw away shattered the moment.

Blinking away the last remains of broken intimacy, Sorcha turned to see her sister racing headlong toward her. She stood just in time to catch Onora in her arms as her younger sibling fairly bowled her over.

"You are free!" Onora's cry of pleasure attracted attention from all around as villagers, her father's men-at-arms and a few gathering nobles from nearby lands turned to see the source of the noise.

Sorcha could scarcely speak from the tightness of her sister's hug, but she laughed with pleasure and returned Onora's enthusiastic greeting as well as she might. What did she care for the curious looks? She had already driven her father to call for her lifelong confinement to the convent. No transgression she made now could possibly make her situation more dire. Although, she supposed, he could yet find fault with Onora.

Before she could suggest they make their reunion more private, however, Hugh wrapped a guiding arm about her shoulders and drew them deeper into the trees at the top of the hill.

Onora did not go quietly.

"You wish to hide us, sir?" She relinquished her tight hold of Sorcha, but did not let go completely.

As Sorcha watched her sibling, noting the new maturity in a face free of all childish softness and the long dark waves that any woman would envy, she could not help but wonder if Hugh would find Onora appealing. The notion made her uneasy. Sorcha told herself that was only because of Onora's untempered youthful passions and Hugh's hidden past.

"I wish to keep the daughters of the king safe from harm during a time of growing unrest." Hugh did not even meet Onora's gaze as he peered out over the fair-day gathering, hand upon the hilt of his sword while his eyes searched for…what?

"You think we are at risk now more than in previous years?" Sorcha asked, already knowing it must be so. However, if Hugh had any particular reason to think the house of Connacht was in danger, she wished to know of it.

"You are wise to the enemies your father makes with his bid for the High King's seat." His sword hand relaxed as he turned back toward them, although Sorcha remained more uneasy than ever.

He'd said he would protect her at any cost and it seemed his actions attested to that. While she appreciated the guardianship, she regretted to think she needed it.

"Do you think Conn is safe?" Her heart ached with a sudden need to be at her son's side. "The cottage is hardly a fortress—"

"Conn is far safer at home where his presence is unknown by all but those closest to the king." Hugh's shoulders relaxed and Sorcha felt some of the tension slide from her own.

"*You* know of him," Onora accused, her rosebud mouth full of disdain as she pursed her lips. "Why should we believe your motives when you are a Norman?"

Hugh cast a smile upon Sorcha. "She bears great resemblance to you in all ways." Bowing, he backed up a step. "Lady Onora, I will leave your sister to address your concerns. If you need me, I will be within shouting distance."

Striding away to speak to Sorcha's groom who had appeared on the hillside, Hugh left the sisters alone in the sheltering trees.

Onora wasted no time.

"Sorcha, I tried to see you yesterday to tell you that Da wishes to send you to the convent with all haste. He says he will not wait until the end of summer and that you must leave before Lammas."

The fear and empathy Sorcha saw in her sister's eyes sent a tremor of alarm through her.

"So soon?" Her heart sank at the thought of leaving Conn before his second birthday. She had thought to have more time with her son before her father imposed the inevitable censure upon her for having a child without the benefit of a husband he chose.

A husband who married her before a real priest with a hundred witnesses.

Old regrets rose high, threatening to pull her under their heavy weight.

"He claims we are both unsafe now. He is to hasten the search for my husband and he will not afford you as much time with Conn as you wanted before you are to—" Onora's voice broke "—depart from us forever."

Tears leaped to her sister's eyes and Sorcha pulled her close to comfort her. Onora made it sound as though Sorcha would be sent to her death. And, in a way, perhaps she would be. She would very likely never see her family again once she was sold into the nunnery. Onora would wed a man from a far-off kingdom for a political alliance. Their father would be embroiled in wars that might last for the rest of his life. Sorcha's youthful mistakes would be forgotten once she was locked away behind the high gates of a priory. Her sole comfort was that Conn would be raised by the king.

Her illegitimate son would find acceptance at last.

But the price for clearing his name of her sins would be high indeed.

"I have always known this day awaited me." Sorcha would not cry in front of a sister already disposed toward giving free rein to her emotions. "In the end, we make no choices without consequences."

The wisdom had come too late to Sorcha, but it might yet aid Onora. Sorcha watched a group of girls chasing butterflies nearby and felt a pang of yearning for those simpler times when they would have joined the village children in such a game.

"But at least they are *your* choices." Onora gazed off into the distance. Nay, she seemed to be staring toward Hugh and the groom. "You did not bend to father's will to wed some toothless old nobleman who would swive with a sheep in the absence of a woman."

"Sister!" Sorcha sought for a sense of outrage with which to chide her, but could not hold back a laugh. "I cannot fathom where you have gained such a wicked mind."

"It is not far from the truth, and well you know it from the men Father offered to you."

Sorcha recalled two different lords her father had suggested as husbands and shivered anew. She had spent so much time these past moons regretting the life she had to offer Conn that she had almost forgotten what made her rebel so strongly in the first place. Would she have been any better off now if she'd dutifully wed one of those ancient noblemen?

"But I have learned that acceptance is more important than you realize." She squeezed Onora's arm to emphasize the point as a nearby children's game grew rambunctious.

Hot cockles always appealed to the most rowdy children as it involved placing a hood over the eyes of a person in the center while others circled him and randomly hit the blinded person until they were identified by name.

Somehow, this round of hot cockles had spread all the way up the hillside as the blindfolded boy listed about, trying to both duck and guess his tormentors' names.

Hugh must have noted the players' advance, for he called out to her from his position farther down the hill. She was about to proclaim her safety when she was struck in the temple and fell heavily to the ground.

Chapter Six

Reckless youths scattered like the wind.

Hugh plowed past them to reach Sorcha, suspicious of every face that streaked by but unable to search for a culprit until he knew the princess of Connacht had suffered no lasting harm. He had been alert for full-grown men who might wish to hurt her or steal her away, not barefoot urchins in the midst of a game.

"Sorcha." He kneeled to the ground beside her, careful not to land on the river of auburn hair spilling out onto the grass.

Her skin was pale, the faint freckles on her nose standing out in sharper relief. He plunged his hand beneath the blue veils hung from her silver circlet, feeling along the back of her head for any injury. Gently, he sifted through her silky hair.

Relief rushed through him when he found no blood, though he discovered a lump just above her ear. The spot was swollen and warm to the touch.

"She said nothing before she fell," Onora told him, her voice breathless. "She merely sank to the ground."

The young groom, Eamon, joined them. Hugh allowed him to be present since he had spoken to Sorcha's party the night before and discovered the king had indeed given him the task of overseeing the princess's safety. A mission far too large for one untrained in the knightly arts, but the move seemed typical of a man who could run a kingdom but didn't know how to handle his daughter.

"She is going to be fine," Hugh assured Onora, willing it to be so.

His chest tightened at the sight of Sorcha's face wiped clean of all expression. He wanted to see her eyes open again, her strong temperament animating her face with stubbornness and determination. He remembered the fierceness in her green eyes when she held her son close the first day they met—as if she would wield a sword herself before she allowed Hugh near.

"I will scour the trees," Eamon announced, his voice firm until Hugh peered up at him and Eamon quickly added, "With you permission, of course."

Nodding, Hugh released him to the task before lifting Sorcha's shoulders so that she reclined in his lap as he knelt beside her. She was warm in his arms, her body delicate and light against him. He was struck anew by the need to safeguard her. An overwhelming urge that went far beyond his sworn duty to her father.

He had come here to protect this woman. He knew it somehow, the knowledge planted deep within him in the way that he'd known his given name even though he remembered nothing else. The rightness of holding Sorcha settled over him, quieting a storm inside him that had been raging for nigh on two moons that it had taken him to travel to Ireland and find her. For just this moment, having Sorcha safe beside him was enough.

"She awakens," Onora whispered, reaching in to touch her sister's face.

Hugh had to fight the urge to wrench Sorcha away. The need to keep her all to himself was so strong it made him uneasy.

"Sorcha." He spoke softly to her, calling her from whatever visions the darkness held for her.

What if she awoke with no memories, the same way he had awakened in a crofter's hut that day two moons ago? What if her mind was as blank as his, her injury stealing all of her secrets and any knowledge she might have of him?

The notion chilled him even as it opened a doorway to intriguing possibilities. A woman who did not know him had no reason to withhold herself from him. Yet, he wouldn't wish this hellish torture on anyone, most especially not this woman.

"Where is Conn?" She pulled her eyes open, suddenly alert. Blinking, she struggled to sit.

"He is fine," Hugh assured her. Clearly, she had not lost her memories. "You are at the festival day and he is home with his nurse."

"Praise the saints," Onora murmured, moving closer to squeeze Sorcha's hand. "Eamon went to look for the person who hit you."

"They were just children," Sorcha protested, prying herself the rest of the way up so that she sat without any support from him. "No doubt it was an accident."

His arms ached from the loss of her in them, but he ignored the sting of it to concentrate on what had happened.

"Did you see any of them armed with rocks?"

"Nay." She shook her head and then stopped abruptly, no doubt in deference to her injury. "They played hot cockles and merely hit one another with their hands."

Hugh recalled the game in which a hooded child attempted to guess the identity of those who hit him. He had a fleeting memory—a scrap so small it could hardly be called a memory since he merely heard the triumphant shouts and goading words of a childhood pastime before it was gone. But he knew his mind was recalling a game he'd played once. A game with family and friends.

His life had become the opposite of hot cockles. He knew the identity of everyone around him but did not know himself.

"Do you know of anyone who might wish ill upon you?" Hugh lowered his voice and spoke close to her ear, mindful of the small crowd that had gathered to see what had happened.

He would have preferred his introduction to the village to be more discreet so that he might study their faces at his leisure and, perhaps, without their knowledge. If he had passed through here before, he might find some who recognized him. Ideally, he could have gauged people's reaction to him while they were less guarded. Now, his presence here would be well known. But the importance of his own mission paled in comparison to keeping Sorcha safe.

She peered back at him now, the color coming into her cheeks.

"No one would wish me ill, sir. My banishment permits me no opportunity to make enemies." She shifted her weight as if to stand. While he would have rather held her there a bit longer, both because touching her was a pleasure and because he wanted her to feel steadier, he helped her to her feet.

Still, he wasn't ready to give her up to her worried sister or the curious fairgoers yet.

"Your lady fares well," he announced to the crowd, gesturing to her as she stood. "I pray you will allow her a few moments to recover her strength."

Onora nodded, biting her lip. Perhaps she thought he did not word his request strongly enough, for she made a shooing gesture toward the crowd.

"Aye. Let us give Lady Sorcha some room, please." She turned to Hugh and spoke hastily, her veils crooked upon her head. "I will fetch her some wine, but keep her still."

Turning on her slippered foot, Onora made a sweeping motion with her hands as if to brush all the remaining gawkers off the hillside as she strode down into the thick of the fair to retrieve a cup of wine for Sorcha.

Hugh guided her toward a large rock as he kept his eyes upon the tree line in search of Eamon. He did not hold out much hope the groom turned man-at-arms would find who was responsible for striking her, but he waited anxiously for whatever news Eamon brought.

"I am well enough to retrieve my own wine," she protested. "I did not make a deal to attend the fair with you only to be shuffled off into the farthest corners where I see no one."

Hugh would not be deterred. No matter that the pink had returned to her cheeks and her eyes blazed with full cognition of her whereabouts, he would not risk anything else happening to her. But he feared that to protect this independent woman, he needed to know far more about her.

"I have reason to suspect someone may want to hurt you." He could not confide the fact that his services had been retained by her father. Nor could he explain the driving need to protect her that was rooted deep within his muddled brain.

"You make too much of an accident." Reaching to adjust her circlet, her gown stretched over womanly curves.

He did his best to prevent his gaze from lingering on her breasts, but with the neckline of her surcoat shifting, a flash of pale skin just below her collarbone was strong enticement.

He cursed his wandering attention.

"You are at risk on the fringes of your father's lands and these are dangerous times." He fell back upon the impending threat of the Normans who would march on Connacht before long. "Any battle tactician knows the value of an important captive and you, my lady, make a tempting catch. Ah—that is, you would command a fine ransom."

She kept her eyes trained on her sister, who hurried up the hill with a fistful of her surcoat's skirts in one hand and a cup of wine in the other. What was it about these ladies of Connacht that they thought nothing of lifting their hems? Hugh did not think he'd ever been a man of great propriety, but earthy manners among beautiful women did not go unnoticed.

His eyes darted back to Sorcha's legs to relive a delectable memory.

"I do not see a need to fear for my safety and one small mishap in a child's game is unlikely to persuade me otherwise." She finished adjusting her veils and brushed back her hair from her shoulders before settling her hands in her lap.

"But you do not think like a warrior to see what an advantage you give your father's enemies with your exile." Hugh considered her situation for a moment and then launched the question that desperately needed asking. "Is there any possibility Conn's father might wish to retrieve his son?"

At the mention of her former lover, Sorcha felt more numb than when she'd first awakened from her faint.

Thankfully, she was saved from having to answer Hugh's question by Onora's arrival. With grateful hands, Sorcha took the cup from her sister and murmured her thanks.

"Lady Onora, would you allow us to speak in private a bit longer?" Hugh framed the request politely enough, but his tone made it a command.

Onora looked ready to argue and Sorcha nodded her consent, unwilling for her sister to overhear a conversation she did not wish to have.

"If you are certain?" Onora asked her, not even pretending to take orders from the foreign knight who seemed eager to take command.

"I will be fine. We can speak tonight at the bonfire," Sorcha assured her.

Below them, the fair was back in progress as if it had never been interrupted. She had hoped to be a part of her family's world if only for the day, but it seemed even now she was the outsider as she remained on the fringes of the group.

Hugh waited until Onora withdrew before he spoke again.

"I ask out of concern for your safety." He seated himself beside her while the scent of cinnamon and burning wood rode the breeze.

No doubt a loaf of sweet bread baked nearby.

The fair swelled with attendants as tradesmen and their families finished morning chores to join the feast day. A minstrel strolled the tents with a flute, sending up a sweet tune as he walked. A falconer from her father's lands had brought a few of his birds to show the children.

"My husband would make no claim to Conn," she informed Hugh, surprised at how easy it was to speak of the son the rest of the world did not want her to acknowledge.

She would far rather be confronted with questions than chilled by icy silence. If only her father had felt the same way during the time she was with child, Sorcha might have been able to defend herself from his anger and assumptions.

And yes, she still called Edward du Bois her husband since she had every reason to believe he was at the time Conn was conceived. Her father had made sure she knew that marriage had not been legally valid as it was performed by a false priest, but he could not take away the fact that she had good intentions at the time. She would not defend her actions to any man—including Hugh Fitz Henry—only to be called a liar.

"How can you be so sure?" His words were gentle as she stared off into the distance, watching her sister move through the crowd of curious and admiring stares.

Had Sorcha been viewed that way once? She could not recall what it felt like to be the envy of everyone around her, but perhaps she had been too concerned with testing her own mettle and proving herself to her father to notice the way others had looked up to her.

Dragging her attention from her sister, she met Hugh's gaze.

"My husband is dead."

Something shifted in his eyes, but she could not read whatever thoughts lurked behind his amber gaze.

"I thought he— That is, your father seemed under the impression that he abandoned you."

Even after all this time, the knowledge of her father's disappointment in her still had the power to sting. But she refused to regret the blissful days that had led to her son's conception and—saints protect him—her son himself.

"I guess, in a way, he did." Sorcha had known Edward

would leave her to wage war upon her countrymen in the south, but he'd sided against her father's enemies and fully anticipated his triumphant return. She might well hate him for playing her false, but she never would have wished him dead. "He went into battle and did not come home."

Hugh's gaze slid away from hers and she watched him follow the progress of a small merlin across the sky, the bird's chains freed if only for a moment. Below them, the falconer watched it circle along with the small crowd who had gathered about him.

"I do not wish to pain you, Lady Sorcha, but was his body returned to Connacht for burial?"

"Nay." Her insides chilled at the question and she suspected he knew more about her past than she had realized. "That is yet another reason my father declared my marriage false. But I begin to think you have already heard much of my personal trials."

Bitterness clogged her throat to think of her father confiding her naive choices to this bold Norman who appeared as if he'd never once doubted himself.

"He said only that the name of your priest proved false, invalidating your union." Hugh picked up her forgotten flagon of wine and motioned for her to drink. "I hesitate to upset you but if an enemy wishes you harm, we would do well to put a face and a name to him."

"Well, clearly it cannot be Conn's father." Grateful to settle that awkward discussion, she did as he bade and drank deeply. She had feared the attraction she felt for this man, but she had not thought to fear his keen intelligence or the eyes that saw too much. He'd dragged the most sensitive issues into the light, hacking through them with unnerving speed to find the answers he sought.

"You mistake my point." He plucked at a far-flung corner of her skirts that had strayed close to his leg, his fingers gently rolling the bright length of embroidered blue linen away from him. "If your priest was false and your husband's body was not returned to you, what reason do you have to trust that he really died?"

Sorcha's vision blurred for a moment as she considered Hugh's suggestion, her eyes unable to focus on the movement of his fingers along some curling stitch of floral decoration near her hem. Dizziness assailed her and she had to replace her flagon on the rock beside her.

"My lady?" His touch fell away from her skirt, a fact she could not feel but somehow sensed.

Pins seemed to prick behind her eyes, her world sliding as out of focus as her vision.

"That cannot be." Everything within her revolted at the idea that pushed Edward's betrayal to a low depth she had never suspected. "I have struggled to resign myself to the fact that I was duped by a false priest and that Edward might have purposely used such a figure to preside at our nuptials because he did not plan to remain in Connacht. But if he allowed me to think he was dead for a convenient way to not face me—to elude my father's vengeance—he is a greater coward than I could have ever guessed."

The world about her spun and she planted her hands upon the rock to steady herself.

"Sorcha." Hugh's voice shot through the dizziness, as strong and sure as the man himself. "You should rest after the blow to your head."

He slid an arm about her back, keeping her upright. His other hand landed lightly on the side of her face, tilting her chin up so that she could see only him.

As if she absorbed some of his strength, she felt strangely improved. The ground beneath her steadied. All at once, her vision focused.

Her senses became sharply attuned to his closeness. The clean scent of his soap. The heat of his skin wherever he touched her. The slight pressure of those touches somehow urged her near. Or was that a fanciful imagining? The air constricted in her chest until she had to take shallow breaths around that tingling knot of intense awareness.

"I am fine," she protested, though the weakness in her voice suggested otherwise. Clearing her throat, she attempted to regain control before she did something untoward like… dissolve into the compelling strength of a stalwart knight. "Truly, it was the thought of being mistaken about Edward's death that made me uneasy, not any pain from my temple."

With an effort, she straightened, drawing herself away from temptations she couldn't afford.

"It is a natural enough conclusion, unless you saw proof of his demise." He eased away from her slowly, as if afraid releasing her too soon would topple her from her seat.

"I have the word of my groom, Eamon." She peered back toward the tree line to see any signs of his return. "We will speak to him at once."

Then she would put to rest this new uneasiness that she had been betrayed even more deeply than she originally thought. Hugh's presence might unleash unwieldy desires inside her, but she would not allow him to resurrect demons from her past when she needed to carve out a future for her and her son.

Chapter Seven

"Curse your eyes, Bartlett. You have all the subtlety of an aging whore." Eamon might not have cared about the oafish attack on Lady Sorcha if Hugh Fitz Henry had not been present. But the astute Norman changed everything.

Eamon could not relax his guardianship of the princess if he hoped to maintain his newly elevated status with Tiernan Con Connacht. For that reason, he was not pleased to meet an old acquaintance in the forest.

"What of it?" Gregory Bartlett was a bowlegged clerk who had risen from duties as a lowly tax collector to become one of Edward du Bois's most trusted servants.

Eamon had met him the year before when du Bois had been in Connacht trying to cause trouble among the Irish kings in the hope of usurping power for a greedy band of English barons. Eamon had been glad to earn some extra coin by helping Gregory and Edward du Bois deceive Sorcha into marriage, but back then, Eamon had only been a groom with little to lose. Now, if anyone from Connacht discovered his treachery, he would sorely regret his rising position. Something he did not think the Normans would match for his service.

Bartlett sat astride a fat donkey now, his mount poised for eating instead of taking flight through the woods, no matter that the rider had just committed a crime by throwing a rock at the princess.

Eamon had not expected to see Bartlett again after the man paid him to lie about Edward du Bois's death. But the clerk had reappeared in the woods near Sorcha's cottage a few days earlier and hinted that they might have further need of Eamon's services. And while he craved the extra money, he could not risk his faithlessness being discovered.

"You will arouse notice from Lady Sorcha's new protector." Eamon planned to spin out his knowledge by slow degrees in case there was coin to be made for the quantity of what he offered.

He'd volunteered to search the woods for the princess's attacker just in case du Bois's men had been at the bottom of this. But in truth, he'd been protecting himself as much as du Bois since Eamon would not give up his new position as one of Sorcha's guardians. If Hugh Fitz Henry had discovered Bartlett in the forest, there was a chance he might have talked. Eamon would not allow anyone to discover his part in betraying the royal family of Connacht.

"She is to wed?" Gregory asked, shifting his portly form on the donkey in a flap of dark robes and weathered sandals.

Eamon arched an eyebrow.

"You do not think I will sell out my lady without good cause, I hope."

"You are more addlewitted than I remember if you think I will place a single coin into your hand without some assurances of your loyalty." Gregory shook his head, dislodging the hood pulled over his bald pate. "You are as guilty as I am of deceiving the princess. Perhaps you should pay *me* for my silence."

Eamon stepped back, abhorring the thought that he could lose his position because he'd been outplayed by a lying money handler who thought nothing of harming a woman. He stumbled over a tree root and quickly righted himself.

"Why have you returned?" Eamon asked, suddenly afraid for his own neck. Had the false-faced clerk come back to tell Lady Sorcha the truth? "You did not tell me anything of substance the last time we met, evading my question at every turn. But I want to know what du Bois's presence in Connacht means."

"Relax, groom." The clerk dismissed his concerns with a wave of a fat, beringed hand. "I am only here to report news of Connacht to my lord. Is it true the princess bore a child from the union with du Bois?"

Eamon wondered how he could fall so quickly from thinking himself ahead of the game to discovering he had been greatly outdone. Worry crept up his back and crawled along his shoulders. He had his ma and three sisters to support since his da died last winter. He could not afford to lose his new rank with the Irish king any more than he could afford to upset du Bois's men.

"Aye. A boy." A child born to privilege even as an exile and a bastard. With a powerful knight for a father and a king for a grandfather, the whelp would never know the hardship of sleeping on a dirt floor in winter as icicles formed beneath your nose. Young Conn would never toil all summer only to have the blight wipe out his crop or a woodland beast devour the fruits of his labor.

Eamon had been poor and a bastard besides—reviled by the stepfather who raised him with his half sisters.

"We can be sure the child is Edward's?" Bartlett pressed as the strains of music from the fair floated on the spring breeze.

Eamon bristled on Lady Sorcha's behalf.

"The princess cried for the loss of du Bois many days after his death." Eamon knew she shed many more tears over the loss of love than she'd spared for the exile most women would have despaired. "She has not let a soul close to her since your lord's departure—"

"You mean his death?" Bartlett grinned, displaying a mouthful of missing teeth.

"Aye," Eamon corrected himself. He'd sworn to Sorcha that he'd seen du Bois's lifeless body, even though he'd known full well that both the clerk and the lying lord had left Ireland after the skirmish that was supposed to have killed du Bois.

"Then I have a great deal to report to my lord." Bartlett lifted the donkey's reins and tugged the lazy creature toward the south. "He is involved in a campaign not far from here and may wish to retrieve his heir. Then again—he may prefer to ensure his future bloodline remains untainted by a youthful indiscretion."

Eamon sucked in air, surprised at what the man suggested.

"In either case," the clerk continued, "we may require assistance with the boy and with the new man she sees. At that point I feel certain we could find an equitable arrangement. As I recall, you have many who are dependent upon you."

Bartlett's narrowed eyes communicated darkness Eamon had not perceived the previous year when he'd been quick to do the man's bidding. Not that he really had a choice. But any man who could harm a child so that some worthless lord's bloodline remained "untainted" was surely the most soulless of men.

"I am at your command," Eamon promised, wishing he'd never chased down the person responsible for throwing a rock at the princess.

In an effort to impress Onora and keep his secrets, he'd placed himself in an untenable position. Now, he also had a long absence to explain to Hugh Fitz Henry. Turning on his heel, he vowed to quickly round up every child who'd played a game on the fair's hillside that morn. He would question them all even though he'd already seen the real culprit. He needed the children's help to adequately account for all the lost time since he'd departed the princess's side.

Hugh strode past the tents as the sun set on the feast day without a word in private to Sorcha's groom.

The lad had sought out all the players of the game on the hillside in the hope one of them might have seen who had thrown a rock in Sorcha's direction. But no amount of questioning had yielded answers. Hugh had left Sorcha in her sister's care by the bonfires where the minstrels played and the dancers whirled while he awaited Eamon to finish his task with the last youth. Sidestepping a silk trader whose cart was full of more ribbons and trim than actual cloth, Hugh attracted the attention of two maids scuttling past, their heads bent in giggling conversation. Or at least they were until they spied Hugh.

One gasped. The other tripped. Each clutched the other.

"Ladies." Hugh nodded a greeting, curious about their reaction. "Have we met?"

"No, but it is never too late," the one spoke up, her white cap sliding sideways on her tousled dark hair. "We can entertain ye for as long as you please. We have a hidden spot awash in soft leaves within yonder trees."

The plump maid—not more than eighteen summers—jerked a thumb toward the place she had in mind. Her friend, a bony blonde with ample hips and a fresh grass stain on her skirt, nodded her encouragement.

"No, thank you." He knew it was not in his nature to rut with one so young, no matter how freely she offered herself. "I only thought you—"

He shook his head, cutting himself off. Apparently he'd misinterpreted the looks they'd given him.

He wondered how long it had been since he'd known a woman.

"Never mind," he told them, wrenching his attention away from them. Their eagerness did not tempt him half so much as the red-haired princess who was as cagey as she was spirited. "Good eve, ladies."

With another nod, he stalked past them, eager to settle the matter of Conn's father with Sorcha. And for that, he required the groom.

"Eamon." He interrupted him at last, impatient with his thorough questioning of boys hardly old enough to wield a rock with enough force required to fell a grown woman. "A word please?"

Reluctantly, the ambitious groom dismissed the last boy. Hugh had asked the king about Eamon and discovered the young man had been enticed into service with the promise of a spot guarding the keep's walls and—perhaps—a chance to prove himself on the battlefield when the Normans came. Something inside Hugh had recoiled at the thought of such a promise to someone untrained in the use of arms. It was one thing to give a laborer the chance to put his natural strength to more challenging use. It was another to place him in a role that required skill and lifelong training to succeed.

Hugh vowed to help the younger man himself, unable to stomach the thought of turning an overeager man out onto a killing field with no notion of weaponry.

Eamon could shape a future for himself even as Hugh did. "Aye?" Eamon joined him outside the empty tent.

All the tents were clearing out as fair attendants proceeded to the bonfires for drinking and entertainment. Watered wine and mead flowed with abandon from the king's storehouse, although the sovereign himself had yet to appear at Erasmus's feast day. The villagers toasted their lord in his absence, all the while whispering among themselves that he'd denied them his presence because of Sorcha's attendance. Sorcha had overheard the rumors and did not try to contradict them. She had not been mistreated after the incident with the rock, but neither had she been welcomed into the fold with open arms by her former people.

"If you would attend the princess by the bonfire, we would like to speak with you." Hugh pointed the way past the tents and stepped into the flow of tardy villagers heading to the celebration.

Even from this far away, Hugh could hear the strains of lute and tambourine music that signaled the start of a dance. Would he remember the steps of a round to perform with Sorcha?

The question brought to mind a memory of music in a quiet pasture played by children and an idle nurse. The scene in his head involved no great hall, but the most rural of settings for a forbidden pastime.

As quickly as the vision had come to him, it dissipated, leaving Hugh with the worry that he was not the highborn knight he imagined but some lowly farmer's son with dreams and ambitions like Eamon's. Had Hugh been raised in the back halls and pastures of some rich lord's keep? Could he have learned his knightly skills by imitation and not training?

"Did you reveal my true purpose to Lady Sorcha?" Eamon asked, ignoring the straggling villagers who sought to capture his attention.

Hugh blinked away his unsettling thoughts, his focus slowly returning to the present. "Of course not." He could not compromise Eamon's purpose without implicating himself. And the more he spoke to Sorcha, the more he became convinced she would not appreciate being deceived.

She'd surely been fed more than her share of lies.

"Then what—" Eamon's words were cut off by Onora.

"Here we are!" she shouted over the music, waving her arms at one end of three bonfires in a row.

Hugh hastened his pace toward the women, eager for answers that Sorcha had a right to hear directly. He had the impression that her father had not pursued enough of the truth a year ago where Sorcha was concerned, and it seemed he'd owed his daughter better than fury and exile.

But then, Hugh sensed a tender place in his heart growing for the fierce princess who'd once thought to protect her son with a small blade and a large share of maternal determination. He could not help but admire a woman who had forged a life for herself with no help from her family. For his part, his brain felt more fractured every day that he found no family. No name. No roots or a past to claim as his own.

Hugh watched her now, her hands clasping her sister's as Onora swept her up into a dance. Sorcha shook her head to deny her laughing partner, but Onora spun her about anyhow and Sorcha's feet found the steps with remembered rhythm, her natural grace apparent in every move.

The bonfire bathed her in bright, warm light, the flames

adding a flush to her cheeks. His gaze slid down her blue surcoat, the rich shade of the dye fading at the seams and at the neck where it hugged her high, full breasts. Her long auburn hair swished against her back as she spun, the breeze catching her veils and revealing the lush hue of her curls.

"The bards say their mother was just as beautiful," Eamon offered suddenly and Hugh realized he had been caught staring.

Then again, Eamon's gaze seemed to be firmly glued to Sorcha as well. A fact that roused a level of fury in Hugh he could not have anticipated. He thought to warn Eamon of the fruitless pursuit of a woman so far above him in station, when the younger man spoke once more.

"They say Onora shares her mother's dark hair." Eamon's gaze lingered on the other noblewoman who twirled Sorcha about. "Although I have heard that Tiernan's lady wife had eyes more like her elder daughter."

Still, Eamon's glance did not leave Onora. And while it might be foolhardy to hunger for a lady who could never return his feelings, Hugh did not feel so compelled to interfere now that he knew where the other man's interests lay.

"Eamon." Sorcha paused her dancing steps, her face losing its laughing lines as she waved the men closer. "Thank you for attending me."

Hugh wished they could retreat for greater privacy, but most of the assembly's focus remained on the dancers and the music. They would be safe enough to speak here, in the shadows beyond the reach of the firelight, as long as they kept their voices down.

"You called for your groom?" Onora asked, peering about. "What need have you of a horse? I thought you would stay with me until the moon rises high."

Sorcha grabbed her sister's arm and spoke low into her ear until Onora nodded, seeming to understand the need for discretion. Her eyes found Eamon and narrowed, as if searching out the truth of answers before she'd asked any questions.

"Let us move out of the way of the dancers," Hugh suggested, taking Sorcha by the arm to guide her around a swath of fragrant smoke from the fire.

"Your questions must be of a serious nature," Eamon observed in a tone Hugh did not quite fathom.

But then, perhaps a man raised up from a low station was never fully comfortable in his new seat. Nervousness played out in his hasty step as he joined them.

"We were discussing the people who might wish to harm Sorcha earlier," Hugh informed him, ready for answers. "And wanted to ask you about the last time you saw Conn's father."

Sorcha gripped her sister's hand, unprepared for Hugh's direct launch into the heart of the discussion. She had been thinking about that fateful winter when her false husband died ever since Hugh raised the question about Edward.

Sorcha's father had been on a campaign in the south where the Irish kings had been fighting for power after the death of the High King. All of her father's best men had attended him in the battle, leaving Sorcha guarded only by an aging nurse, a doting steward and a handful of the youngest knights, many of whom had been playmates of hers since childhood. Slipping from the keep to the village and then outside the town walls had never proven a problem. Especially with the enticement of Edward, who had rescued her from a band of forest outlaws. She'd trusted him so easily, but then, he'd protected her honor when it would have been easy for him to take her innocence as reward for dispatching her attackers. Instead, he'd wooed her for weeks while her father was away, always proving himself a gentleman when she'd bestowed ardent kisses upon him.

Instead, he'd asked for her hand after the waning and waxing of a moon cycle. He'd imposed upon a cleric whom she thought was known to Edward. Only after Edward's untimely death did she discover the priest was not listed in any church's records as a man of God. The vows she'd taken under the stars with the deer and hares as witnesses had turned out to be as false as her marriage. What had always troubled her was the role Edward had played. Had he understood the full extent of his friend's deception?

"I do not know what I can tell you that I have not already related to Lady Sorcha and her father." Eamon bowed his head in a gentle show of respect.

Sorcha appreciated the groom's kindness toward her. He'd always been wise beyond his years with a charm that made him a favorite in her father's court.

"A few points call for clarification." Hugh's jaw tightened, his face cast in flickering shadows from the play of the bonfires nearby. "Did you see the man's body for yourself?"

Eamon shifted uncomfortably and Sorcha guessed he did not wish to upset her.

"I am prepared for your answers, Eamon," she assured him. Although she would have appreciated a bit more wine to steel her. She'd felt shaky ever since she'd been struck by the stone, but she wasn't sure if that was because of her injury or the worrisome turn Hugh's thoughts had taken about her safety since then.

She would not be so frightened if she was the only party

at risk. But the thought of anything happening to Conn concerned her greatly. Did Hugh care about the boy because he might be a relative? Or could he truly care about them simply because he wanted to court her? Sorcha did not trust her judgment anymore when it came to men.

"I saw Edward du Bois struck down two days after his arrival on the battlefield in Meath," Eamon explained. "I dared not venture close to his body since he fought with the Normans for the southern kings against my own lord."

Sorcha had known Edward was Norman, of course, and thus more inclined to support her father's opposition. But when he'd left her that winter, she thought he went to discuss a peaceful resolution. She never knew if he'd taken up arms anyhow, or if he'd been killed while seeking peace.

"Then it's very possible that du Bois fell but did not die." Hugh's hand moved to her back, a steadying touch she hadn't realized she needed until this very moment.

Beside her, Onora squeezed closer, still holding her hand in sisterly support. All around them, a cheer went up for the minstrels as one rousing tune ended and another lively round began. The dancing took place closest to the central bonfire while Sorcha's party huddled near the farthest fire to the east. Nearby, she could see couples sneaking away from the fire to find privacy in the forest, a reminder that they needed to keep their voices low for a sensitive discussion.

It also reminded her of the forbidden pleasures she would never enjoy again once her father installed her at a convent. She was certain she had not discovered the full extent of what delights a man and woman might share behind closed doors with Edward, but her small knowledge of a man made her curious to learn more.

"But I saw the blow delivered with my own eyes," Eamon insisted. "It was a grave strike to his head."

"His head?" Sorcha straightened, setting aside her imaginings about the couples who stole off into the woods behind them.

She'd thought Eamon told her father that Edward had been struck in the heart.

"Aye." Eamon nodded, his eyes steadfast upon her as if he recalled the detail very clearly. "He did not arise after the blow to the back of his head."

Sorcha wondered how she could have confused such an important fact. Sure, she had been upset when Eamon had delivered the news and then recounted it again for her father many months after the king discovered her condition. Her unhappiness at the time must account for her muddled memory. And no one else save her father would have heard Eamon's account since they had strived to keep the whole incident as quiet as possible.

Onora had been purposely left out of such discussions so as not to upset her or, as Sorcha suspected, so as not to romanticize an unsanctioned affair.

"I have witnessed a man suffer such an injury and live through it." Hugh's certainty of this fact gave her pause.

Eamon, on the other hand, appeared less certain.

"Have you?" Sorcha watched him carefully, alert to some change in his demeanor, some subtle shift in his expression. "Was it someone close to you?" She did not think about the personal nature of such a query until it hung in the air between them.

"Nay." His golden eyes went blank and she knew it was no trick of the firelight that made them thus.

Hugh did not wish to reveal any more about the incident

that she would wager her cottage had happened to someone very close to him.

"What does it mean if du Bois is alive?" Onora asked, her tone impatient. "We are not even sure of his real name, you know, since our father went to great lengths to find his family and let them know about Sorcha."

"Did he?" Sorcha's heart lifted at the news. Even if her sire's efforts had been to no avail, they demonstrated a desire to believe her story about her unwise "marriage."

"Of course he did," Onora admonished, releasing Sorcha's hand to swipe away a fly buzzing about her head. "I am certain I disclosed as much to you on one of those early visits to see Conn."

Before Sorcha had banned Onora altogether for fear of the risks she took.

"If du Bois is indeed alive, we must question why he would not contact Sorcha in all this time." Hugh sidestepped some children hurrying from the woods with sticks and leaves to toss into the flames. "We must also question his use of a false priest. Perhaps at the time he only intended to play a sordid game with a young woman's affections. But if he lives and has discovered the existence of his son, he might wish to claim the child."

Sorcha's heart stuttered in her chest. Could Edward be alive? Hugh genuinely believed that to be so. If it was true, it meant Conn could be in danger and that was a consequence she refused to suffer because of her starry-eyed foolishness. She would protect her son and she would start by making completely certain her new suitor didn't have any connection to the man who'd lied to her in the past. The man who bore too much resemblance to the golden-eyed knight by her side.

Chapter Eight

"We should seek an audience with your father at once." Hugh gripped Sorcha's hand to lead her away from the feast-day dancing.

If there was a chance the father of Sorcha's child yet lived, Hugh would need far greater resources in order to keep her and the boy safe. Since he had naught to his name and no promise of coin until the summer's end, he had no choice but to inform Tiernan Con Connacht of this new suspicion.

"Wait." Sorcha dug in her heels and refused to join him, her lips pursed in a small frown while the firelight limned her auburn hair in an even more fiery shade. "May I speak with you privately first?"

"I know there is no love lost between you and your father but—"

"You're wrong." She withdrew her hand from his and folded her arms. "There is a great deal of love lost. But I would like to talk to you before you seek out the king. And besides, I am not ready for my first night of freedom to end quite yet."

The plea persuaded him like no other would have. He admired the graceful way she'd adjusted to life as an exile and he did not wish to rob her of this night when she'd already lost part of the day to her injury and the ensuing search for a guilty party. He would wait a bit longer to speak to the king.

"As you wish." He searched the revelry for a private place, his eyes lingering on a kissing couple stumbling backward into the forest.

The vision spurred a hunger for Sorcha he had no right to act upon. That knowledge did not stop his brain from imagining what she would feel like pressed up against him, her soft curves yielding to his roaming hands. Her lush lips parted for his kiss. He could picture the feel of her hair between his fingers. The scent of her fragrant skin as he bent to taste one creamy breast.

"Perhaps we could retreat to one of the vendors' tents?" Sorcha suggested, her eyes darting away from the amorous couples blending into the shadowed woods.

"Follow me." His voice scratched his throat with the hoarse response, his whole body attuned to Sorcha's every move. He took her hand again, careful not to touch her breast as he unwound her folded arms. One false move would surely be his undoing. "This way."

The tents were a good idea. There was at least some light upon them from the torches lining a path between the kitchens and the fair. People walked along the small thoroughfare, some carrying game boards or flagons of ale while others danced in drunken abandon or carried sleeping children home to their beds.

"The cook's tent had a table." Sorcha pointed to the right. "In here."

He slowed his pace to enter a low canopy raised on skinny, young trees that had been cut and stripped of their leaves for the occasion. The scents of sweet cakes and ginger still lingered even though the cart was empty now. In the back of the tent, a table and bench sat vacant, though a chessboard of rudimentary pieces remained ready for players.

He pulled the bench out for Sorcha. Her skirts caught on a rough edge of the bench as he sat and he tugged the soft fabric free, draping the wayward material on her lap before he took a seat beside her.

In the dark.

They were far enough off the path that no one would notice them unless they came looking for them. And although they were no more alone now than they'd been at her cottage the day before, Hugh had grown far more aware of her in that time. He'd touched her scalp in his search for injury. He'd held her hand in his own. He'd learned more about her passionate, impulsive side.

And he grew more and more convinced they shared a connection she did not want to reveal.

"Tell me of your family." Sorcha peered up at him in the darkness, her features visible only by the grace of a fickle moon concealed, at times, by patches of clouds.

"My family?" He had no notion what could have brought this on, but he was instantly on alert.

"Aye." She grinned up at him. "You have seen so much of my feuding clan and yet I know nothing of your people. I should like to know more about the man who would pay me court."

He wished he could see her better to gauge the sincerity of her words. Was that truly why she wished to know? Or had she begun to suspect something was amiss?

Or—if she had known him in the past—did she seek to test him somehow?

"I thought you would not even consider courtship." He delayed his response, unsure how to tread.

He debated kissing her instead of answering, but feared he would not be able to stop himself, when he needed to maintain his position with the king.

"Nevertheless, we are here together this night." She reached to toy with one of the simplest of figures on the chessboard that he assumed must be a pawn. "I find myself curious about the Fitz Henry family seat. Are you a knight beholden to an overlord or do you make your home with your kin?"

Warnings flared up in his head like a watchtower blaze. Did she play a game to trap him? Or was her interest an innocent diversion to prolong her escape from exile?

She twirled the game piece in her hand as if contemplating her next move. Her profile took on a snowy hue in the moonlight, her creamy skin appearing unnaturally pale. One wavy lock of hair fell forward over her shoulder to slide along the bared skin below her collarbone. And while her blue surcoat was completely circumspect, her lush figure created an enticing shadow at the base of the neckline, a valley where the lock of hair disappeared from view.

"As a mercenary, I belong nowhere." That much was true enough. He knew the answer would scarcely satisfy her.

"But you did not spring to life bearing arms. Where were you raised?"

He told himself she was interested because he'd presented himself as a suitor. But something about the timing of her questions put him on guard.

"North of London." It was where he'd awoken from his

memory loss. "But I became a mercenary to forge my own way in the world after a rift with my family. I prefer only that which I've achieved on my own."

He sent up a silent prayer of apology if he had loving parents somewhere.

"What of Conn's father?" she asked, shifting the chess pieces around the board as if to begin a game anew. "Edward du Bois was—or is—a Norman like you. Is his family name familiar to you?"

Perhaps this was her larger purpose then. Some of the tension went out of his shoulders.

"His family was very prominent," Sorcha continued. "In fact, Edward once received a post with the king's seal upon it."

He watched the chessboard, realizing all at once that she wasn't rearranging the pieces to start a new game. She was playing a game herself—a fast-moving affair in which she made her plays as well of those of her opponent. Moreover, she seemed to be playing quite well on both sides. Her easy mastery of the board stalled out, however, as one side checked the other.

Hugh knew she was sharp. Sorcha's understanding of politics and her ability to read and write were proof enough. Seeing her game strategy played out on the board only confirmed Hugh's instincts about her. If he denied knowing a prominent Norman family, would she call him out for an impostor?

"His name is du Bois?"

"Aye."

"I do recall a family with that name," he lied, his memories wispy bits of nothing that formed disjointed pictures in his mind.

"Truly?" She gripped a chess piece in midair, her fingers obscuring the shape.

"I did not know them personally," he clarified. "I merely recognize the name."

She rocked the game piece back and forth faster.

"You would be the only one then."

He stilled. "What do you mean?"

"After Edward died, my father sent secret missives all over your native lands." She plunked the piece down decisively on the board. "And no one acknowledged knowing any family called du Bois."

He reeled at the revelation, seeing his misstep. Recognizing her trap too late.

"And since you don't know the names of the country's most prominent families, I would guess that you are not a knight of any consequence, the way you would have my father believe." She backed away from the table and rose from the bench. "No matter how you look at it, you are most certainly lying about who you are."

Hugh straightened, recognizing the need to settle this matter immediately. Before she went to her father. He reached for her as she turned to depart.

"Wait—"

"Too late, Hugh." Her shoulders were rigid where he touched her. She shrugged him off. "Checkmate."

Sorcha had always wanted an opportunity to put her former deceivers in their place. During the long months of her confinement, she'd dreamed about taking revenge on that fat priest for lying about his status as a holy man. She'd also imagined herself confronting her false husband with the fact that he'd given her a name no one recognized and claimed a fake priest for a friend. In her imaginings, her self-righteous triumphs raised her up and made her feel strong. Empowered.

Her victory over Hugh's lies had no such effect. She picked her way through the darkness with Eamon on her return to her secluded cottage dwelling, her mood darkening more with each step when she should feel glad that she'd discovered Hugh's deception. He'd asked for a chance to explain himself, but she'd been in no mood to hear more untruths. When he'd insisted she at least speak to her father about obtaining better protection for herself and her son, she'd refused to do so with Hugh at her side, but had promised to send her father a note in the morning to inform him. She would be sure to mention Hugh's perfidy as well.

And where, at one time, she would have reveled in the chance to show her father how unsuitable his choices were for men to court her, now she felt only deflated. She had wanted to like Hugh.

"My lady?" Eamon's voice interrupted her thoughts just as she'd reached a humiliating conclusion.

She seemed to still be attracted to the wrong sorts of men.

"What is it, Eamon?" She allowed her courser to lead the way. The animal knew well how to find its oat bin. Sorcha might not be allowed far from her cottage, but the horses were kept exercised thanks to Eamon.

"He follows us." The groom kept his voice low as he leaned closer in the darkness.

"Who?" She peered behind them through the trees, but all she could see was a vast darkness.

"Fitz Henry."

She pulled up sharply. "What?"

"Hugh Fitz Henry follows us, my lady. I assume he wants

to ensure your safe arrival at the cottage, but if you would like me to call to him—"

"No."

"Very well then." Eamon slid from his horse. "The cottage is just ahead. Shall I take your mount?"

Sorcha was disoriented, not having seen her small home through the trees. Her father's keep could be seen from many leagues distant, the ramparts a beacon to travelers throughout the kingdom. Even at night, torches flickered from the central watch posts. Her cottage was dark as a new moon; the squat design backed into a hillside so that a traveler might never spot it if not for the bright flowers Sorcha had trained around the door. Even the garden walls, while high, were covered in ivy and stacked with natural stone that used no mortar. The whole structure hid within the forest as if it had grown up from the earth.

"Yes. Thank you." Sorcha swung a weary leg over her horse's back.

"Good night then." With a soft command to her courser, he led the animals away for the night.

"Good night, Eamon." She stretched up on her toes to ease her legs, not used to such full days of revelry and riding. Though, in truth, she was more heartsore than physically tired. Between Onora's insistence that Sorcha would be leaving at the end of summer, Hugh's deceptions and his suggestion that Edward yet lived, her mind recoiled from all she needed to worry about. She could not wait to see Conn and hug the warmth of his tiny body to her breast before he fell asleep. Each moment with him was all the more bittersweet now that she knew he might soon be taken from her forever.

Picking her way over the forest floor, she lifted her hem so as not to catch her skirts on the undergrowth. There were soft deer paths winding around the cottage, but she tried not to take the same trails time and again to prevent any one from receiving too much wear. Clear paths brought unwanted company—beggars, outlaws, hungry travelers seeking a meal.

"Sorcha."

Hugh's voice rumbled shortly behind her, all the more surprising for the fact that she hadn't heard him approach.

"You move well through the forest for such a large man," she remarked, hoping to hide her trepidation at seeing him.

"I grew accustomed to it on my journey here. When you are a party of one, it's best to avoid confrontation altogether, even for a knight." He fell into step just behind her, perhaps because the trees were too close together to allow them to walk beside one another.

"How can I be sure you are even a knight of the realm?" She did not think he could have fooled her father into thinking he was a warrior without demonstrating some sort of skill, but then again, her father's thoughts were on his wars and not his wayward daughter's suitors. "If you are not who you say you are, how can I be certain of anything you have told me about yourself?"

Her voice had risen by the end of her query, her frustration surely evident. They paused in front of the cottage, while in the distance, Eamon secured the horses for the night. His quarters were behind the small stable, so unless Sorcha called out for him, he would not return.

When Hugh did not respond immediately, she continued to spill her concerns.

"You must see where I would be cautious about deceptive men." At least she was now. She'd never known a moment's caution prior to Edward's death and the ensuing discovery that she had not been wed by a real priest.

"Of course. But my circumstances are most unusual." He drew her toward a bench tucked up against the cottage wall, a small space she had arranged to enjoy her roses on summer mornings before the sun had risen over the high garden walls.

She refused to sit seeing the conflicting emotions in his eyes, sensing she should have never trusted him for a moment. Cold dread pooled in her belly.

"Explain yourself, sir."

He hesitated. A dark shadow crossed his face as he studied her.

"I do not know who I am."

Chapter Nine

Sorcha slumped back against the rough-hewn wood of the cottage wall, trying to absorb Hugh's revelation.

A few thorns from the climbing roses pricked her skin through her surcoat and she straightened, perplexed. "I do not understand."

"I experienced a grave injury before I left England. A blow to the head from which I awoke confused." He did not join her on the bench beside the cottage, but chose to pace the distance between a pair of young saplings bending gracefully in the night breeze.

"You did not remember how the injury happened?"

"I had no recollection whatsoever. I awoke in a crofter's hut among simple peasants who had found me bleeding in a ditch and tended me for two nights until I regained consciousness." He stilled his pacing and turned to study her, his stance wide as he crossed his arms over a formidable chest. "I had worn out their hospitality, rightly so considering their livestock shared their home. They planned to dump me in the village square and wash their hands of me, but I left the home first, fearing I'd be taken for an idiot if I appeared not to recall my own name."

Was it possible? She had heard of such odd happenings in the stories of the troubadours, but thought loss of one's memories was a fanciful storytelling device dreamed up for dramatic effect. She did not give it any more credence than witches stealing children from their beds or goblins arising from graveyards at night.

"Actually," Hugh continued, perhaps seeing the startled expression that must have crossed her face, "I feel certain I am called Hugh. But as for family ties and allegiances or even the whereabouts of my true home—I am afraid I remember nothing."

"Why call yourself Fitz Henry?" she could not help but ask, curious about this man anew. If he was creating an elaborate lie, he'd certainly chosen a difficult story to support.

"Why not?" He lowered himself to the bench beside her, bringing to mind the small size of the seat. "The name is common enough. Unlike du Bois. If anyone sought to know more about me, they would find plenty of persons who share this name."

For a long moment, they took each other's measure in the moonlight. The clouds had drifted away from the orb for the moment, spilling a soft white glow on them.

"Suppose I were to believe you." She could not fathom what it would be like to awaken with no memory of the past, although she could imagine well enough what it felt like to feel alone in the world without an ally. "Why would a man with no discernible roots cast his fate to a foreign country or offer to court an exiled princess?"

She could not understand what he would gain. And mostly, she wanted to shout, *why me?* Was their meeting a random accident? Or had he been counseled that a fallen princess could be had by any knight willing to overlook her dubious virtue and another man's son?

Thinking about it steeled her emotions.

"The boy who stabled my horse before I met with my injury assured me I spoke of a journey to Connacht when I first arrived in the small town."

"What if someone told him to tell you that?" Sorcha put aside her doubts for the moment to follow his tale. "Perhaps you met with some foul play in the town and the people who harmed you paid the boy to get you well out of the way?"

Hugh shook his head, but she could see the doubt pass through his eyes as surely as the clouds moved across the moon again.

"I have staked all on his story. I believed the truth in his eyes."

"And how can one judge such a thing?" Sorcha rose, unable to wade through his tale or the events of the day that weighed heavily upon her shoulders. "I thought I had that power once and it turned out to be the biggest mistake of my life. I hope for your sake you do not suffer the same fate."

Hugh stood, too, his large frame and battle-hardened body assuring her that—no matter his name—he was indeed a warrior to be reckoned with.

"Will you keep my secret?" He stood close to her in the darkness, the warmth of his body making her shiver. "If only for a short while?"

"Secrets are dangerous," she warned him, wishing she had listened to that counsel when her old nursemaid had bestowed it upon her long ago.

She should not have hidden her relationship with an unknown Norman from her father's advisers while the king was off fighting foreign wars. Sorcha should have shared her worries and fears, enlisting the aid of those wiser than she to make the best decisions.

"Aye. All my life is a secret to me and it puts me in danger every day." The heat behind his words presented an illusion of truth. He spoke like a man tormented by demons of his own.

"I owe you for helping me rejoin the world today, if only for a few hours." She had enjoyed the intense interest he seemed to take in her, the dark worry over her safety as well as the insistence that she seek better protection from her father. "I will keep your secret until we may speak again."

She might have more questions. And perhaps, with a little ingenuity, she might discover if his story was one more embroidered tale.

"When will that be?" he prodded, seeking answers she did not have.

"You may return to the cottage in daylight, but—" she pulled a wool shawl up from her waist to cover her shoulders "—let us not meet under the cover of night anymore."

There was an intimacy about it. A sense that they shared more than secrets in the darkness.

"On the morrow then." He nodded.

She thought he would turn on his heel and leave. He must have a horse tied nearby for him to have followed her all the way from the fair. But his feet remained rooted to the spot and—oddly—so did hers.

"It was a pleasure to be with you today."

The simple compliment touched her. Then, with slow deliberateness, his hand was upon her shoulder.

In a flash, she recalled the way he'd held her earlier. The way his hands' fingers had sifted through her hair in a search for injury. She had been half-conscious at the time, alert to nothing of the outside world, yet strongly aware of this one man.

"On my oath, I have told you the truth." He held her spell-bound with words while his face lowered closer to hers. His golden eyes did not fall victim to the bluish pallor the moon cast. They remained keen upon her, his gaze heated from the inside out.

Her breasts tightened beneath her surcoat, her body far too aware of him.

"Hugh—" She opened her mouth to protest, but he chose that moment to seal his lips to hers.

He had no right to kiss Sorcha.

Hugh guessed at another time in his life that would have mattered to him, but he refused to care now when her lips were soft and yielding. When she'd given him the unexpected gift of keeping his secret for at least a little while.

But what he'd intended as a chivalrous thank-you turned sensual when her mouth parted beneath his. He'd not been expecting that. Perhaps neither had she. But he was powerless to stop himself from drawing her close and savoring the taste. Powerless to ignore the feel of her womanly form against him.

The scent of roses clung to her, permeating the night air. She tasted like sweet wine and temptation, a combination that burned clear through him.

"No!" She wrenched away from him so hard he thought they must be under attack.

"What is it?" His skin burned with the desire to feel her next to him once more. He reached for her, on instinct.

"Nay!" Her voice was less certain this time. More desperate. "What if you are wed to another?"

She stepped backward out of his reach. At least he had his answer. She was not frightened of a marauding army or hungry wolves. She was merely scared of being deceived.

"I do not have the sense that I left a family behind, but I do not blame you for your concern." He bowed, ready to ride out of here and run his horse until the night air cooled his over-heated desire. "I'll return in the daylight hours as you suggest."

She nodded, her eyes round with worry and lingering passion. He could see her heartbeat throb at the base of her throat, a fast-paced pulse that soothed any regrets he had about breaking off the kiss. She'd been as tempted as he had.

But rather than admit anything of the sort, she turned and entered her cottage, closing the door quickly and sound-lessly behind her. He was left with no more answers about his past than he'd had at the beginning of the day, yet his heart felt lighter than it had in months.

Sorcha ingen Con Connacht kissed like an angel. Perhaps her mouth was all the sweeter since he could not recall any other woman's lips. She had, essentially, just given him his first kiss all over again.

And no matter how their pasts were intertwined, he had the feeling no bumbling experience he might have had as an awkward lad could compare to the taste of heaven on earth he'd just received.

Hugh did not go far from the cottage.

He'd sworn a duty to the king to protect his eldest daughter and that meant day and night. The previous evening he had established a camp some distance away in the woods where he remained close enough to watch the main path that ambled nearest Sorcha's home and still view the cottage as well. The spot required him to camp on a hilltop, a position that made him slightly more vulnerable to the outlaws and thieves that sometimes populated a forest, but he'd rigged several spots nearby to trip up those who approached. That would at least give him warning if someone tried to attack him with stealth.

Now, hours after he'd left Sorcha, he felt secure enough to sleep fitfully on the ground beneath the stars. Eamon was accustomed to rising early, so Hugh knew Sorcha would benefit from his protection while he rested. He would see the king later to speak to him about Conn's father, and at that time, Hugh would suggest a man-at-arms to take another shift of the watch.

Sleep claimed him quickly, but his rest remained fitful. Although he was used to slumbering on the forest floor, he was aware of every rock and tree root beneath him now. Even his dreams were confusing scenes that plagued him with a nagging sense they were all too real…

A sword hovered above him.

Hugh tensed in anticipation of the blow, his fingers clenching in the dirt beside him as sweat poured from his forehead. The drink he'd taken in a nearby tavern had been fouled, the hostile brew dulling his wits and churning uneasily in his gut. If not for that tainted ale, he would fight this opponent. Claim victory. He'd battled multiple enemies with fewer weapons than he now possessed. But his drink had been marked, his enemy the lowest kind of coward.

Why could he not see the attacker's face?

Time stood still for one godforsaken moment as Hugh realized this was the end. His head would be cleaved in two by a man he should recognize. A man who seemed to know him all too well.

"See you in hell, Hugh," the false-faced dog above him shouted as his weapon fell, the whole scene far removed from him in his haze even as it played out inches away.

He had not fulfilled his life's dreams. Had not prepared for such an end. Too die ignobly was a warrior's worst fear.

At the last second, he realized the snarling murderer did not swing the blade end of his sword. Instead, it was the heavy hilt that lowered.

When the weapon connected with his skull, he cursed his enemy with his last breath…

Hugh awoke with a start, dripping sweat the same as in his dream. Slowly, the trees around him came into focus, the sound of a brook rushing nearby reminding him he camped just upstream of Sorcha's cottage. His dream remained vivid, the sensation of betrayal and cunning around him strong. His gut instinct told him the dream had been an actual memory, a piece of his past surfacing through the murky darkness of his mind.

But why couldn't he recall the attacker's face? Had he not distinguished the man's features even at the moment he'd been assailed? Perhaps the fouled brew he consumed had blurred his vision. Still, in his dream he felt certain he'd known the man. There lurked a sense of betrayal so deep it had to be rooted in a close relationship. A friend or trusted servant. He found it difficult to believe a fellow knight would choose such ignominious tactics for battle, but he would not rule that out either.

Someone close to him had wanted him dead. Had they wished to prevent his trip to Connacht? The idea spurred him to think about what an enemy of his might mean to Sorcha's safety. Had he brought further danger to the princess's door without realizing it?

Straightening, Hugh brushed off the leaves and dirt of his short rest and whistled for the horse the Irish king had lent him. He would retrieve Sorcha at once and bring her to her father's court. If the old man was so concerned about keeping his eldest daughter safe, why would he leave her in a tenuous outpost of his kingdom with no guards but a stranger and a groom with little training to keep her safe? Hugh intended to find out precisely what sorts of threats the monarch perceived against Sorcha.

After Hugh's dream, he could not help but think the princess and her young son were both at risk for more reasons than those the king already feared. Hugh may have unwittingly drawn a dangerous old enemy to Connacht, and he was at a treacherous disadvantage since he wouldn't even recognize the man if he came face-to-face with him.

Chapter Ten

Sorcha could not decide which unsettled her more—facing her father for the first time since their heated argument over a year ago, or sitting next to Hugh after sharing an unexpected kiss the night before.

They waited in a small antechamber outside the keep's great hall, a room she had never spent much time in when she lived here since she'd never been a guest. Even after seeing her at the fair the day before, the servants did not seem to know how to treat her. They nodded awkwardly and mumbled their greetings, perhaps afraid of embracing the spurned daughter of the man who supported their livelihood.

"Is it his habit to make his guests wait?" Hugh asked, refusing the bread offered by a young maid Sorcha did not recognize. His legs sprawled from the seat of a narrow wooden chair that usually accommodated fleet-footed messengers instead of hulking knights. His fingers flexed against the arms of the seat, his jaw tight with frustration.

"That is not his intention, but it is frequently the case." Sorcha was surprised by a desire to smile at memories of her father that were not overshadowed by their final argument. "He is a well-meaning steward of these lands, but not always an organized one. He tends to listen long and hard to whomever has his attention at any given time and woe to those who had legitimate appointments."

In the years that she had helped him run the keep, she had spoken to him more than once about his tendency to make others wait—even when they were important visiting knights or barons. But no matter that her father agreed with her in theory, he still tended to get caught up in whatever situation arrived under his nose. That inattention of his was the only reason she'd managed to hide her impending babe from him for so long.

"We need to speak privately afterward," Hugh told her, rising to his feet in the chamber that boasted only one small tapestry of a battle at sea and a few worn rush mats that desperately needed changing.

"I have not spent much time with Conn," she fretted, regretting that she'd left the cottage before her son awoke this morning.

"This won't take long," he assured her, his hand resting on the hilt of a sword bearing her father's crest.

Hugh must have truly impressed the king to have gained a horse and a blade. It was highly unusual for a royal house to arm its knights or its men-at-arms—except when they were mounting a large campaign and needed extra warriors.

Could Hugh have made arrangements with her crafty sire that she knew nothing about?

While she hesitated, one of her father's men—Donngal— appeared in the doorway.

"He will see you now." His expression was hard. Hostile

even. Or at least it seemed that way to Sorcha until he looked at her.

He blushed then and turned on his heel.

Ah, she had hurt him once and had not intended to. He had wished to court her before she met Edward, but she had been opposed to showing interest in any of her father's men and had surely rebuffed him with unnecessary vigor. She regretted that now, knowing how a person's pride could be as fragile as his heart.

Hastening forward toward the great hall, Sorcha smoothed her skirts and straightened her veils, but she did not bow her head as she entered the large, airless chamber that could be sweltering hot in the summer and frigidly cold in winter. Even now, on a lovely spring day, the hall was still and stale smelling. A few ashes from the fire pit blew around the hearth in the only indication of a draft somewhere.

Her father was seated in his usual place, upon a small dais where he held court once a month to dispense justice to the villagers and collect accountings from the various men he'd put in charge of his mills and farms, sheep and dairy. Today, however, he merely met with a handful of knights whom he was in the process of dismissing.

Sorcha strode directly to the dais, ignoring the knights to present herself to her father. Tiernan Con Connacht was not so different from her in his temperament and the way he took his measure of people. She knew he would not respect meek humility from her even after all she'd done to irritate him. He had not raised his daughters to stand in the shadows and hope for acceptance, although Sorcha had been forced to take just such a position with his exile plan.

"Good morning, Father." She ducked a shallow curtsy, greeting him the same way she had countless mornings of her youth, then took a seat that one of the knights had just vacated. The rough trestle bench snagged on her worn surcoat, threatening to tear right through the silk that had been washed too many times over the last year. Sorcha had not been able to take the full extent of her wardrobe with her when she was banished, let alone all her furnishings and other possessions. Therefore, the garments she had taken with her had to be tended carefully.

The king's eyes followed her progress before he gave a bark of laughter.

"Cheeky wench," he pronounced at her modicum of deference, although he did not speak unkindly. His attention then turned to Hugh.

"Your request sounded urgent. Dare I hope you have made progress wooing my headstrong daughter so quickly?" The king raised his bushy eyebrows in a suggestive manner.

Embarrassment burned her skin as the other knights, except for Fergus, made their way out of the great hall. She could not help but see a couple of them chuckling at her expense as they adjusted their swords and pulled short capes over their tunics. Sorcha wrestled with an urge to leap to her feet and defend herself, but the king's watchful expression warned her perhaps this was some sort of test of her composure. She did not wish to give him the satisfaction of flying into an outburst.

Before she could think of a coolheaded rejoinder, Hugh stepped closer to the king to speak.

"I find it difficult to court a woman who is in grave danger. Perhaps we would meet with more success if Sorcha was not living on the fringes of the kingdom, prey to every outlaw, thief and invading enemy that patrols your borders." He took a seat on a trestle table, but instead of settling onto the bench, he made himself comfortable on the eating surface, putting him at almost eye level with the king. "Did your men tell you of the injury your daughter sustained last night at the fair?"

Her father's expression clouded. This was new terrain for them. Having an intermediary to intercede on her behalf could have felt like a loss of independence. But instead, she appreciated the presence of someone who could hold his own with the formidable Tiernan Con Connacht. The king's will was as renowned as his temper and Sorcha had gone toe-to-toe with her sire enough times in her life to appreciate a second line of defense. Or even, as in this case, a first.

"I heard she became unwittingly embroiled in a raucous children's game." He snapped his fingers for one of his hounds and the dog came forward immediately.

Sorcha could not help but think he would be more satisfied with his lot in life if everyone would respond to his orders so readily.

"We stood far from the tents, up on the hillside, and still she was a target. I do not think it a coincidence."

Her father's attention moved from Hugh to her.

"And I suppose this means you seek refuge in my keep?" He lifted an eyebrow, frowning as he motioned for his dog to sit beside him. The big hound settled on the floor, as quiet as Fergus in a chair near Sorcha.

"You told me to leave this keep, Father. I would never ask to return where I am not wanted." She regretted the words almost as soon as she said them. She should have used the opening to ask for Conn's safe return to the keep instead of marching out her pride.

"I think it would be wise to keep her where there is the necessary manpower to guard a princess." Hugh gestured to the great hall around them where extra weapons and fighting men sat during most hours of the day. "Either that, or assign men-at-arms to guard her at all times."

"Out of the question." Her father banged a fist on the arm of his chair, causing the hound to jump with a start. "I must prepare for war. I cannot spare any men to chase ghosts at the forest's edge."

It was what she had expected, although she could tell Hugh was surprised.

"Perhaps you are unaware of the dangers she faces alone." Hugh's voice became low and lethal. "I have reason to believe her son's father may yet live. He could pose a serious threat if he wishes to claim his child."

At the mention of Edward du Bois, her father's complexion mottled and then turned completely red. He gripped the arms of his chair and she half feared he would draw his sword.

"You will never speak to me of that Norman dog again." He raised his voice, blaring the message throughout the great hall. "Do we understand each other?"

Hugh narrowed his gaze. His silence spoke louder than her father's bluster. Fergus straightened in his seat as the confrontation tensed. The hound bristled and the fur on the back of its neck lifted.

Sorcha had not seen her father draw a blade in his own hall since she was a child, but the act was not unheard of. And she truly believed no topic had ever made him as angry as this one.

"Father, neither of us saw the body. And after hearing Eamon describe the blow Edward suffered in battle, Hugh believes it might not have been mortal." She hoped to share their concerns now, before her father became too enraged to be reasonable. "You know I do not ask for anything for myself. But I do not believe Conn should be placed in danger on the outskirts of the kingdom because of your anger with me."

Her father leaped from his chair in a swirl of crimson and blue robes that matched his scarlet tunic and azure-colored hose. His neck bulged with taut veins as he swallowed his anger down past a thick gold torc about his throat.

"All the more reason you should make ready for the convent and my grandson will take his place in my household." His icy glare froze her insides as she realized he meant every word. "I will write to the good sisters at once and see if they will accept you as soon as I can deliver you hence."

The words wounded her as no others could have. A cry of pain wrenched free from her lips.

"Sire," Hugh interjected, "if du Bois knows about his son, he will not rest until he leverages that connection by fair means or foul." He slipped off the table to stand on the same footing as the king. Hugh towered above him by a head, his easy stride at odds with her father's restless roaming about the chamber. A maid entered with a platter of food, but Fergus shook his head ever so slightly, sending the woman scuttling back to the kitchen with the breads and cheeses.

"That bastard will never breach these walls so long as I draw breath," the king swore.

"But will he breach the convent walls?" Hugh pressed, circling an abandoned pile of minstrels' instruments off to the side of the dais. "Your enemy could hold your daughter captive until you give him his son. Will you be able to turn your back on her so easily when she is threatened?"

Sorcha's belly tightened with a whole new fear she had not considered. She had been so focused on keeping Conn safe she had not thought about what lengths Edward might go to in order to obtain the boy. Her eyes flew to her father's face, unsure what his response might be and half-afraid to find out.

"My father would never barter away my son," Sorcha declared, saving her father from having to make a choice. Or, perhaps, saving herself from hearing her father make the correct choice. "Conn is worth ten of me, and no one knows this so well as the king."

Rising from her seat, she hoped this meeting had accomplished all Hugh had hoped for, since she could not sit still in her father's great hall for even one moment longer.

Without looking at Hugh, she simply turned and walked toward the door.

"I have tried to protect you, Sorcha," her father called. "You have never made it easy to keep you safe, but I have tried."

There was a weariness in his voice she had never heard before, a note of regret that plucked at her heart even after all this time. He was telling her that he had given up on her. But perhaps he did so with some misgivings. Hesitating, she slowed her step.

"I know. But some of us find it harder to be ruled than others." She knew it was nowhere near the apology and begging for forgiveness he'd always sought, but it was as close to an explanation as she'd ever attempted to make for her actions. "In that small way, at least, we are alike."

Striding away without another backward glance, she hoped Hugh would follow her out. It was enough that she'd been assured Conn would have a place in the kingdom. Now she knew for certain her father would accept him, and after the way he had banished her, that was more than she'd dared to hope for.

At the age of twenty-two summers, she had already betrayed her father by denying him the political alliances that should have been his by right through her marriage. She had borne a child without the blessing of a legal wedding and brought shame onto her family's name. Her sister might never make a good marriage because of her. True, she had delivered a beautiful boy into the world, but at what cost to everyone around her?

Out in the courtyard, she peered back to the keep to see Hugh approaching. And for the first time, she did not see a man who looked like Conn's father or a man who wanted to court her.

As her gaze roamed over his battle-hardened frame, she saw only a man who had kissed her. A man who cared enough about her to ask her father to relent on his terms for her exile.

No matter that Hugh did not know his name or his past, he had attempted to intercede with the king for her in a way no one else had ever dared. And looking at him right now, she could no longer see a man to be wary of.

Instead, she spied a knight who would be the last man to court her before she was sent to the convent. Her last chance to know some taste of passion before she relinquished all claim to worldly pleasure.

And suddenly, she no longer feared the temptations he'd shown her the night before. A more sophisticated woman now than she'd been after her false marriage, Sorcha understood what to do to prevent another pregnancy. Her midwife and her wet nurses had given her most valuable information on that score. Right now, with the upheaval of the meeting with her father still squeezing her heart tight, Sorcha longed for nothing more than to fling herself into Hugh's arms with all possible haste.

* * *

It took a supreme effort to unclench his fist as Hugh stalked back into the great hall for a word with Tiernan Con Connacht. He knew Sorcha was in a hurry to return home to her son, but he had made an excuse to return to the hall privately, explaining that her father might listen to reason if he could speak to him alone. She'd nodded an unhappy consent and he'd wasted no time retracing his steps.

"Sire." Hugh reentered the hall without an escort, ignoring the heated conversation the king seemed to be having with the knight closest to him. Fergus.

Both men looked up at him. Hugh didn't give them a chance to return to their conversation.

"I do not understand your actions." Frustration beat an angry rhythm through his veins. "You wished me to protect the princess without her knowledge because you said she is opposed to your guards. But she recognizes the dangers and came with me today to ask for protection, so why do you not—"

"Did she?" The king's expression darkened. "I heard her request protection for her son, not for herself. She is as obstinate as ever and I will not bring a willful and arrogant lass back into my keep. Her sister is young and impressionable, and I will not allow her chances of a good marriage to be compromised by Sorcha's influence."

The king glared at Hugh and then glared at Fergus, dispensing his warning looks equally. Had Fergus argued for more leniency with the princess as well? Perhaps he was an unexpected ally.

"So do not bring her to the keep. I merely ask for assistance in protecting her at the cottage." Hugh could not understand the old man's motives. "Whether or not you care for her any longer, she remains valuable to your enemies. If for no other reason than that, you should—"

"You will not tell the king his business." Tiernan flew out of his chair, his hand on the hilt of his sword, his face flushed with rage.

Hugh knew a moment's temptation to draw his own sword, but he was a more temperate man than that. He would not embroil himself in a civil uprising or international politics by pointing a blade at a sovereign king.

"As you wish. But I cannot fathom why I should pretend to court your daughter when we both know what she needs is a guardian at all times." The ruse made no sense and he resented deceiving her, especially after last night's kiss.

After her experience with Edward du Bois, Sorcha deserved better from Hugh than more lies.

"Well, you would not have gotten anywhere near my daughter if you had arrived at her gate with my blessing as her protector." Some of the flushed color drained from his face as he rocked back on his heels. The anger transformed into a self-satisfied smirk so fast that it made Hugh uneasy.

Suspicious.

"Nevertheless, there is no need to pretend now." He could not risk kissing her again while this untruth sat between them.

"Then you shall leave my lands as much a pauper as you entered them." The king returned to his seat beside Fergus, his fur-trimmed robe draped carelessly over the arm of his chair. "You are free to choose, Norman."

Hugh could not afford to choose freely. With no memory, no past and no home to return to, he had to rely on his reward to buy him the freedom to recover his identity. Having coin in his pocket would help assure he was not taken for a madman when he returned to England.

"Will you at least consider making Eamon a man-at-arms?" Hugh knew the groom had not been properly outfitted as a warrior.

"He has little training," Fergus entered the conversation for the first time and Hugh wondered if the knight was in charge of training the keep's fighting men.

"He is sharing the watch with me. He needs a fast horse and more weaponry," Hugh insisted, determined to wrest some compromise from this stubborn monarch. The maid returned with the tray of breads and cheeses and Fergus waved her deeper into the hall. The scent of the food reminded Hugh he had not eaten since yester eve.

"Aye," the king finally agreed. "I will see it done today if you send him to me. Onora will sew my crest upon a banner for him. Take Sorcha some food before you leave."

The king pointed the maid toward Hugh and she held out the platter to him. Sweet and savory breads had been cut into slices beside three kinds of cheese. Seeing that the food and a few more weapons was all he was likely to get out of the Irish king, Hugh helped himself to the maid's tray and turned to leave.

He was no closer to understanding the king's design, but at least he knew to expect no help from that quarter. Sorcha's mistake would be held against her for as long as the king's disappointment with his daughter remained. Judging by what Hugh had just heard, that could be a long, long time.

Still, Hugh was only obligated to protect Sorcha until she left for the convent. And it sounded like that time would approach much faster than either of them had originally thought.

He should be relieved that he only had to pretend to court her for another sennight or perhaps a fortnight at most. But given that Sorcha had been the only person in Connacht to betray any hint of recognition when they'd met, Hugh was not eager to lose his connection to her.

Besides, after the kiss they'd shared, he couldn't help but think that locking up such a beautiful, passionate woman for the rest of her days was too cruel. Sorcha was a devoted mother. A beloved sister. She did not deserve the fate her father would banish her to.

As he exited the great hall and spied her seated on a bale of hay near the rings where the horses were tied, Hugh promised himself he would thwart the king's plan for as long as possible. Even if that meant deceiving Sorcha against his will.

Chapter Eleven

"What would you do if you knew you had only a sennight to live?"

Sorcha had worried the question to pieces the whole ride back to the cottage, unsure how to handle her final days of freedom.

Such as it was.

She was an exile, banished from her home and her family. So it wasn't as if she could enjoy all the normal experiences she had grown up with—such as the early-morning breakfasts with her sister sneaking rolls from the kitchen before the household awakened. She could not sit at her favorite loom in her mother's old solar, weaving her daydreams into the bright colors her father's wealth could afford. Nor could she practice her skill with a crossbow in secret behind the keep, her aim a source of pride among the few men who'd been with her father since he was a mere baron with naught but a few farms to his name. She no longer had the luxuries she used to or the run of an extravagant household. But she did have her son and her own modest home. They had brought unexpected pleasures that surpassed many of her old experiences.

And yet, she did not know how to construct memories that would last her a lifetime in this short window she'd been given before she was handed over to the good sisters at a local abbey.

"I cannot answer well without knowing who I am," Hugh answered finally.

Sorcha had been so lost in her own thoughts as the trees grew denser near the cottage that she'd scarcely recalled that Hugh had been taking a long time to respond to her question. Now, she half regretted her query since it must call up frustrating reminders for him.

As Eamon approached them to take their horses, she asked herself how *would* a man spend his last days of freedom if he knew not his family, favorite activities or his most beloved friends?

"It was thoughtless of me—"

"No." He silenced her with a look as Eamon hastened his pace, his hand extended to take the reins while Hugh leaped to the ground. "Thank you, Eamon. You're wanted at the keep today. I will watch over things here if you can make haste to leave."

An unfathomable expression crossed Eamon's face. Worry? Sorcha was uncertain.

"I think my father wishes to reward you for your service," she assured him, not wanting him to dread the meeting the whole way across her father's sprawling lands.

The groom nodded his thanks but did not look as reassured as she thought he might be. Nevertheless, he held the reins for her courser as Hugh helped her down.

She noticed the feel of Hugh's hands upon her waist.

Though he touched her with quick efficiency, the warmth of his palms seeped through her gown to heat the skin beneath. Each finger left an enticing imprint before he released her.

Surely it was only because she had allowed herself to think about indulging in such pleasures during her last days outside the convent that her mind ran so quickly to fleshly desires. Because if not for the sudden knowledge that her time as a layperson was almost over, she would never consider inviting a Norman into her bed again.

As Eamon departed with their mounts for the stables, Hugh's palm landed on her back once again.

"Are you all right?" His voice stroked her senses like a minstrel's fingers plucked his instrument, coaxing a sweet, singing response that fairly vibrated right through her.

"Fine," she blurted, unsure of herself. Of him. She had merely opened a mental door when she thought about making a forbidden memory with Hugh. She had not committed to the idea in fact.

Had she?

"You look a bit nervous. I hope you do not doubt my ability to keep you safe."

Ah, she did not doubt this man's ability on any level. Therein lay the problem. There was a subtle self-assurance about Hugh's touch. His speech. The way he moved through the world. She admired the way he had confronted her father, even if he had not won all he wished. Edward had not the courage to seek out her father during battle to ask for her hand. He had merely solved the problem by marrying her quietly.

Hugh would have never settled for such a solution, and she appreciated his stalwart strength. His determination to follow through on what he felt was right.

How many men could have made the journey he had—

with no memory of the past—and land in the good graces of a notoriously temperamental monarch?

"I trust in your sword arm." She looped her hand about his sleeve, reminding herself of his capable power. Her hand strayed onto hard muscle, the delineations apparent through the thin fabric of his soft linen tunic.

"Sorcha." He halted their progress toward the cottage when they were a stone's throw from the riot of budding roses around the front door.

He said nothing for a long moment, merely staring at her with his gold-flecked eyes that seemed to glow from within. All at once she realized what her touch had done to him. His face wore an expression not unlike the one it bore the day she lifted her skirts to catch Conn's kitten.

Only now, the look did not scare her away.

"Aye?" She let her fingers trail along his forearm in the subtlest of caresses, taking in the warm, virile strength of him as if she could absorb his might right into her skin.

"You play with fire," he warned her, his gaze flicking down the length of her body with a slow, measured stare. By the time his glance returned to hers, she was fairly humming with awareness. "But I think you already know that."

"I have been thinking about how I would spend my final few days of freedom," she confessed, keeping her voice down in case Conn's nurse lurked near an open window.

"And what conclusions have you reached?" He halted her roving fingertips by clapping his big hand on top of hers, imprisoning her between his arm and his palm.

Her heart stuttered in her chest because she knew he had guessed her wayward thoughts. She bit her lip, less sure of herself as she stood so close to him, enveloped in the heat of frank, masculine interest.

"I have not." She swallowed back the other words that had warred for dominance on her tongue. "There are so many reasons to consider besides what I would like."

His dark eyebrows lifted. She had caught him off guard. He recovered quickly, however, and he leaned closer to speak softly in her ear.

"If I were you, and I faced life within an abbey's walls, I would not consider anyone but myself. And, Conn, of course," he clarified, his words a heated rasp against her ear. "But until you can be certain about what you want, you would be wise not to stoke fires that will burn you unnecessarily."

She nodded her understanding, but the movement was jerky. She tried to blink away the sensation he stirred inside her, but found her eyelids heavy.

Spellbound by the man and the moment, she splayed her free hand on his chest. Just to steady herself, she thought. But she ended up leaning closer, her mouth watering for another kiss that would help her make up her mind—

The cottage door unlatched from the inside. The scrape of metal against wood warned her away from Hugh and she stumbled back.

"My lady," Conn's nurse greeted her, the woman's eyes drooping with exhaustion. She held Conn in her arms, and the child whined pitifully. "I think he misses you."

Immediately, Sorcha relinquished her hold on Hugh and she hurried toward the cottage.

Hugh could not imagine that he had been a father, since Sorcha's instant abandonment of him for her child felt highly foreign to him.

Unlike swinging a sword or kissing a woman, being

tempted sorely one moment and then overlooked for a chubby and bleating little boy was not familiar ground for him. And while the abandonment was not exactly flattering, he admired her gentle way with the child.

"Of course he misses Mama," Sorcha cooed, holding her arms wide to receive her son. "My precious boy!"

Hugh bit back the tide of lust that had been sweeping through him just moments before. Fascinated by Sorcha's transition from a sensual woman into doting mother, Hugh followed her into the cottage past the bleary-eyed nurse. The woman picked up a satchel from the floor by the door and bid goodbye to her mistress before heading toward the stable. Did the nurse have quarters there as well?

He might have asked, but Sorcha was busy juggling her son from one hip to another, keeping up a running commentary about everything from how much she'd missed him to how strong a knight he would make one day.

"…and he will carry the broadest sword and rule with the bravest heart," she told the wide-eyed little boy who bore more of a resemblance to his dark-haired auntie than Sorcha herself.

Conn, for his part, seemed more interested in seeing how tightly he could wind his mother's long, auburn curls around his plump fingers. Clearly, Hugh had lost his chance to be alone with Sorcha. But perhaps the anticipation would make the pleasure stronger if he got another opportunity.

"…and they will bow low to their king," Sorcha told Conn, bending forward as she said it so that the boy's baby-fine hair nearly brushed the straw mats on the cottage floor.

While the boy squealed with delight, Hugh did not bother to hide his interest in the curvy, delectable picture Sorcha presented with her antics. She was too overcome with motherly joy to notice where Hugh's eyes lingered anyhow.

"Would you like to speak in the garden, Sorcha?" he asked, helping himself to the sideboard where the nurse must have laid out some ale and a few berries in a heavy stone bowl. "I will bring you something to eat."

He still had the bread and cheese her father had insisted he take, although he'd have to visit the stables to retrieve them since he'd left them tied to his horse's saddle.

"That would be lovely." She smiled at him over her shoulder, her mood brightened immeasurably by the child she held in her arms. She did not seem to notice how the boy tugged her head sideways with the fistful of luscious red curls.

"I'll meet you outside in a moment," he assured her, patting the boy's silky head before peering out a small window to gauge the distance to the stables. He could not roam too far from the woman he needed to protect. Her father might not take the threat against her seriously, but Hugh damn well did.

Laughing and playing, Sorcha wandered off with her charge, her hips swaying as she walked barefoot into a private chamber away from the main room. The cottage was small, but it had been cleverly designed to afford private sleeping quarters between the main room and the walled garden. A small cluster of buildings ringed the cottage but at a fair distance. Besides the stable, there was a kitchen with little more than a storage cellar and a hearth for cooking. Hugh assumed the other shelters were living quarters for guests and perhaps a garderobe. All of the smaller buildings bore thatched roofs like a crofter's hut, the materials blending into the hilly landscape so well they weren't apparent until one strayed close to them.

Leaving Sorcha to share a moment with her son, Hugh

hastened to the stable. True enough, he wanted to retrieve the food stores. But he had left them purposely to speak with Eamon privately.

When he entered the stable, however, the groom did not appear overly eager to make his trip to the king's keep. He had backed Conn's nurse against a wall, his hands thrust into the bodice of her kirtle to free generous breasts. The woman's cap had fallen off and her fair hair spilled over her shoulders to shield most of her nakedness. Only a hint of pink nipple jutted through the flaxen veil as her lover rammed his hips tight to hers.

Thankfully, the lad's braies were still tied about his hips.

"Eamon." Hugh didn't care what the man did on his own time, but he did not consider this to be an hour of leisure for the groom. He should be seeing the king to arm himself for guarding his mistress, not losing himself in a woman.

The thought reminded Hugh how close he'd come to losing himself in Sorcha's kiss just moments before.

The nurse squealed her dismay as she struggled to cover herself, but Hugh had no interest in her embarrassment. At least Eamon had the sense to look shamefaced, his cheeks flushed with more than thwarted lust.

"I am leaving for the keep immediately," he sputtered as he yanked the ties on his tunic to pull the garment into place.

"A word with you first, please." He eyed the woman, who appeared frozen in place now that her clothes were on once again. "Alone."

The nurse sprinted for the door, her coarse leather shoes slapping the dirt floor as she ran out. Hugh took a moment to tamp down his anger while he watched her depart.

Eamon cleared his throat. "The woman does not know of my role in protecting—"

Hugh raised his forearm to the groom's throat and backed him into the stable wall. Eamon's head whacked into the worn boards, his eyes wide as Hugh's arm pressed against his throat.

"You will not forsake your duty to the princess again or I will ensure you never serve the king in this lifetime." He lifted his arm enough to put some pressure on Eamon's jaw, tipping his chin up so he could look Hugh in the eye.

Hugh would make sure his message got through to the lad.

Eamon made a gurgling noise, his face suffused with more color than his guilt had given him earlier. Reluctantly, Hugh released some of the pressure on his throat.

"Are we clear about that?" he asked, needing confirmation that Eamon understood exactly what was expected of him.

"Aye." Eamon gave a small nod, his movements still impeded by Hugh's grip.

"Excellent." Hugh stepped back, knowing he'd taken out more frustration on the groom than was necessary, but when the king refused to protect his own daughter with any more men than Hugh and one undisciplined youth, it made him angry. "Leave now so you can take a watch by nightfall."

Eamon pushed himself off the wall and wasted no time heading for his horse. Hugh watched him leave as he retrieved the food stores still tied to his saddle. Clearly the groom had done little more than undress the nurse since they'd returned from their trip.

Fuming silently, he left the stables and returned to the cottage, determined to keep a closer eye on Eamon and knowing well it wouldn't be easy to do when Hugh needed to keep an even better watch on Sorcha now that he knew Eamon was more interested in his own needs than the princess's.

He could only hope that the king's faith in Eamon would give the younger man a new appreciation for what a large opportunity he was being offered to raise himself up in the world. Because Eamon's sword arm and attentive watch might one day be the only things that stood between Sorcha and the enemy that lurked ever closer.

Why did Hugh remain here?

Sorcha watched the hulking warrior make a tentative peace with her son. Conn had been intimidated by Hugh at first, holding tight to her skirts whenever she placed him on the ground during their small meal. But Hugh seemed to be winning the boy over with a gentle game of chase through the fruit trees, where Hugh would hide behind the trunks until Conn caught up, keeping the distance between them close. Conn laughed with childish delight each time Hugh disappeared and then reappeared from behind a tree.

All of which entertained her with a bittersweet reminder of what her son was missing in life by not having a father. But the pleasure she took in the game did not account for Hugh's continued presence. Surely chasing a wee babe through the gardens was not the sort of pastime most men would prefer while courting. So what was his true motive?

Hugh darted and feinted from one side to another as the two of them squared off beside a small sundial covered in moss. Conn made to move to the right, and Hugh followed suit, now on his knees. Then Conn hopped to the left on his wobbly, baby legs and Hugh did the same. Mostly, Conn giggled and held his belly until Hugh toppled over as if defeated by a stronger foe.

Sorcha studied his face as he mimicked minor death throes that did not even fool a child. She wondered if he had children in his native lands, since she could not envision any man playing so easily without having some experience at the games that would amuse a little tot. The thought sobered her good humor until she rose from the ground to scoop up her son.

"Did I scare him?" Hugh asked, sitting up suddenly from where he'd been convulsing so recently. "I did not mean to give the boy a fright."

Her mother's heart warmed at his concern and for the first time, she wondered if she should consider Hugh's courtship after all. Perhaps he played with her son to demonstrate his ability as a father, and his seemingly natural ease with Conn had all been carefully orchestrated to persuade her.

"Nay, you did not frighten him." She kissed Conn's warm cheek and stroked his baby-soft hair. "I only thought he might be ready to nap now that he has eaten and played. I do not wish to detain you and I know you hoped to speak with me."

That was only part of the truth. The other was that it tore at her heart to go through the motions of a family tableau, knowing they might all be separated in another fortnight.

Conn's nurse emerged from the cottage before Sorcha could seek her out and she handed over her son. The nurse was unusually quiet as she took him, her eyes darting over to Hugh before she ducked back into the doorway with the boy in her arms.

"We wish to speak privately, Enid," Sorcha called after the younger woman. "You may rest after Conn falls asleep."

"I did want to speak to you," Hugh answered as he rose from the ground and dusted off the dirt and leaves clinging to his tunic. "But I did not mean to send Conn away early. He is a sweet lad."

"I cannot help but think a man might say as much if he hoped to woo a mother," Sorcha replied cautiously, walking closer to where the remnants of the meal still lay upon the ground. As much as she had begun to consider the option of an alliance with Hugh to escape her fate in a convent, Sorcha knew she must question her every impulse when it came to men.

She had been so wrong on so many levels last time. It was one thing to consider a dalliance with a man as a last selfish act before entering a nunnery. It was another entirely to bind her life and Conn to him when he might be as untrustworthy as Edward. She had no reason to suspect Edward would deceive her. So it hardly mattered to her now that she had little reason to mistrust Hugh.

He laughed now as he lowered himself to the ground beside her.

"You are probably right, but in this case, I stand by my assessment. Your son is a good-natured lad, and I think you must know it's true enough. If I had raved over his disposition while he cried and pummeled me with tiny fists, you would have better reason to suspect my words."

Hugh stretched his long legs in the direction of the catmint and parsley. He'd situated himself close to her, but not so close she could take offense at his presumption. He leaned to one side to retrieve the wine he'd placed in the brook during their meal. The water was shallow, but it was spring fed and cold, providing the cottage with a fresh supply.

"You wished to speak with me," she prodded, unwilling to be lulled into thinking a future with Hugh would be the romantic haven she'd once dreamed her parents had enjoyed.

"Yes." He held the wine aloft, letting the water roll off the jug for a moment before settling it on the turf between them. "More wine?"

She knew strong drink should be consumed in moderation, but if she joined the local priory she would have the rest of her days to contemplate moderation. She nodded and held out her cup, a bone-and-jeweled receptacle that had belonged to her mother's wealthy family before finding their way into her dowry.

And all at once she understood her importance to Hugh.

"What has my father promised you if I agree to marriage?" Just this morning her father had asked Hugh if he had made progress wooing her. No doubt her crafty sire had merely pretended not to endorse the Norman mercenary's courtship.

In truth, he would gladly hand her off to anyone who was not a common peasant for a hefty sum of gold. While she'd lost much value for many good political alliances, she might be worth enough coin for Hugh to reclaim a life as a knight, even if he never recalled his past.

"We have not discussed marriage." He drank directly from the jug since he had not been able to locate a second cup when he brought out their meal. "How could we when I do not know my own past? I could not even claim a keep to house you."

Sorcha sipped the cold wine, allowing the flavors to flood her tongue as she watched Hugh, more confused than ever. She thought about his resemblance to Edward and weighed the consequences of confiding that small piece of information. What if Hugh was related to the man she'd once called husband? Could Hugh have come to Connacht to reclaim Edward's son for him? Perhaps that had been his mission and he simply did not remember it. If so, would he turn on her once she confided her fears?

Or was there a chance—given how vehemently he'd

pleaded her case in front of her father—that he would continue to protect her no matter what dark alliances his past might hold?

"Tell me, Sorcha." Hugh had set down the jug and he reached for her now, his hand settling on her arm with a gentle heat that muddled her thoughts on contact. "Do you wish to wed?"

Chapter Twelve

He hadn't intended it as a proposal.

Hugh could see that Sorcha had taken it that way at once, however. Her green eyes widened in surprise, her lips parting with a small gasp. Some vein close to the surface of her skin leaped in nervous protest at her throat.

Or did her heart pound for other reasons altogether?

Hugh had been fighting his attraction to her all day with little success and the sparks leaping between them now could hardly be denied.

"My father wanted me to wed one of his allies once. A gouty old king in the south who used to visit our keep and pinch me through my surcoat long before I became a woman." Sorcha told the story without prelude, the words tumbling from her lips faster than he could take them in. "I ran from the threat of that marriage into a false union that has caused my father grief and shame. I do not think I can trust his judgment or mine when it comes to nuptials."

"So you do not wish to wed anyone?" He found her response curious. Even if he hadn't meant to propose a match between them, he was very intrigued about what she wanted. "Not even if it meant avoiding the convent and having a chance to raise your son?"

His hand moved over her arm without his permission, indulging in her softness. He'd felt protective toward this woman from the moment they'd met and now, having seen her spar with her father and shower her son with love, his emotions for her were even more complex. All he understood for certain was that he admired her.

And, yes, he wanted her.

"I want to be with Conn." She spoke softly, but he heard her conviction resonate through her voice. "But if I make a bad marriage, I will have the rest of my days to contemplate it and only a few years to enjoy the comfort of seeing my son grow. He will be taken away to be fostered and then I'll be at the mercy of whatever man has settled for me. Do you think a fallen woman will be treated well by her new husband? For that matter, do you think my son will be treated well?"

"Your father would never allow harm to come to—"

"Will he not? He allowed me to birth my son in the middle of the woods with no company save a young, inexperienced nurse. I do not trust him to intercede for Conn against a stepfather, especially one who did him the favor of marrying his banished daughter."

The bitterness in her voice sliced through him and he wondered what it would have been like to meet this extraordinary woman before life had dealt her such blows. He fingered a tiny bow sewn on the shoulder of her surcoat, a silken extravagance grown limp with many washings.

Exile might have left her old gowns faded, but it had not dimmed her spirit.

"You should be ruling a kingdom instead of languishing in a remote cottage."

"Pretty words for a warrior." She cocked her head sideways, as if seeing him anew. Only then did she seem to become aware of his hand upon her shoulder. Perhaps because his errant fingers had untied the ribbon there.

Their gazes met. Held.

The air in the garden grew thick and combustible.

"I speak the truth." He skimmed a finger along the ribbon that edged her bodice, following the binding down her collarbone to hover just above her breast. Only the soft creamy linen of her kirtle prevented his finger from brushing her bare skin.

"Men do not speak the truth, but rather what is expedient." She lifted her cup to her mouth and took another sip of wine before replacing the container nearby. "I believe you would tell me whatever might land you in my bed right now."

Surprise glued his tongue to the roof of his mouth. The cheek of her. But was she correct?

His restless touches certainly supported the theory.

"I do not seek to seduce you." He pulled his hand back, relinquishing his hold on her with more than a little regret.

"Perhaps you have forgotten the nature of seduction along with all hints of your past, because I assure you, those touches are hardly accidental." Her surcoat slipped off her shoulder where he'd untied the ribbon, leaving a small patch of skin clad in no more than a kirtle so thin he could see her flesh beneath it.

His mouth dried up at the sight. His whole body tensed as he realized she did nothing to replace the fallen garment. She merely gazed back at him with all-knowing green eyes that seemed to issue him a challenge.

Or was she merely testing him?

"I want you, Sorcha. But I have nothing to offer you until I recover my memories, and even then—" He might be promised to another. He could not forswear himself by making vows to one woman if he'd obligated himself to another.

"You're wrong." She leaned back on her elbow, half reclining on their soft turf blanket while the brook babbled nearby. "You have something I want very much."

Everything inside him stilled. Waiting.

He watched as she turned on her hip to face him, her long, siren's hair cloaking her in fiery softness. She toyed with the ribbon he'd loosened, her fingers trembling ever so slightly as they plucked at the free end. Her eyes remained downcast, giving him no hint what she had in mind.

"I would know all the mysteries of physical pleasure before I must leave the secular world forever." When she met his gaze, it was through the veil of her long lashes. The glance seared him, her desire as plainly written as any missive.

Words eluded him. Thought pretty much shut down too, leaving him burning up with the need to give her exactly what she'd asked for. Honor held him back. But he sensed those chains were more fragile than the delicate blooms that blossomed all around them.

"Surely you have not forgotten how to please a woman?" she teased him, her tone sweetly chiding. Yet he sensed a new worry underneath it, an insecurity she would not want him to see.

"I—" The sound came out with feral edge and he swallowed it. Tried again. "I think it's like fighting. I have no specific memory of training or any battles. Yet I know well how to wield my sword."

Her grin fanned the flames inside him as a wicked glint lit her eyes.

"I would like to be the beneficiary of your skill with a weapon, I think." She leaned closer, her hand landing on his chest to graze the ties of his tunic.

Heaven help him. If this was not a wise act, he required divine intervention. Quickly.

His heart thudded beneath Sorcha's hand, his whole body straining toward her. His fingers aching to tunnel through her hair and cup the back of her neck. He wanted to kiss his way down her bodice and peel away her garments to lay her bare on the grass for his pleasure. He wanted to spread her thighs and taste her desire until she bucked beneath him, shaking with need for him.

Then he wanted to bury himself so deep inside her he'd replace every forgotten memory with the vivid image of Sorcha wrapped all around him, his name on her lips…

And then he recalled her request and the careful wording of it.

I would know all the mysteries of physical pleasure.

"Did you not know pleasure in the past?" He restrained from touching her, unable to place his hands upon her until he was certain that touching her was the right thing to do.

He guessed that the next time his hands strayed to Sorcha's delectable body, he would not be able to remove them until he'd wrested heated sighs of completion from her full, pink mouth.

Her hands were another matter.

They traced intricate patterns on his chest, unfastening the laces of his tunic to brush teasing caresses along his bare flesh.

"I do not think so." She bit her lip and frowned. "Either

that, or the joys of coupling were vastly overestimated in the stories I have heard."

Ah, Hugh did not think Hercules himself could have accomplished the feat of leaving now. Her son was safely asleep in the cottage with his nurse while Hugh watched over Sorcha in the enclosed garden. They were as safe from harm as possible and he fulfilled his duty. What man could leave an experienced, passionate woman questioning the enticements of sexual union?

Sorcha did not seek to trap him into marriage. She knew of his circumstances and his lost memory. She only wanted a taste of pleasures her oafish first lover had not bothered to give her.

Hugh could not begin to deny her.

For the second time in her life, she was going to commit the rashest of acts.

But it hardly seemed fair that she had taken such a chance last time and was still paying the consequences, yet she'd never been fully rewarded with the joys. If she was to be punished until the end of her days for letting her passions get the best of her, she would at least be able to say she'd wrested every drop of pleasure from the experience.

Hugh covered her hand with his, pressing her fingers to his chest with firmer pressure. He held her there for a moment, allowing her to feel the fierceness of his heartbeat.

She braved a glance up into his amber eyes and knew at once he would give her everything she wanted and more. He might not recall any lover before her, but he knew precisely what to do. And the knowledge set all her secret places to humming with anticipation.

He could not have excited her more with a physical touch.

"I will please you," he vowed, releasing her hand to trace the binding along her bodice the way he'd done earlier.

Only this time, he did not stop when his finger reached the curve of her breast. He gripped the heavy silk of her surcoat and tugged it down, exposing her breast cloaked in naught but the creamy linen of her kirtle.

She gasped at the sensations. The rough and the gentle. The gallop of her heart and the shallow, tiny hitch of her breath. Her eyes drifted closed and her other senses sharpened. The scent of flowers and grass floated over her as Hugh's mouth nipped the aching fullness of her breast through the kirtle.

"Oh!" She clutched his shoulders, arching into him, but he would not be hurried.

He nipped her again, always just missing the tight, beaded crest that rose up for his kiss.

For a moment, she considered making her expectations for pleasure a bit more clear and precisely drawn out. But then his mouth clamped around her nipple, his tongue laving the taut point through the fabric and she nearly screamed with the lush pleasure of it. Her hands stroked his hair, her fingers winding through the silky dark mass to hold him where she wanted him.

He groaned against her, his tongue vibrating with the sound in a way that sent sweet shivers to her feminine core. She wriggled closer, pressing her body against his chest as he tugged off more of her surcoat and unveiled her other breast.

With a stretch and a roll of her shoulders, she edged the kirtle down to fall away from her chest and bare her completely. Her garments hung loose about her waist, twisting about her hips as she whimpered with the feel of his teeth gently scraping along her sensitive flesh.

"Hugh." She sighed his name with a throaty plea, infusing all her longing into that one word.

Losing her virginity had been painful after a reasonably exciting build-up and she did not want to topple from this heady precipice when Hugh had built her anticipation so thoroughly.

"I want to reach the same dizzying heights of pleasure that a man can," she confided, her thoughts crystallizing in a way she hoped he would understand.

He chuckled softly as he lifted his head and stared down at her, the sunlight playing beautiful shadows across the stark planes of his face.

"You are still worried, Princess?" He reached to gather the hem of her skirts and slowly raised the fabric up.

"You may remember the basics of—um—swordplay. But since you have no *particular* memories to go by, I do not want to risk being disappointed." Her legs trembled as he released the hem of the surcoat to pool the fabric behind her.

Next he tugged her kirtle up.

She shifted her legs together, clamping her thighs tight to hold on to the pleasant tingles their play incited.

"You are right. I have no woman but you to think about now. No woman but you to remember." He rolled her onto her back so that her raised skirts made a bed against the grass for her bare skin. "Do you know how much a man wants to please the first woman he's with?"

His gaze lowered to take in her mostly naked body in the warm sunlight. With her gowns twisted about her waist, the lower half raised and the upper half lowered, she was thoroughly exposed.

And desperately eager.

"I have heard that a man is often overexcited with his first woman." She had probably listened to far too many maids' tales when it came to coupling, but she had wanted to be sure she pleased her husband. Those same maids had told her how to prevent pregnancy, but the instructions had come after she had been expecting Conn. She saw no cause to hide her knowledge with Hugh.

And perhaps she took a little pleasure in surprising him.

His gaze lifted to hers, his eyes narrowing as he raised himself over her and lowered his hips to graze lightly over hers.

"Ah, but a man is also stiff as a scythe handle and strong as an ox with his first woman, so I still say, you will not be disappointed."

The long, hard length of him tantalized her right through his braies. She could not play at teasing him any longer. Her thighs were damp with moisture from between her legs and she could not hide how much she wanted this.

Wanted him.

Reaching between them, she stroked him through the heavy fabric, her palm massaging him from base to tip. The strings had come undone at some point, but whether she had untwined them or he had, she could not recall. Once she noticed the gap, she freed him, unleashing his shaft to rest on her thigh.

She edged downward, more than ready to open herself to him. Already, her experience with Hugh was so much more intense than her first time. She knew the rest had to be better. More delicious. More decadent.

"Just a moment," he cautioned, holding her wriggling, panting, restless body in place with one broad hand planted on her belly. The heel of his hand grazed the curls between her legs, the warmth of the touch making her squirm.

"Yes?" Her hips arched in spite of herself. But she would not let anything stop this sweet, swelling feeling inside her. And if Hugh needed a few reminders along the way about what a woman liked, she was more than prepared to give them for the sake of a memory that had to last her whole life.

"I am fiercely thirsty." His eyebrows scrunched as he wet his lips and, lifting up on his elbow, he peered around for the wine cup.

She wanted to shriek with the frustration of waiting, but she felt around the grass until she found her cup and handed it to him with a wellspring of patience she did not know she possessed.

He settled between her thighs in a way that struck her as more than a little unseemly, his chest level with the thatch of red-gold curls between her legs. He studied her for a moment, his face inscrutable.

All the while, she willed him to lift the cursed cup to his lips.

Instead, he positioned the cup just above her mound. Too late, she saw his intent. One strong arm pinned her hips to the ground as he lowered his mouth to her…

Oh *my*.

He tipped the cup to pour the liquid over her slick, secret places. With his tongue, he caught the wine in great, messy laps, stroking her sex.

She squealed because it was unexpected. And then she squealed because it was the most exquisite bliss. Hugh set aside the cup at some point, but his bold kisses did not cease. He covered her mouth with his hand, perhaps to quiet her, but she could not help the urgent sounds she made.

She turned her head from side to side on the grass, searching for some relief from the knot of sweet tension building inside her. She'd never known such delicious distress, but not for all the world did she want it to cease. Her nails grazed Hugh's shoulders, her hips twisting against his chest to accommodate the breadth of him. Or, perhaps, to increase the pressure of his mouth as he lapped the most sensitive spot.

All at once, the urgent build inside her paused. As if she ran toward some precipice and then hesitated at the last, everything within her stilled for a long moment. The day burned itself into her memory in that instant, and she knew she would never forget one detail of this decadent revelation.

Then, the momentum of their passion shoved her over the edge, catapulting her into a sea of dark and heady sensations. Her body convulsed with wave after wave of luscious pleasure. The tide carried her deep into the bliss she'd been seeking, only the feeling was like nothing she could have imagined. The carnal joy of it blinded her, blocking out everything except the sensations causing a fiery riot within.

Hugh held her through it all, his body the rock she clung to while passion had its way with her. His legs tangled with hers, his arms wrapping around her to anchor her tight. It took a long while for her to catch her breath, but when she did, she did not hesitate to urge him on. She knew he had not reached the amazing heights that she had. While ending their tryst now might leave her both satiated and safe from the consequences of further intimacy, she would not repay this man's generous tutoring by sending him away frustrated.

For that matter, she would not risk sending him into another woman's arms to assuage his hunger.

"I am well pleased," she whispered in his ear, stroking

her fingers through his dark hair then edging lower to caress his shoulders. His back. His hips. "But until I benefit from all that hard strength you spoke of earlier, I do not believe we are finished."

Chapter Thirteen

No man's loyalties should be so divided.

Eamon did not care greatly about the Irish king or the Norman knight who wanted him to steal Princess Sorcha's child. But he cared very much about choosing the path that would win him the most gold. The most envy of his peers. And right now, with the king holding his new weaponry for him and new orders from the Norman knight that instructed him to bring the little boy into the woods with all haste, Eamon could not decide which task to take on first.

The king was notoriously fickle and impatient.

The Norman was notoriously dangerous.

Turning his horse back in the direction of the cottage, Eamon prayed he could accomplish both duties without either party being the wiser. With gold from Bartlett and du Bois, plus a horse and the trappings of a knight from Connacht, Eamon would be dining in the great hall and swiving every wench from dairy maid to lord's daughter in no time.

Urging his mount faster, he knew the time was opportune. The boy's nurse had panted after him like a bitch in heat. She would be easily managed. As long as the princess and her new protector were otherwise occupied, he could meet Bartlett at his encampment and still reach the king's keep by nightfall.

"Eamon!"

A feminine cry echoed through the forest. Only, the sound did not come from in front of him where the cottage sat. No, this call came from somewhere behind him.

Reining in, he turned. Perplexed.

He was far from the king's courtyard. Far from the road. He did not expect to encounter anyone save the occasional outlaw or beggar. Neither of which should know his name.

"Here!" The sound was closer this time, the voice mingling with the pound of hoofbeats through the woods.

He recognized the sweet tone of the lady's voice at the same moment he recognized the complete lack of caution. The innocence blossoming into feminine wile.

Considering all he needed to accomplish this afternoon, she was also quite possibly his worst nightmare.

"Lady Onora." Slapping the reins lightly, he walked to meet her as she slowed her palfrey to a trot. "Where is your escort?"

He did his best to appear disapproving, but in truth, he could not help but admire the lady's boldness even as he acknowledged her foolhardiness. She was utterly vulnerable to any unsavory types in the forest. Thieves and outlaws. Ambitious grooms whose needs for willing female flesh had been thwarted by Hugh Fitz Henry.

Eamon ground his teeth just thinking about how close he'd come to burying himself between the plump thighs of the wet nurse.

"I cannot stay long." Onora peered over her shoulder. "I

thought you might escort me back to the keep since, as I understood it, you were on your way to see us anyway."

A secretive smile graced her features, lighting up her lovely face. She had always held him at arm's length before, burying her obvious interest in him as a man beneath the cool disdain of her lofty position. But something seemed to have shifted in her attitude today. Some restraint had been lifted.

"It would be an honor—" except that he needed to kidnap her nephew "—except that I must return to the cottage first. I do not know how soon I will be able to depart for your father's lands."

She peered around the wood as if taking stock of her place in it. Her dark hair had fallen free of some of the plaits holding it back and her circlet was askew. She was more than passing fair; her creamy skin and wide, blue eyes were often heralded by troubadours and lovesick squires. Any man would hasten to do her bidding. Except for him. Except for today.

"We are not far. I will come with you and see my sister before we head back." She smiled prettily, seemingly unconcerned with her disheveled appearance from what must have been a hard ride through the woods. "Perhaps you have not heard what good news awaits you."

Her coy glances were not the practiced flirtation he was accustomed to, but that did not dim her appeal in the least. The fact that she would pay attention to him reminded him of the pleasures that would be his if only he could appease two competing masters.

Unfortunately, her timing could not have been worse. Stealing away Sorcha's brat would have to wait.

"I have received all the good news I can hope for in

meeting a lovely lady in the forest." He rode closer, holding his hand out to her to see what she would do.

Was the younger sister as passionate as the elder? Perhaps he wouldn't have long to wait to find out.

She stared at his hand for a long moment, biting her lip with sweet indecision. Then, at last, she extended her fingers, allowing him to kiss the back of her knuckles in a courtier's greeting. He kept it short, unwilling to rush this newest conquest that could turn out to be the biggest prize of any he'd sought yet.

Because if he was able to bed the king's daughter, he wouldn't think about faking his death to escape the consequences the way the Norman knight had. Nay, Eamon would hold out both hands and let the king rain a small fortune on his head to wed the eager maid.

"I pay no attention to your idle flattery, Eamon," Onora chided. "We meet each other in this wood often enough when I leave gifts for my sister. I bring tidings that offer much better news than my presence."

She tossed her head and withdrew her hand from his, but he could see his compliment did not leave her cold. He rode as close to her as he dared on the path back to the king's stronghold, his thigh grazing hers for an instant as they squeezed between two fat hawthorn trees.

"I find that hard to believe," he lied, entertaining himself by pulling off her garments in his mind.

Saints above, perhaps he had been setting his sights too low all this time. What if Onora Con Connacht was within his reach? Eamon would be the king's son-in-law. For that matter, if Eamon helped kidnap Sorcha's child, one day perhaps Eamon's own son would be in line for a kingdom.

A fortune. A powerful future.

"But it's true," she argued, peering at him over her shoulder. "My father has asked me to work on a banner bearing his colors for you."

Her lush figure swayed enticingly as her horse picked its way through the dense forest. Somewhere in the trees, Bartlett awaited Eamon's arrival with the boy. He hoped the fat clerk saw him riding with Onora to give him an idea that he was not some lowly groom to order about anymore. He was well on his way to bigger dreams than mere knighthood. By seducing a princess, he would gain untold power. Lands.

And a future no mere groom could have ever imagined for himself.

Sweat trickled down Hugh's back as he lay, legs twined, with the most tempting woman imaginable.

He had been entrusted with her protection, but somehow he had allowed his ruse of courting her to spill over into his true feelings. And he didn't have a prayer of calling back those emotions now. Not when she had just offered him sweet release after holding back to give her the pleasure that must have eluded her with her first lover. She gazed at him now with a mixture of wonder and determination in her green eyes.

"I can walk away now," he assured her, hoping and praying that was the case even though the thought of ending this interlude struck a blow more vicious than the one he'd endured in the dreams of his past. "I would not be responsible for more years of exile, Sorcha. Not every man is so selfish." Although, by the saints, he wouldn't mind being selfish once in a while.

Now.

"Nay." She shook her head, eyes glittering with the knowing of Eve. "I have learned how to prevent more children. You have merely to—"

"I recall." He wondered for a moment how he remembered, but then decided to trust his knowledge. "There are some things—like wielding a blade or riding a horse—that come naturally to me, even if I do not recall how I know them." He saved her from having to share her wisdom since he wasn't sure he could listen to any more explicit talk of withdrawal without making this a lot harder on himself. "But are you certain?"

He stroked a silky strand of the long, auburn hair snaking down her shoulder to spill over the grass. She smelled like roses and herbs and springtime, her skin as sweetly fragrant as the garden all around them. Sunlight splashed along her fair skin, highlighting faint freckles he would have never seen otherwise. How many other mysteries lurked inside this strong woman who hid her vulnerabilities so well?

"I want you, Hugh." Her hands stirred on his hips, caressing his flesh with the lightest of touches. "By any name, you are the noblest man who has ever attempted to court me, even if you are unsure why you sought me out."

He wanted to be honest with her. He would be honest with her if not for the restraints her father had placed upon him. Still, he would explain himself to her if only she would reveal the rest of her secrets. Why she had seemed to recognize him that first day.

"Perhaps I sensed a connection between us that goes deeper than either of us have guessed." His body pulsated again, aching with need, tired of holding back.

She wanted him as much as he wanted her and he didn't stand a chance of walking away now. Maybe sharing this with her would allow him to see past her defenses, to understand the woman beneath.

Tilting her chin, he aligned her mouth with his. Her breath came fast, her desire still hot even after he'd taken the edge off for her. And wasn't that a rich reward for a man? Sorcha was not merely seeking superficial thrills. She wanted to explore the heat between them as fully as he did.

"Perhaps we are not connected enough," she teased, reaching around to stroke his shaft with the most tentative of caresses.

Just like that, she burned away all doubts and reservations. They were destined for this moment. This union. He'd known it deep within himself from the first time he'd seen her.

"You are a temptress and a sage, Princess." He closed his eyes against a wave of heat that threatened to pull him under at just that one, small caress. "But you must be cautious with a man who has never lain with a woman before, lest you spoil the fun unwittingly."

Her eyes went wide and he could tell he'd surprised her despite her need to tout her experience. Clearly, she had not spent days abed with the man who'd tricked her into marriage or else she would have known whereof he spoke.

Instead, she blushed the prettiest shade of pink, her cheeks matching the pale blossoms floating down from the trees nearby.

"Then show me," she said softly, her fingers halting their dangerous glide along his sex.

Grinding his teeth against the pleasure, he wrapped his hand around hers, guiding her up and down his shaft with mind-numbing pressure. He stifled a groan at the feel of her cool, tender skin all around him, her eyes watching him intently.

Every man should be blessed with a second "first time"

with a woman. Hugh knew without question his experience with Sorcha would outshine any awkward fumbling on some maid's pallet that had come before this.

"You are so hot," she marveled, amazement in her voice. "How would you taste with wine? I wonder."

His eyes flew to hers and he found her peering down at him with an utterly serious expression, as if she would actually commit such an act. His body jerked in her hands, eliciting a girlish squeal that reminded him she had no business attempting such tricks when she had so little experience in pleasure herself.

"You would likely get more than you bargained for," he growled, tugging her hands free before he lost what restraint he had left.

Sealing his mouth to hers, he kissed her, silencing any further ideas she had. Her words were as powerful as her delicate touches and he could bear no more. Lightly, he imprisoned her wrists to either side of her head, pinning her to the soft grass while he aligned their hips.

She sighed into his mouth and he caught her tender cries, tasting her pleasure as she shifted restlessly against him. Her thighs teased him, clamping lightly against him until he released her wrists to gently part her legs. She broke the kiss to fix him with her gaze.

"It hurt other times," she confessed in a breathless rush. "I don't want—don't let anything ruin this."

He wondered if she had any idea what she'd entrusted him with. Ah, curse the man who had treated her with so little care. Even Hugh, for all that he had no recollection of being with any one particular woman, maintained a keen grasp of how to proceed gently with a woman. He knew her pleasure came first if a man hoped to increase his own.

That understanding seemed as basic as breathing, although, heaven help him, he wished he could recall when and where he had acquired such knowledge. Still, he would not mind making all new memories with Sorcha. The thought teased him with enticing possibilities.

"Never," he promised, slowing himself down enough to touch the slick flesh between her legs. He tweaked the swollen folds, playing there for a long moment before he slipped a finger inside.

She arched her back to grind her hips against him, assuring him she was more than ready.

"Hold on to me." He wrapped her arms around him, needing her close, wanting to feel every hesitation, every slight nudge and roll of her hips to understand what pleased her best. "Don't let go."

He felt more than saw her nod. Her head was tucked up against his chest, her cheek pressed tight to him. Holding her hips still, he steadied himself, wanting her to feel only pleasure.

"I've got you," he crooned in her ear, finally allowing himself to edge his way inside her.

She was wet. Snug. Perfect. He fought the urge to bury himself deep and fast like an untried youth, to explore every secret inch of her until release rocked him. But he hadn't waited this long to wreck the moment now. He would not hurt her the way another man had.

Sweat streamed down his back now, the slow trickle turned to a hot rivulet as his heart thrummed him like an ax against a shield.

"Hugh." She breathed his name against his skin, a warm and damp invocation. "More."

Even knowing it might be too soon, Hugh could not help

but answer her call. With a groan, he pushed himself deeper, surrounded himself with her sweet feminine flesh. His forehead fell and he rolled onto his back, keeping her tight against him as he brought her with him. He wanted to relinquish control. To allow Sorcha to take her fill as she learned what pleased her best.

But then he recalled his need to pull out before the end and he rolled them right back. He had no choice but to maintain control. By the saints, he owed that to her.

For her part, Sorcha panted and squirmed. Her mouth came alive against his neck as she kissed and licked him, teasing her tongue over his throat.

"You are a treasure." He realized that even if he never received the reward her father had promised him, it was enough to have this time with this amazing woman.

He would find some other way to finance his return to knighthood. He would deceive Sorcha no longer.

The need for her crawled like a fever up his back, and his hips moved faster. Each thrust brought him new pleasure, each withdrawal a unique pain. He wanted her to remember this moment, remember him forever. Even if he never recovered his past, he wanted this one woman to feel as if she had known him in full measure. He would hold nothing back.

"What are you doing to me?" she whispered, her fingers losing their grip on his shoulders as he accelerated his pace and then slowed it again. "I have never felt—"

He did not know what she'd been about to say, but whatever it had been, he was certain he understood. Desire swamped him. Pummeled him. Demanded release.

Her body spasmed around him, squeezing tight with her fulfillment. And although he would have given anything to experience that pleasure in full measure, he had no choice but to pull out.

To let his release spill harmlessly into the grass.

He mourned the loss of her all around him, the chance to share something monumental. He could not even catch his breath as he rolled her to one side and held her in his arms.

Felt her heartbeat. Inhaled the rose-tinged scent of her, mingled with…

Smoke?

Shoving up to his elbows, Hugh scanned the horizon. Through the trees and bushes, he could already see the source of the smoldering scent.

Flames shot out the cottage windows.

Chapter Fourteen

Sorcha didn't recall rising, but a moment later, she flew across the garden with Hugh sprinting ahead.

Her bare feet hardly registered the rocks and thorny branches she trampled along the way. All her attention fixed on the corner of the cottage where Conn would have been napping. As she dragged her surcoat up to cover herself, she noticed the thick gray smoke hissing out a small window of the stone-and-timber lodging. The wind blew away from them, no doubt carrying the earliest warnings of the fire on a breeze in the other direction.

Guilt stabbed her even as she careened into Hugh's back.

"Go!" she shouted, her hands grasping the fabric of his tunic to tug him aside, the heat from the flames warming her now that they stood closer to the structure. "I need to find my son. Go or get out of my way."

Stumbling into him, she tripped on a timber that outlined the herb garden. Hugh's arms were there to catch her, keeping her upright.

"Conn!" she shouted between cupped hands. "Enid!"

Hugh grabbed her hand and dragged her away from the front door where the roses shriveled and blackened in the heat.

"I am going in the back window." He raised his voice over the dull roar of the flames and pointed to a small opening on the side of the cottage where Sorcha normally slept. "Stay right under the opening in case I need to hand him out to you."

She nodded numbly, quivering inside with the thought of her precious child hurt inside the roaring blaze. All around her, the trees shrank from the fire, the leaves disintegrating into nothing next to the flames raging up through the wooden roof. The stone walls fared better, but they radiated heat.

Could anyone survive inside the small building?

"Would the nurse remain with him while he slept?" he asked as he reached for the window's ledge, his arms impossibly strong to pull himself up to the opening.

"Sometimes." She had not required Enid to sleep beside him, but oftentimes, the nurse fell into slumber while rocking the boy.

She watched Hugh haul himself up onto the window ledge, using his cape as a blanket to protect himself from the hot stones. Why had she taken her eyes off her son for a moment? She had been living in denial by raising him here, far from her father's armies and the protection of a well-guarded keep.

"Conn!" Her voice failed her, coming out in a half sob, her throat raspy from shouting and inhaling fumes. "Hugh?"

Stepping closer to where Hugh's feet had disappeared through the cottage window, Sorcha leaned in to touch his cape, but she was not tall enough to see inside when she stood close to the wall. Backing up again, she watched anx-

iously as angry red flames danced all around the cottage.
Somewhere nearby, timber cracked and creaked, a shrill cry
from the structure that the whole thing might fall.

Above her, a piece of the roof crashed in, showering her
with sparks. Small burns peppered her skin. She drew the
skirt of her surcoat up over her head like a hood to prevent
her hair from catching fire.

Fear twisted in her gut, spreading into all-out black panic.

"Here!" Hugh's voice was suddenly beside her ear and
she had to turn to see him around the fabric she'd drawn up
over her head.

And there, at the window, was her son.

Swaddled in blankets, Conn peeked out from a woolen
wrap that covered his head, his hands and his feet. With a cry,
Sorcha reached for him, relief swamping her so hard she
feared she would fall to the ground from the force of it. The
weight of her son's body—alive and wriggling inside his
shell of linens—was the most welcome burden she'd ever
carried.

"My boy." She prattled and cooed and stuttered through
words of reassurance that were as much for her as for him. "I've
got him," she called into the cottage to Hugh. "Can you get
out?"

"I can't find the nurse anywhere." He coughed as a wave
of smoke blasted out the window. Behind him, another beam
from the roof caved in.

Hugh stumbled forward, his shoulder raking down the
stone wall just below the window ledge.

"You can't stay inside." Sorcha hesitated between the
need to run clear of the building with Conn and the desire
to haul Hugh out with her own hands before the whole
cottage collapsed. "Perhaps she is already out."

"Enid!" Hugh shouted, his voice gritty with fumes as he raised himself up again.

Sorcha spotted a burn festering on his shoulder already, his tunic charred away and sealed to the skin around the edges of the burn.

"Come out!" she demanded, scared and desperate to run from the cottage. "She might have taken some air outdoors."

Although wouldn't the nurse have run back to the building if she'd seen it smoking? Sorcha prayed the young woman was somewhere safe.

Hugh appeared unconvinced, but before he could sprint off into the burning building again, the structure shifted again, showering her with more sparks.

"You must come out!" she cried, unwilling to be responsible for Hugh's death.

Nodding, Hugh hefted one leg over the window ledge, his cape slipping off the rocky wall as he did so. Sorcha held Conn in one hand and pulled at Hugh with the other, closing her eyes and averting her face to avoid the heat of the fire.

"Let go and run!" Hugh yelled, glaring at her with the eyes of the damned.

Still, she yanked at his leg, praying and pulling with all her might.

Finally, his other boot appeared and he half leaped, half fell to the ground beside her. No sooner had he escaped the inferno when the rest of the ceiling caved in with a horrible whining crack of wood.

Soot and sparks chased them as they ran deeper into the garden enclosure away from the fire. Sorcha bent forward around Conn to protect him from flying debris while Hugh tucked her to his side, shielding her with his body in much the same way.

"It's all right, baby." She rambled soothing words in her son's ear, praying they were true. "We are safe."

Beside her, Hugh slowed his pace to look back at the burning cottage.

The acrid scent of smoke hung thick in the garden that still swayed with blooms of every hue. The blossoming trees and babbling brook made a strange frame for the ugliness beyond the enclosed garden.

"Is there any way out of the garden besides through the cottage?" Hugh's gaze swept the stone walls that circled the private retreat that had been such a source of pleasure for her during her exile.

"No." Heart in her throat, she tried not to mourn the loss of material things inside the cottage. None of it mattered as long as they were all right.

She prayed Enid was all right.

Still, seeing the cottage in flames made her think about how much time she'd spent there. How many important events had taken place inside those walls. The birth of her son. Her slow realization that she didn't need a husband to be happy.

And of course, there were the material things. Tiny blankets she had woven herself for Conn, the imperfections a part of their appeal since she had improved her skills greatly during her banishment. She'd had such incentive to weave and sew when it was her child who would reap the benefit.

Now, all those precious little things she'd worked so hard on were gone along with a few of her mother's treasured possessions. Sorcha had only brought the items that meant the most to her into exile—her mother's silver comb, a golden brooch, an embroidered veil that she'd worn on the day of her marriage to Sorcha's father.

The price of their loss was a small one to hold her boy safely in her arms.

"Then we will have to scale the wall." Hugh guided her toward a young pear tree with low-hanging limbs. "If you let me hold Conn while you climb, I can help you up and then hand him to you while I follow."

Her arms tightened around her son instinctively, even as she saw the wisdom of the plan. With a kiss to Conn's forehead, she passed him to Hugh. Perhaps he was too young to be frightened by the fire because he went willingly to Hugh, holding his arms out through the blanket that had come loose around him. Sorcha's heart clenched to see her son reach out to the warrior who looked so much like his father.

The man who had more than earned the right to know of the resemblance.

She vowed to confide the truth in him as soon as they were free of the fire and certain that Enid was all right.

When they reached the top of the wall safely, Sorcha turned to repeat the process for lowering themselves to the ground. She moved to hand Conn to Hugh so that she could descend first. But Hugh shook his head.

"Wait here until I am sure it's safe." He edged down the wall, lowering himself slowly.

"I do not think the fire will spread this far." Frowning, she turned back to see the cottage from her bird's-eye view on the wall. She kissed Conn's head absently, wondering when she would feel safe to ever be apart from him again. "We are well away from it now."

The cottage stood in ruins, the structure flattened from the blaze while the wood burned to nothing.

Hugh gripped her ankle with one hand before he went any

farther and she tore her attention from the smoldering debris to discover an intent look on his face.

"Sorcha, there is a chance that fire was set on purpose." His hard look didn't startle her nearly as much as that terrifying possibility. "Think about it. No hearth fire burned. No candle would have been lit at midday. The kitchen is not near the cottage and in fact, that building remained untouched by flame off to one side. We must consider that this could have been a purposeful act, and if so, we need to take care the person responsible does not lie in wait to finish his job."

Hugh would not allow the king to turn his daughter away this time. Tiernan Con Connacht should not have sent his daughter out into the woods with no more protection than a lone knight and a groom more concerned with bedding women than guarding them. And Hugh should not have allowed it to come to pass.

He nodded to the guard in the gatehouse as they approached the keep. The drawbridge was lowered unless the king was under attack, so taking shelter inside the stalwart walls was easy enough. Convincing the king to allow Sorcha to stay within the walls might prove more difficult.

But that's exactly what had to happen.

The courtyard teemed with activity. Masons applied their craft to the outer stone ring, strengthening the castle's defenses. Maids carried milk from the dairy while young boys hauled wood in for the day. Horses drew carts full of hay in from the fields toward the stables, the rhythmic clop of their shoes ringing on the cobblestones. In the distance, the grind of metal on stone suggested a blacksmith was hard at work.

"Sister!"

From across the courtyard, Onora waved to her sibling.

The dark-haired young princess held a bright length of cloth in one hand as she spoke with Eamon. Too bad Hugh had encouraged the groom to make haste for the keep today or he might have seen who had set the fire.

Sorcha hastened into Onora's embrace and only then did she allow someone else to hold Conn. Hugh had offered numerous times to take the child on their tense ride through the forest back to the castle, but Sorcha had been pale with worry and insisted on carrying Conn. He was relieved to see her take some aid from her younger sibling.

"What happened?" Onora's startled blue eyes roamed the three of them, no doubt taking in the burned clothes, soot-covered faces and the thick scent of smoke.

"We must see the king at once," Hugh told her, ushering the group toward the entrance to the keep. "There's been a fire."

Onora's cry of dismay did not distract Hugh from observing Eamon's reaction. The groom may not have been overly vigilant in his duties, judging by his lack of haste to see the king earlier today.

Yet the quick loss of color in Eamon's face told Hugh he was as upset by the news as Onora. Perhaps the realization of how grave the consequences could be for losing focus would spur him to be all the more committed to his duty.

It was a lesson Hugh took to heart as well. He had not forgiven himself for allowing those moments in the garden with Sorcha to undermine his watchfulness.

"How did it happen?" Eamon asked at the same moment Onora hugged Conn tighter and asked, "Are you unharmed?"

"We are fine," Hugh assured her, hastening their pace through a narrow alleyway that led into the keep. He bypassed the waiting area for visitors, determined to see the monarch immediately. "I will tell you all I know at the same time we tell the king."

They passed a troop of servants bringing jugs of wine up from a storage area, while young girls skipped ahead of them with clean rushes in hand, presumably for the hall floor.

"What is afoot here?" Sorcha asked. "There is so much activity. Has the meal not been served yet?"

Hugh had expected to see the king after supper and was surprised to think they hadn't even served the food yet. He hoped that wouldn't prevent the king from sending men to the cottage to search for Enid and look for clues about how the fire started.

"We have an *honored* guest tonight," Onora informed them, her eyes narrowing with clear disdain at the mention of the guest. "We play host to the king of Breifne, and Father hopes to arrange a marriage for me to the ancient drunkard who is as known for his temper as he is for outlasting his wives."

Hugh guided the party into the hall and was disappointed to note the king had not yet taken his seat.

"Where is he?" Impatience simmered along with anger. At the king, at himself, at the notion that he could not claim Sorcha even if he wanted to, since Hugh wasn't even certain he had the means to support a family.

After what had happened between them, he feared he owed her his name as well as his protection. But what if those things meant little? What if he had other commitments at home? Of course, the time to consider those things had passed when he pulled Sorcha's garments off and succumbed to temptation.

"I think Father is in his chambers," Onora answered. "Let us go up and see him together."

Hugh nodded, appreciating the young woman's fast assessment of the situation. Then again, perhaps she was only too glad to put off a meal that might end with her betrothal to a quick-tempered old man.

"Hugh." Sorcha hung back as Eamon, Onora and Conn led the way up a staircase at the back of the great hall.

Hugh paused and waited for her to catch up, although their delay allowed for a good distance between them and the others.

"What is it?" He hated seeing the worry in her eyes, the soot smeared across her pretty face. He had failed her on so many levels this day.

"We had never met before you arrived in Connacht a sennight ago. But I can explain why I might have seemed unsettled to see you that first day in the forest."

His foot missed a tread on the narrow stone staircase dotted with arrow slits and hidden alcoves for knights to surprise invading forces.

"I thought you recognized me." He recalled how her reaction had demanded he remain in Connacht as much as his gut instinct that he was meant to be here.

"You bear a striking resemblance to my false husband," she confessed.

Hugh's thoughts spun with the admission. He'd wanted some hint to his identity, some clue to his past. But not like this. Not when the only link that came to light marked him as—what? Kin to a lying, cheating bastard?

Worse still, might Sorcha have lain with him only because he reminded her of another man? The idea bludgeoned the feelings he was beginning to have for her.

"I did not remark on it because I was unsure if you were here on his behalf. I thought you might be a brother or—"

"Sorcha!" The king's voice boomed from the private chambers above. His footsteps fell heavy on the stairs and he intercepted them before they could reach the apartments. "What happened?"

Above them, Eamon and Onora stood on the landing with Conn between them. The boy's blanket had slipped to the floor and he appeared eager to pet a fat gray cat winding about his chubby legs.

Hugh was grateful for the king's interruption, lest he reveal some of the tumult of his emotions. He planned to step back from Sorcha on a personal level even though he'd resolved to protect her physically.

"I am fine," Sorcha asserted, stiffening at her father's approach. "The cottage burned to the ground. Hugh rescued Conn, but could not find Enid. You must send men to search for her."

The king hugged her, his scarlet robe wrapping around her like exotic wings. Sorcha wavered on her feet but softened, leaning into the father who had banished her.

"Of course." The king raised a hand and Fergus appeared on the stairs, squeezing his large frame past them. No doubt he went to do as Sorcha had suggested.

Hugh still reeled with Sorcha's admission about his resemblance to Edward du Bois, but as Fergus stomped past him, he recovered himself enough to stop the descending knight.

"There is a chance the fire was purposely set," he told Fergus, recognizing the man's intelligence. He was obviously well trusted by his overlord. "There were no fires lit within the cottage and the blaze did not start in the kitchen. Given the threats we have feared to the princess's safety, you might search the surrounding area. If you have men who are accomplished trackers, take them with you."

Fergus looked to the king, but Hugh could not discern the glance they exchanged.

"Let us speak privately," Tiernan proposed, steering Sorcha up the last few steps. "Onora, you must ready yourself for our guest tonight. Eamon, you may remain."

The protest from Sorcha's younger sibling was evident even before she opened her mouth to speak. The bright cloth she'd been holding fell from her hand and Hugh realized it was a banner bearing her father's standard.

"I have been separated from my sister for a year." Onora's voice wobbled, but Hugh suspected it had more to do with anger than tears. She clutched her father's arms with both hands, attempting in vain to gather up the old man's attention when he peered away from her with studied effort. "You cannot mean to ban me from her presence now when she could have been killed in that godforsaken outpost you've punished her with."

The king pried her hands gently off his shoulders, his ringed fingers strong but insistent as he nudged her toward the door.

"I have already lost the chance to make one political alliance with my eldest. I will not lose another when we are so close to meeting the terms of your marriage."

Hugh wondered if anyone else noticed the tears Onora blinked back or the blind fury that darkened her features for a fleeting moment. The king certainly seemed oblivious as he thrust her toward the blue velvet curtains covering the heavy wooden door to his apartments.

"You will not send her away without allowing me to see her again," Onora told the king.

"You do not rule here, daughter," he informed her, closing the door with a thud behind her.

Ensconced in the king's private antechamber, Sorcha lowered herself into a seat near a low window looking out over the village's main gate. Eamon retrieved the banner Onora had dropped, tucking it into his coarse woolen cape before settling onto a simple bench in front of a tattered old tapestry.

Hugh tried not to think about what it meant that he resembled the last Norman Sorcha had cared about. Right now, he needed to convince the king to allow for better protection for Sorcha.

Before he could speak, her father turned to him.

"You must wed my daughter and leave this night."

Hugh knew he must have heard the man wrong.

"Sire—"

"Take Eamon with you," the king continued, "and put as much distance between you and Connacht as possible. We've heard a Norman army approaches and I've got my hands full with an upcoming battle. I cannot look after Sorcha if the father of her child launches his own attack."

"I will not wed again," Sorcha protested, rising from her chair. She wavered on her feet and Hugh realized she must be overwrought from all that had happened.

And, perhaps, she would never bind herself to a warrior who might be related to a man who had deceived her. At very least, Edward du Bois had not admitted his true identity when he married her, lest the king find his family through diplomatic connections in England.

"Then Hugh can deliver you to the convent." The ruler turned on Hugh, dark accusation apparent in his angry gaze. "It's the least he can do for allowing your enemies to burn your house down around your ears while he was present and paying court to you."

Hugh wondered how the wily old king had managed to maneuver him so skillfully. Had the monarch marked him for a husband to the fallen princess all along? Or was this idea of marriage a mere convenience when the Irish overlord did not have enough manpower to protect his keep let alone manage a daughter with a mind of her own?

But then, what did it matter when the old man was right? The crafty ruler knew without question that Hugh would make sure Sorcha was safe.

"It is not time for me to enter the convent yet," Sorcha argued, her green eyes lit with fear and worries she should not have to bear. "I will not be separated from my son so soon after he had such a frightening experience, especially not when I had no plans to leave for another fortnight at least."

"Would you prefer to remain here where battle is imminent?" her father shouted, stomping about on a dusty rush mat in a narrow chamber crammed with furnishings. "I am sending Onora away in the morning with the man I hope will be her groom. I will not have my daughters here when Connacht is attacked by invaders."

Suddenly, all the activity in the courtyard and the frantic efforts of the masons made sense. The king prepared for war. He had not bothered to attend his own village's fair because he had been too busy making hasty preparations to marry off one daughter and send the other into the care of the nuns because his reign might very well be finished.

But even if Hugh could bring himself to trust Sorcha's safety to someone else, he needed to stay close to her when she might very well hold the key to his past.

"I will take her with me," Hugh agreed, suspecting the king had foreseen exactly how this meeting would unfold.

Perhaps the cottage fire had only hastened along the end result he had fully anticipated from the start.

"I will not leave my son," Sorcha protested, turning the full impact of furious green eyes on him.

"We will bring him with us," Hugh assured her, watching Conn squeal with delight as the gray cat batted the laces of the boy's tunic. "I will not take you to the convent."

The anger in her gaze switched to confusion. Surprise.

And, at last, betrayal.

"I do not understand." She bit the words out between clenched teeth.

"We will wed." He was no more prepared for such an event than her. He did not know if he had other commitments or if he had made promises to someone else at another time. But he would not let her remain here with a father determined to send her away with anyone willing to have her.

At least this way, he knew she would be safe from harm and free to help him uncover the mystery of his past. He could not leave Connacht without her when she was his only link to his identity.

But he would not bed Sorcha again until he was certain she was free of any romantic feelings for the father of her child. After all, he couldn't discount the notion that she'd allowed her broken heart to dictate her actions with Hugh, sleeping with him without telling him of his resemblance to du Bois. Only a fool would subject himself to the kind of intoxicating passion Hugh and Sorcha shared if there was any chance those powerful feelings were one-sided. So, no matter how much the effort cost him, Hugh would not touch his new wife.

Besides, whether or not Sorcha realized it, their vows would not even be legally binding since they could not be married under his rightful name. No marriage was lawful when conducted under a false identity, a fact Sorcha should know all too well after her brief marriage to the elusive du Bois.

With that settled, Hugh only wanted to depart Connacht. But seeing the fury return to Sorcha's expression, he anticipated the battle she created over this union would soon rival the advance of the Norman army on her father's gates.

Chapter Fifteen

He took a huge risk.

Eamon slipped from the keep at sunset, unwilling to watch the princess Onora's public courtship by a foul-mouthed lord. More importantly, Eamon needed to find Gregory Bartlett in order to discover who burned Sorcha's cottage to the ground. So Eamon galloped past the outlying villages near the king's lands to roam the empty forests of Connacht. He knew the direction of Bartlett's encampment and he wore no colors to identify him as one of Tiernan Con Connacht's men. He should be able to slip into the Norman camp quietly.

And then, he would have his answers. Did du Bois and his men set the blaze? And if so, had they set it in retaliation for Eamon's failure to steal the boy?

If that was the case, they had taken a deadly chance. The boy could have been killed. Sorcha and Enid could have been killed. Thankfully, Enid had been found by the king's men, exhausted and overcome by fumes, frantic about the safety of her young charge.

Still, Eamon had been livid to think the fat clerk would undermine his efforts that way. Besides, he did not wish any harm on the child. He would find Gregory if it took all night since Sorcha and her son would leave Connacht two days hence.

If Eamon hoped to gain the coin from handing the boy over to his father's men, he needed to do so with all haste.

Nearby, he heard a shout go up from a small group of men—perhaps fifteen or twenty voices raised in cheer. Steering his horse toward the sound, he slowed the animal to a walk, treading carefully so as not to be overheard.

Soon, he came upon the Normans. Many of the knights stood around another brightly dressed warrior seated on horseback, a leather glove in one raised hand. The mounted knight whistled an elaborate call and Eamon spied a prized white gyrfalcon flying overhead, a fresh kill in its talons.

Clearly, one of the men had brought his falcon to provide sport and entertainment. The cost of keeping such a bird was vast at home, requiring a falconer to train it and hunt regularly, as well as an aviary and special equipment. On the road, the cost must be prohibitive for all but the wealthiest of men.

Perhaps he had found du Bois.

Turning, Eamon hoped to avoid seeing Sorcha's onetime lover. The man whose fortunes had paid Eamon to falsely swear he'd witnessed du Bois's death. Taking care to move silently through the wood, Eamon slid off his horse's back to lead him around the encampment in search of Bartlett.

He never saw the trip wire or the men who lay in wait holding the ends.

In an instant, he fell to the ground, dragging his horse's bridle as he tumbled. The animal reared, pawing and snorting above him as he scrambled out of the way of the hooves. But free of that threat, he landed into another. A heavy hood descended on his head, covering his eyes and stifling his nose and mouth.

Like a falcon returned to its master, his world went black.

"I will not wed him!"

Onora's words echoed what churned in Sorcha's own heart.

The sisters sat together in the small solar they had shared before Sorcha's exile. Since the evening meal, they had been preparing for the quick nuptial ceremony that would bind Sorcha to Hugh the following day. Onora's future groom had agreed to wed her as well, but not as quickly as her father had hoped. The visiting lord had only acquiesced to the match on the condition he could bring his new bride back to his Breifne home for the wedding that would ally the Connacht and Breifne lands. Onora's future husband hoped the union would soothe his restless knights and tenants who feared the Norman invasion and—perhaps already made plans to welcome a Norman lord.

Now, while Conn slept on a pallet nearby, Sorcha sorted through her old wardrobe to find garments to pack for beginning a new life with Hugh. A life that would begin with a journey to—where? She wasn't sure even Hugh knew where they would settle.

"I do not see how either of us can avoid it," Sorcha counseled, refusing to give in to her own childish urges to run away from what was expected of her.

And yet, wouldn't she have reacted the same way as Onora two years ago? In fact, she had reacted precisely the same way and look at all the heartache she had caused with her rash, reckless decisions.

"But you will marry a man who has shown you nothing but honor." Onora jammed a needle through a thin piece of silk, her stitches bound to reflect her angry state as she sewed flowers on a veil she would wear for her marriage ceremony. "I will wed a man who groped me under the trestle table. And then again in the corridor on my way to the garderobe. And once upon the darkened stairwell on my way to my apartments yester eve."

She fumed with her anger, and Sorcha's heart ached for her sister. Sorcha set aside her packing, her small trunk already stuffed with all the garments it would hold. She knew Onora required comfort to face the lack wit she would wed. Sorcha recalled too well when their father had threatened to wed *her* to such a lecherous lord some two years ago and it was after that debacle that Sorcha had attempted to form her own alliance with Edward while her father was off on a military campaign. Of course, her own machinations had hurt her as much as they had wounded her father and robbed him of his right to benefit from her marriage.

Time had taught her well that she did not have all the answers. She also knew happiness could not be found by running away from one's responsibilities. Sorcha had an obligation to her son now, and that was something she would not forsake, even if it meant marrying a man who did not care for her. The betrayal in Hugh's eyes had been all too apparent when she'd confessed his resemblance to Conn's father.

What might life have been like if she'd met Hugh before Edward du Bois entered her life? Back when she'd had the chance to marry a man based on her own whim? Ah, but it did no good to look back and wish. She would wed Hugh now because he could keep her son safe. And that ability was worth far more to her than her own happiness.

"True enough." Sorcha took the small sewing project from her sister's hands before Onora tore the delicate veil. "But at the time I thought I was marrying Edward, he had shown me nothing but honor as well. Some men hide their shortcomings and deceits better than others."

Hugh seemed to be a man full of honor, she thought as she smoothed the fabric Onora had crinkled. Hugh also seemed to be a man who would live up to his promise to protect her son. But until he remembered his past, how could she be completely certain? If he harbored some relation to Edward du Bois, Hugh might find he'd been sent to Connacht for the most underhanded of purposes.

Would his loyalties shift forever once he remembered his true identity? She had not told anyone Hugh's secret, although it occurred to her confiding the truth to her father might be her only way out of the marriage now. But given the king's distracted state and his haste to send his daughters away before war broke out, Sorcha feared he might choose a husband even less suitable. At least with Hugh, there was a chance he would retain some of his protectiveness of her. Or some of the tenderness she'd seen in his eyes before he discovered the guilty secret she carried around with her.

Remembering the way he had looked at her on the stairwell jabbed at her heart more than she would have ever dreamed possible given how short of a time they'd known one another.

But that magical time together in the cottage garden had bound them somehow. Even though their bodies were no longer physically joined, there was a connection between them that could not be undone simply because they walked away from those heated moments they'd shared.

"You could take me with you tomorrow." Onora tugged Sorcha's arm, destroying the stitch she'd been in the process of making.

"Have you lost your wits?" Sorcha set aside the veil, regretting neither of them would be able to wed using the veil their mother had been married in—the veil lost in the fire at the cottage. "Father would disown us both. He would be within his rights to withhold my dowry if my husband protected his other daughter from making an advantageous marriage. I do not think Hugh would thank us for bringing another small war to his gates."

"Please?" Onora rose from the small cushion where she'd been working and lowered herself to sit at Sorcha's feet. Draping an arm over her sister's knee, Onora turned pleading blue eyes on her. "Can you not at least ask Hugh? You know how wretched I will be wed to Rory of Breifne. Did I mention he is rumored to have driven his other wives to early graves?"

"People gossip to that effect whenever a man outlives his bride." Sorcha knew it to be true, but that didn't prevent guilt from twisting her insides.

In Onora's place, she had avoided marriage at all costs, hoping to find the kind of love her parents had known. But her recklessness had hurt everyone she loved. And perhaps it would be her son who suffered the most from her rash act. If anything were to happen to him—

Sorcha could not think of it.

"But *you* would not wed Rory of Breifne. You ran away from just such a marriage when you wed Edward while Father was off on campaign." Onora picked up the wedding veil Sorcha had set aside and flung the expensive silk clear across the chamber to land in the woodpile near the hearth.

"And I do not see why I should wed a lecherous old drunk either."

"But could you honestly be happy being banished from everyone you care about? Knowing you caused your father such disgrace and disappointment? It is easy enough to threaten disobedience and another to feel strongly enough to carry it forward despite all the hardship." Sorcha peered over at Conn's sweet baby face, knowing she could not have withstood the seclusion if not for him. "I have often cooked my own meals and baked my own bread, lest I subsist on cold food alone."

Onora pouted, her blue eyes still dark with anger and resentment.

"But Cook brings you food every Saturday."

"Aye. And it isn't warm even on Saturday. By Wednesday, that food is gone and I must prepare something from what meager supplies I keep in stock." She had spent hours attempting to learn how to prepare meals when she'd first been banished. Shortly afterward, she'd realized the importance of having a garden and taking care of it. "I have to wash my own garments. Entertain myself even though there are no instruments, no games, no guests or diversions, save nature and Conn."

Onora tilted her head to one side, considering.

"You realize it is likely I will never see you again?"

The stark truth hit Sorcha like a lightning bolt. They had not even gotten to share the last year and a half together, as their meetings since the banishment were hasty and infrequent.

"I will try to see you," Sorcha promised, not knowing how she could make it happen, but vowing to make an attempt.

She owed Onora that much. Her baby sister did not even

have the warm memories of a mother that Sorcha did. Because of that, Sorcha had always tried to spread some of that happy contentedness to her younger sister the way their mother seemed to be able to lift others up just by being around them. Sorcha experienced a deep grief at the loss of time with her sister—time she would never retrieve because of her long exile.

An exile she'd been as responsible for creating as her father had been. Today more than ever, Sorcha realized how much unhappiness she had caused by her selfish decision to thwart her father's attempt to marry her off. Now, Onora would never know the brief glimpses of happiness that Sorcha had—first in the hopes she'd had with Edward, even if they proved to be false. And later, in the moment of passion she'd shared with Hugh.

For that, and so much more, Sorcha vowed to do whatever she could to visit her sister after her wedding.

Nodding, Onora swiped a hand over her eyes and stood. "I will try, too." She moved to Conn's bedside and kissed her nephew. "But by the saints, if he beats me, I will not care what disgrace I bring to our father's house. I will learn to cook and do my own washings and gladly live like a hermit."

"I pray it does not come to that." She could not envision Onora thriving away from the entertainment of a big keep.

"Hadn't you better prepare for tomorrow?" Onora scooped up Conn and brought him over to Sorcha.

Sorcha hated to leave Onora so soon, but understood her sister's wish to be alone. Taking her son, she clutched him close to her heart.

"I thought we might visit longer since, as you said, we may not see each other for a long time after tomorrow morning."

Onora nodded, but opened the door to Sorcha's tiny bed-chamber off the shared solar.

"So much is happening, I fear we both have many plans to make." She kissed Sorcha's cheek and sent her on her way. "I want you to have the veil for tomorrow. And I need to pack my own things, too."

More guilt weighed on Sorcha's shoulders and she wondered how Onora could go from swearing she would not wed to packing up her things in the course of an hour. Perhaps her sister was not as rash and reckless as Sorcha had been. A dose of practical sense would bolster Onora far better than any foolish bravado might.

"Sleep well, sister," Sorcha told her, cradling Conn close and thinking this would be her last night as an unwed woman.

"I think we will all feel better tomorrow once the dreadful waiting is over. Perhaps half the fear is not knowing what will happen."

Sorcha smiled. "Wise words."

They said their good-nights, but as Sorcha settled down to sleep, she feared she had missed something. Onora's mood had shifted during their conversation from despair to resignation. It had happened too quickly. Too easily. Would Onora attempt to run away during the night to avoid the marriage?

Worry knotted her belly. As if she didn't have enough fears with an impending marriage to a man she didn't really know, someone trying to hurt her and possibly Conn too, and an uncertain future in the land of her father's enemies. Now she needed to think about what Onora might do to avoid a wedding.

Settling Conn on the bed alone, Sorcha rose to listen at

the door, hoping that if Onora made a move during the night, Sorcha would be there to talk sense into her.

The vows had been blissfully short.

Hugh had taken no pleasure from standing beside Sorcha earlier that morning, knowing she resented his unexpected proposal and the marriage she had little say in. They rode away from Connacht now, their marriage only a few hours old, their traveling party a small retinue of three retainers to protect the new couple. The king had demanded Hugh accept the service of three men-at-arms including Eamon, all of whom Hugh planned to send home once he regained his memories.

Once he found a destination to bring his new bride to.

All night he had feared she would demand to be taken to the convent rather than bind her life to his forever. She had hardly spoken to him since their meeting with her father after the fire, but he suspected she had given ample consideration to life in the nunnery. She had no reason to think she and her son would be safe traveling with a man who had no home, no troop of loyal knights, no secure keep with a moat and portcullis to fend off invaders.

Worst of all, perhaps, was her suspicion that he was somehow related to the father of her son. But the news didn't sit any easier on his shoulders than it must have weighed on hers. It could not be a coincidence that two Normans of similar looks would visit a far-flung Irish kingdom within such a short time span.

"My lord," one of his men called to him from a clearing ahead. The eldest of the trio acted as scout, setting the company's course and ensuring they did not come across the Norman army by mistake.

Hugh had taken the northern route to the sea to avoid the invaders, but there was a chance straggling recruits or new armies could be riding from most any direction to join the larger force marching on the northern kingdoms.

"We can arrive at seaside by nightfall. Shall I ride ahead to search for a boat to make the crossing?"

"How is the lay of the land?" Because Hugh had taken the southern route on his journey through Ireland, he could not envision the terrain ahead. "Is it favorable to predators or will we be able to see our enemies approach?"

"It is hilly, but the trees sit back from the road. You cannot travel anonymously through the wood, but neither can anyone seeking attack." The man-at-arms—Robert the Red—wore the same dark colors as the rest of the party. They sought to hide their Irish affiliation, shedding their colorful robes and tunics for more somber shades. No torcs adorned their arms or necks. No music hummed from tuneful lutes to entertain the travelers on the long journey.

"Very well. Ride ahead and see if we can find a boatman to take us. Tomorrow morning, if possible." Not that Hugh knew where he would head once he reached the shores of his homeland. But with trouble dogging their heels, he thought it best to leave Ireland behind.

"Aye." Robert nodded and sped off, his horse carrying the least of the supplies to facilitate his task.

Hugh peered back to another man riding beside Sorcha. Peter was an experienced and strong fighter who had seen combat numerous times in the king's army. He took his mission seriously, keeping a wary eye on the tree line ahead and behind the princess at all times.

Sorcha rode near him, cradling a sleeping Conn in her arms. She had to be exhausted and the day was not half finished yet. The child was not heavy, but no woman should have to carry that kind of weight on horseback for hours on end. She had to be uncomfortable.

Unguarded, she appeared worried. But Hugh knew as soon as she caught him staring, her expression would turn hard. Defensive.

He wondered if he would ever again see her as open and unyielding as she'd been in his arms before the fire broke out.

Behind Sorcha, Eamon brought up the rear. He'd been assigned to ensure they were not followed, but he'd had so little time as a man-at-arms, Hugh was not sure that he served the purpose all that thoroughly. Hugh did not understand why the young man seemed so distracted, but his attention did not appear to be on keeping Sorcha safe. Perhaps he missed Enid back in Connacht, but Hugh would not hesitate to send him home if he could not carry his weight.

"Hugh."

Sorcha's voice surprised him. She had not spoken to him more than was strictly necessary since he'd come to terms with her father about a wedding. He had thought about visiting her chamber the night before—not to claim her, of course, but only to discuss his plans for the future—but thought better of it. Talk of Hugh visiting her bedchamber might have stirred trouble, when the princess had already been banished for allowing her passions to rule her. Besides, he had been up most of the night making preparations for the journey, pressing the king to supply him with as much as possible to maintain Sorcha's safety.

"Aye?" He'd been tempted to call her wife, just to try the name on for size, but guessed the word might not yet be welcome.

He would not push her patience when she had willingly chosen him over the convent.

"I ride no farther until you tell me where we are going, when we arrive and what accommodations will be at the other end for my son." Her green eyes glittered with thinly veiled hostility. Dark shadows beneath them suggested she had not slept any more than Hugh had the night before. "It is not too late for me to ride to the convent if you are not going to consult with me on our future plans."

Hugh could not tell what surprised him more. That she expected him to consult her or that she would wave the empty threat of the convent at him.

"Do you not think it's a bit late to change your mind about taking a nun's vows?" He reined in, waiting for her to catch up to him. "I do not think you can promise God a life of chastity when you have promised yourself to me in front of witnesses."

Hugh noticed Peter never varied his watchful observance of the woods around them during the exchange. Eamon was too far behind to hear what was being said, so did not concern him.

Sorcha slowed her pace as she reached Hugh's side, shifting Conn's position from her arms to one shoulder.

"You think you have fooled me as easily as my father?" She fluffed her long, red hair out behind her, a bright auburn banner in the sunlight. "I only ride with you for as long as it pleases me, sir, since I am bound to you by no other obligation than my goodwill. I have promised myself to Hugh Fitz Henry, a man who does not exist."

Chapter Sixteen

Sorcha had never camped beneath the stars.

The experience appealed to her old adventurous self with the crisp night air tickling her nose and the moon bathing the trees in pristine white light. Her father's dark and damp keep kept out most natural light with its need to maintain defenses, while her cottage had sat in the shadow of the high garden walls. The moon would have only been visible from a window for a few scant hours.

But as much as the natural setting appealed to her wilder instincts, Sorcha could not stifle the sense that they were followed. Watched. She had not voiced the concern, knowing Hugh had posted Eamon behind the rest of the party to ensure no one came upon them unaware. But that did not dim the voice in her head that told her eyes looked out at them from the forest.

At least Conn slept peacefully. Her son had weighed heavy in her arms all day on horseback, but he'd been a very good boy, tolerating the unfamiliar discomforts with only an occasional cry. Now she hoped she could join him in slumber before too long to keep her mind off her second biggest worry.

Hugh.

She rearranged a blanket beneath her head, trying to find a comfortable position that would also prohibit her from peering over at the knight's strong, imposing form resting nearby. He had hardly spoken to her since they'd exchanged vows, refusing to rise to her bait when she'd informed him they weren't legally wed.

Of course, she understood he couldn't do anything about the false marriage since he didn't know his rightful name in the first place. But understanding that did not stop a certain sadness that not one but *two* men had avoided real marriages with her by using false identities. At least this time she could be assured the priest had been genuine. Father O'Reilly had been listening to her confession since she was old enough to understand the nature of sin.

"Do not leave—"

Behind her, Hugh mumbled in his sleep. The words were muffled, half of them incomprehensible, but she thought she understood that much.

Do not leave?

She wondered if he spoke to her in his nighttime imaginings. Lifting up on her elbow, she veered away from Conn to hover closer to where Hugh lay.

"Hugh?" She did not keep her voice down, as Conn usually slept heavily and the men-at-arms had been placed in a strategic circle around them. "Are you all right?"

No response.

Her ears strained to hear any other noise, but the only sounds around her were the distant crash of waves on Ireland's northeast shore, the hum of night bugs and Hugh's even breaths.

Sorcha lay back down, certain she would never rest this night. What if the men-at-arms grew tired and did not hear an attacker's approach? She peered over at Conn's small hand peeking out of the blankets and rested a finger in his tiny palm. He gripped it reflexively, holding her tight.

He held her heart just as securely. She leaned in to brush a kiss on his forehead, vowing to keep him safe.

"Rosa." Hugh's voice sounded again, only this time it was sharp. Clear. A name spoken with a world of meaning.

Freeing herself from Conn's grip, Sorcha crawled the few feet between her bedroll and Hugh's, knowing he would want to hear about this new clue.

Did he know a woman named Rosa in his old, forgotten life?

"Hugh." She shook him gently, her heart stirring at the sight of such a big, strong warrior so vulnerable beneath her hands.

How many other women had seen him thus? She could not deny a peculiar sense of pride that he trusted her enough to sleep with his back to her. He might have felt betrayed that she did not confide in him about his resemblance to Edward, but clearly he did not think her capable of any dark deeds.

"Hugh," she repeated, squeezing his arm through the chain-mail shirt he wore even in sleep.

Her fingers pinched between two of the metal links.

"Ro—" He woke up with a start, his shoulders springing up from the ground as his hand went for his sword.

Sorcha placed a restraining hand on his chest, hoping to claim his attention while his thoughts still drifted close to whatever dream he'd been having.

In an instant, he was on top of her, pinning her to the ground with one hand, his blade drawn with the other. She stared up at him in the moonlight, a wildness seizing his eyes for a moment until he tossed the knife aside.

And kissed her fiercely.

He pushed off of her again, gasping for breath as he rolled to one side and sat up. Her head was spinning, her own breath ragged, to say the least. She was stunned that he could arouse heat in her after brandishing a weapon at her.

"I could have killed you." His voice was a hoarse whisper. "My instincts—"

He broke off, hanging his head between his knees as he seemed to struggle for control.

She touched her lips with trembling fingers, remembering more tender kisses. And yet, even at his most intense, she did not recoil from his touch. His taste.

"A warrior is always alert. On guard."

Nodding her understanding, she remained as confused as ever inside. While she didn't blame him for what had happened, she questioned her own heated response to him that had not dimmed since he had vowed not to touch her.

"I tried to wake you because you were dreaming of someone." She spoke softly, not wishing to startle him any further. And, in spite of herself, she reached out to touch him. To reassure him she was safe. "Can you recall who she is?"

His heart beat beneath her hand, the drum of it forceful enough to thrum right through the chain-mail shirt.

"Rosamunde." He sounded certain as he picked his head up, his eyes locked on some distant point in the past. "She betrayed me."

His gaze moved to Sorcha, his focus sharpening. She eased back on her heels, her hand falling away from him.

"I woke you because—" She felt out of sorts. Unfairly accused. "I thought it would help you recover a lost memory."

"I did." He nodded, his attention moving back to the canopy of trees overhead as he lay down again.

"What do you recall?" She could not deny a wave of jealousy churning in the pit of her belly as she asked. Who was this woman who claimed Hugh's past?

Hugh swallowed hard, the planes of his face hardening into those of a stranger.

"I can recall this woman well. And I know she was promised to me, but she betrayed the betrothal by taking a lover before we were to wed."

Sorcha recoiled, seeking comfort in the warmth of her bedroll from the bitterness in his voice. And, perhaps to a greater extent, from the hurt she felt upon hearing he'd been betrothed to someone else.

"Where are you in your dream?" She tried to think about him and not the ache in her heart for what might have been between them if they had not met each other after such painful experiences. "Can you see what is around you?"

She hesitated from asking him directly if his memories had returned, afraid to put too much pressure on a difficult process. Perhaps she was a bit scared of what other hurts those memories might bring. Would he be the same man she knew once he reclaimed his past?

"Nay." His voice threaded through the darkness, winding about her and awakening feelings she could not name. "I see only the woman."

It was strange speaking to a man while they lay so close in the night. A man she knew so well, yet not at all.

"Is she well garbed?" Sorcha tucked her head close to Conn's to remind herself of her son's presence. To remind herself that she could not afford to indulge tender emotions for Hugh. "Recalling her adornments might help you discover your station in life."

"She wears a bright blue robe trimmed in ermine. And there are jewels—" He closed his eyes and shook his head. "I can't remember any more than that. The dream is fading."

"If she was not a dream, but a true part of your past, you must be a wealthy man." Few women could afford the garments dyed in a blue hue, let alone a rich shade of it.

"Not so wealthy that she feared the consequences of breaking our marriage contract."

"Will you be quick to break ours when your memory returns? I wonder." She turned on her side to face him and old leaves crinkled beneath her blanket despite the spring weather.

He turned to study her in the moonlight, his face only partially visible in the shadows that separated them. He was not close enough to touch, but she found her hand stretching toward him anyway, her fingers coming to rest in a patch of grass between them.

"I could ask you the same question, Princess." His hand extended to the same piece of earth, his fingers a mere hand span from hers. "You already threatened to do so this afternoon when I refused to tell you my plans."

She had been scared all day, unsure of their destination and worried for the safety of Conn.

"I fear for my son," she told him honestly. She saw no need to hide the truth from him any longer. She'd already revealed the only real secret she'd ever had from him. "If someone wishes harm upon us—on him—I am afraid we are vulnerable on the road."

"When my memory returns we will have more men to guard him and the safety of castle walls around us."

"What if it doesn't?" She had attached her name and her future to his. Regardless of the validity of the actual ceremony, she had still publicly tied her future to his. There would be no hiding this marriage as there had been the one that produced her son. What would become of her and Conn if Hugh's past remained a blank slate? They would have no family to call upon for help. No home.

And no matter the appeal of sleeping under the stars on a clear spring night, Sorcha would not wish for such a vagabond existence every day for her child.

"I will remember. The memories are closer every day. My dreams bring back small pieces like a puzzle."

"Memories like Rosamunde." Speaking the woman's name aloud brought with it a unique pain, reminding Sorcha she could not shut off her feelings for Hugh just because they were dangerous to her heart. "You cannot recall her surname?"

Helping Hugh recover his memory would help Sorcha in the end, so she would trudge through the painful parts concerning other women if it meant Conn would have a safe home all the sooner.

"Nothing." He shook his head, his dark hair lit with moonlight as he shifted. "I cannot remember anything else."

An owl hooted a forlorn cry in the distance.

"Perhaps if you return to sleep you will remember more." She hated to send him back to Rosamunde, but considering the lie of their new marriage and the distrust beneath the surface, Sorcha knew she could not be the right woman for him.

"Good night then, Princess." He rolled away from her, taking his hand that had languished in the grass so close to her own.

She regretted the loss of his nearness along with her inability to surmount the wide chasm that now yawned between them. The lingering heat of his kiss made that distance between them all the more painful.

"When I was devastated after discovering a false priest had performed my marriage ceremony, my confessor told me that sometimes, legal marriage may be recognized on the basis of—" she searched for the least awkward phrasing "—consummation."

Silence moved in like a shadow across the moon. Finally, he turned back around to meet her gaze.

"I do not think we will have to worry about that. I do not plan to touch you—"

"I did not mean for that reason," she hastened to interrupt, embarrassed and shamed that he did not want her. She pressed a cooling hand to her warm cheek, grateful for the dim light that rendered everything gray and white. "I referred to my questionable union with du Bois. If he is alive the way you believe he might be, I fear my marriage to him could still prove legal because of Conn. Your contract with my father could be declared invalid."

"I've made a terrible mistake."

Onora shivered in the night air, wishing she'd thought to bring along blankets for her escape. She rubbed her arms to warm them and tucked her gown more securely around her ankles where she sat in her bed of dried leaves a league behind her sister's traveling party.

"Should I have revealed your presence to the others?" Eamon asked, taking her hand in his. Presumably, he only wished to warm her skin. But Onora felt guilty about meeting with him secretly, and she feared the repercussions of any untoward behavior on top of the grave sin she'd committed by running away from her father's keep.

She had not fully appreciated the consequences of leaving home until she'd spent all day eluding view from the traveling party she was attempting to follow. She hadn't brought adequate food rations for herself and she would run out of supplies for her horse as well. As the rear guard for Sorcha's retinue, Eamon had spotted her early on in the journey, but she had begged him to keep her presence quiet.

Now, holding hands with him in the moonlight when no one else knew of her whereabouts, she realized the vulnerable position she'd put herself in. Thankfully, she'd known Eamon most of her life. He would treat her honorably.

"Nay." Onora shook her head, wishing she could go climb into Sorcha's bedroll with a fur blanket and two other bodies to share warmth. "Hugh would only send me home. They cannot discover my presence until I am safely across the sea and standing on English soil."

She'd envisioned that moment in her head all day long. The sunset slipping into the sea behind her. The freedom of knowing her betrothal contract was broken and that her sister would take her in.

"I will help you any way I can," Eamon swore, his thumb stroking lightly along the back of her hand.

She'd dreamed about such touches many times. And certainly that brief, gentle caress pleased her more than her oafish betrothed's groping. But, perhaps because of the groping, she found it difficult to see even this simplest of touches as romantic. Or even friendly.

Besides that, Onora did not know what to make of Eamon's solicitous concern. Whenever she had sneaked over to the cottage, he had chastised her as one would scold a child. But now—when her transgression had been far more dangerous—he had offered to keep her secret. Did he do so to be noble? Or did he only keep quiet for reasons she hadn't quite put together yet?

"Thank you." She withdrew her fingers from his grip. "I appreciate your protection."

For a moment, she thought she spied something unseemly in Eamon's expression. But it was dark out, she rushed to assure herself. And after her experience with her betrothed, it was only natural to perceive threats everywhere she looked.

"Are you sure you will not take my blanket?" He had offered it to her twice already. "Your father would have my head if he knew I could have made you more comfortable and failed to do so."

"I will be fine." She drew her cloak up to her chin and tried not to shiver. There was something far too intimate about sleeping under a man's bed linens. "You may attend your duties. I will see you tomorrow after I find a way to hide myself upon the ferry before it departs."

He rose from the forest floor to stand. Relief raced through her.

"I will give you some privacy." He bent over her with a bow. "But I cannot leave you unattended. I will guard you from a short distance away so I can hear you if you call for me."

Onora watched him stalk off into the night, chiding herself for her foolishness. Eamon didn't mean her any harm. He had been looking out for her for years.

Scraping a few extra leaves over her cold legs, she settled down to sleep. From somewhere in the forest, Eamon's eyes followed her. Protected her.

And until Onora could be certain Sorcha wouldn't send her back home, Eamon's protection had to be enough.

Hugh was not a superstitious man—or at least, he didn't think he'd been one in his life before he lost his memories—but he had a bad feeling about this crossing.

The ship he'd hired waited in deeper water while a smaller craft ferried their trunks and horses out to the vessel. The captain appeared able enough, his experience in making the trip obvious from his knowledge of the winds and tides. So it wasn't necessarily the crossing itself that concerned Hugh.

Perhaps his unease came from his certainty that enemies lurked on both sides of the sea. At least their time on the ship would give him a chance to speak with Sorcha and find out everything she knew about du Bois. Hugh would unearth every clue she could give him about a man who resembled him—a fellow Norman who visited Connacht shortly before Hugh's arrival.

It could not be coincidence.

"My lord." Eamon approached Hugh as the nearest to last ferry went out with their horses and two of the men-at-arms.

Hugh had debated sending Sorcha and Conn earlier, but he trusted his own sword more than the others and had decided to keep them with him until the last.

As he turned to the new man-at-arms, Hugh noted Eamon's ashen face. His unsteady gait.

"What is it?" He peered around the small stretch of beach and saw nothing amiss. Sorcha and Conn were right beside him. "Are you unwell?"

"It is Lady Onora."

Beside Hugh, Sorcha drew in a sharp breath. Her hand clutched his arm.

"What of the princess?" Hugh had left behind that particular problem in Connacht.

"She followed us from the keep." Eamon shook his head as he speared his fingers through his hair. "I saw her last night, but she begged me not to tell you."

"Where is she now?" Sorcha cut in, her slender shoulders edging between the men.

"I cannot find her." Eamon gestured toward the woods. "I watched over her while she slept last night just to the west of where you camped. But I left her side to help load the ferries and now she's gone."

Anger twisted his gut at the ignorant man's actions. Later, Hugh would consider all the ways the man should be punished for his oversights, but right now, he had to find Sorcha's sister.

"Perhaps she secured a place for herself on the ferry during one of its runs," Sorcha offered, shielding her eyes from the sun glinting off the waves as she peered toward the ship.

"Nay." Eamon shook his head and lifted a dark leather satchel. "I found her bag in the forest. She would not have left without it."

Beside him, Sorcha made a strangled sound. Hugh sensed her wavering on her feet and he wrapped an arm about her waist to steady her.

"I will find her." His head reeled with possible scenarios, all of which required his horse and more men. "But I cannot run off into the forest with no mount and no one to protect you and Conn."

"No." She gripped his tunic, her face white with fear. "What if she has been taken by crude men with no chivalry?" Grabbing her sister's pouch out of Eamon's hand, she waved it for emphasis. "They did not even take her bag. They cannot want her for her riches. She could be assaulted even now."

Her rant dissolved in another indiscernible cry and Hugh knew he had no choice but to make some effort to search nearby until the ferry returned with his men.

Even now, the small vessel returned, empty.

"Eamon, go see if you can shout for the men and the horses to return right away." Perhaps the ferryman would hear across the distance and could turn around before he got too much closer to the shore. "Sorcha, I can help Eamon look for her, but that leaves you and Conn at risk. Do you really want me to walk away from Conn right now? There's a chance that whoever took your sister counted on me to do exactly that."

He scoured the shoreline with his gaze, hoping for some sign of movement somewhere. Had he ever been so exposed from a tactical standpoint as he was right now? He might as well have been standing with his braies about his knees and his sword out of reach.

Sorcha swiped away a rogue tear with a shaking hand.

"Do you have a weapon I might use?" She cradled her child close to her chest and the boy protested, his little legs in motion as if he would run the whole shoreline if he could.

"Aye." Hugh took the smaller of his blades and handed it to her. "Do you recall how to hold it?"

He remembered their conversation the first day they met when she'd been hiding the dagger in her sleeve.

"Aye." She gripped the hilt and held it in front of her, away from Conn. "But this time, I will not hide it. I will brandish it well if anyone comes near, I promise you that."

Fierce maternal instinct sparked in her eyes, reminding him of a mother protecting her cub. Hugh could not help a tug of admiration for this fiery Irishwoman even as he hated that she'd been put in this position.

"Then I will do as you wish." He leaned close and kissed her on the cheek, unable to stop himself. "Fare thee well. And tell the ferryman to take you out to the ship as soon as he brings those men to shore."

Nodding, she backed toward the water. Her eyes held his, forming a bond between them that felt all too tangible.

"Godspeed, Hugh."

Against every instinct, he turned away from her to search for her sister.

Chapter Seventeen

The forest seemed unnaturally quiet.

Sorcha's heart beat louder than the soft roll of waves behind her or the mild breeze sifting through the trees in front of her. She kept her back to the water, knowing she was safe from that side. Hugh's men were loading the horses onto the ferry for the return trip. And while not all the animals could make the journey at once, at least Hugh would have his horse and another mounted guard to search for Onora. The last man-at-arms would accompany the ferry back to retrieve Eamon's horse and his own.

But until the first ship reached the shore, she needed to watch the trees for any sign of movement. She'd thought about hiding in the woods with Conn, but what if they were being watched? Besides, by entering the thicket, she'd be that much easier to kidnap without any of Hugh's men seeing where she went. At least if she or Conn were accosted here, the others would see who took them and what direction they went.

But for now, the tall pines swayed peacefully in the gentle

wind blowing off the water. Their dense branches interlaced to form a thick cover over the forest floor, shading all but the nearest lands from her view.

"Ba, ba, ba." Her son chortled baby sounds from his place on her hip, his fingers preoccupied with the gold thread surrounding a jewel on the shoulder of her surcoat.

Absently, she kissed his forehead, her gaze never leaving the trees. If Onora came to any harm, Sorcha would blame herself for the rest of her days. Sorcha had blazed a path through her father's household, defying him daily in a thirst to be recognized for her strength and intelligence instead of her value as a marriage prospect.

Even before she'd run off and wed a man without the king's knowledge, she had sneaked out of the keep to ride on campaigns with his men. She had never fought a battle, of course, as she had never been able to convince any of the men to teach her to fight. But she had thrilled to the challenge of a more adventurous life.

In turn, she had set an example for her impressionable younger sibling that might well have brought Onora to harm. No wonder their father had wanted to banish his eldest. In hindsight, she wondered if he had not made a mistake in failing to exile her earlier in life.

"I pray your aunt is safe," she whispered over Conn's head before risking a glance behind her to see where the ferry was.

The vessel was halfway back to the shore and some of the fear went out of her. But even if she and Conn had weathered the most dangerous moments alone, she still feared for Onora.

And why couldn't she see any trace of Hugh and Eamon in the trees? Turning back to study the forest, Sorcha heard a rumbling in the woods.

The sound started off like a distant drum, but quickly

grew into a thundering beat that made the ground tremble beneath her feet.

Horses.

The noise echoed around the small beach area, bouncing off the water so that she couldn't tell what direction it came from. Fear clogged her throat and buckled her knees. She remained standing on sheer force of will alone.

All at once a riding party broke through the trees. Six men on horseback barreled onto the beach from the south. Their dark robes bore no distinguishable colors or heraldry and they carried no banner.

She launched across the beach in the other direction. Sand kicked up from her feet as she ran, her elbow pumping for more speed. If only she could reach the trees, she could delay them. But would it be enough to allow for her guards to save her? And how would two fight against six?

Leaping over a piece of driftwood, she spared a glance back. One of the riders had already fallen, his body lying half in the waves rolling up to shore.

Her guards must be firing arrows from the ferry. Hope surged for a moment, but as the deafening roar of hoofbeats grew closer, she knew her men would not be able to take down all six of them before—

Hands reached out from behind as if to scoop her up onto a horse.

Tossing her knife aside, she fell purposely to the ground, doing her best to shield Conn from the impact. She hoped the tactic would give her guards more time. But as she blinked sand out of her eyes and rubbed it off her mouth, she saw a huge warhorse rear up, its hooves dancing dangerously close to her head. Conn was crying and clutching her shoulder, but she did not think he was hurt.

Yet.

Looking up at the monstrous knight with rotten teeth atop the destrier, Sorcha feared she and Conn could both be dead before night fell.

Rolling out of the way of the hooves, she braced herself, holding her baby tight. When the weight fell on her back, it was not the impossible blow of an animal's shoe.

But rather the body of a man.

Screams tore from her throat. She tried to scramble out from underneath him and as she shoved at the limp, heavy weight, she realized the warrior with the rotted teeth had been shot in the chest. The arrow protruded from between his ribs, the end scratching her arm as she eased her way free.

"Sorcha!" Hugh's voice filled her ears, his presence offering a thread of hope in the midst of horrifying mayhem.

"Here!" she cried, frantically waving a hand to show her whereabouts among the crush of scared horses and fallen bodies. All around her, members of the riding party had been taken down by a rain of arrows from the men on the ferry and—perhaps—Hugh and Eamon. Thanks be to God that their aim had been sure and true, given how close she and her son stood to the downed man.

"Are you hurt?" His voice sounded closer now, but she still could not see him through the press of bodies. The stench of sweat and fear threatened to gag her.

There were shouts nearby and she thought they might be from the guards arriving on the ferry. Closer to her, men groaned in pain and Conn cried. She was grateful, at least, for the noisy wail of her son since it assured her that he was well enough. Gently, she rocked and shushed him, extricating herself from another man's leg.

"Don't move, Princess."

A blade nicked her back before she could stand, the point stabbing right through her surcoat and kirtle to scratch her skin.

Turning, she saw the man who had performed her first marriage ceremony, the fake priest she had known as Father Gregory. His forehead was covered in sweat as he sat on the sand. An arrow protruded from high on his thigh and the wound bled profusely. She did not think he could give chase if she ran, but she was exhausted and bruised. Besides, her arms ached from carrying Conn and she would not risk a knife anywhere near him if she could not make a clean getaway.

Where was Hugh?

"Who are you?" Hugh's voice rang out at the same moment a sword whipped through the air. The blade was still quivering with the fast splice as Hugh pointed it at the false priest's head. "I know you work for du Bois."

Gregory's eyes bulged from his head, his fear creating an acrid stink that mingled with the metallic scent of blood.

"He's not called du Bois any longer." The corpulent thug loosened his hold on the blade he pointed at Sorcha and she edged forward, away from him. "You honestly do not recognize him, do you?"

Sorcha's gaze flew to Hugh's face while she rocked her son. Did he know Conn's father? When Hugh said nothing, the dying man laughed with a raspy wheeze.

"You have me to thank for your life, you know. I was charged with killing you but thought poisoning you would be less painful than running you through. I thought I was doing you a favor by slipping the potion into your drink and I figured if I struck you in the head, you'd be able to crawl off into an alley to die. I thought for sure I gave you enough poison to bring down an ox."

Sorcha winced at the thought of what Hugh had been through. No wonder he'd lost his memory with his body sustaining so much torment. However, she didn't understand why these men would wish to kill him.

"Who is du Bois?" Hugh rose up, frighteningly intense as he pressed his blade harder on Gregory's forehead.

The effort didn't even make the man flinch, and Sorcha suspected he was halfway to dead.

"Edward du Bois is your cousin." The dying man's eyes closed.

Sorcha feared they would never know the rest. She snatched the weakened man's blade and leaned closer to his face.

"Why would he harm Hugh?" she shouted, moving closer to the fallen enemy. "What is Edward called now?"

"Mont—" The sound was little more than a whisper before the man's head cocked sideways in a lifeless slump.

She watched his chest. No sign of rise and fall. He was truly dead. And with him died any other information he may have known about Hugh or Edward.

"Mont what?" she asked, desperate to have answers about why anyone would hurt her and hurt Hugh purposely. Why anyone would want her precious son dead.

Why did Edward wed her falsely and convince her of his death? Why come after her now? So many questions and the danger growing by the hour.

"Montaigne."

Hugh's answer silenced the questions racing around in her brain. She peered up at him. Hopeful.

"What?"

She saw a new set to his shoulders. A powerful presence that blocked out the sun behind him.

"I am Hugh de Montaigne." He sheathed his sword, his expression grim. "I remember everything."

Hugh waited to speak to Sorcha until after everyone had been loaded onto the ship, his newly recovered memories swirling around his head.

He'd found Onora before the riders had descended on Sorcha back at the beach. She'd been tied to a tree, but aside from some scratches, she had not been harmed. Hugh had debated sending the reckless girl back to her father, but deemed it too risky when the king might already be embroiled in battle. Ireland was crawling with Normans.

So he'd ushered the women and Conn onto the ship along with his men and the horses. He took some of his enemies' mounts as well, though he did not have enough room on board for all of them. He'd paid the captain with two of them, which had saved him gold in the end.

Now Hugh sat on a trunk in the bow of the ship, away from the animals at the stern. Eamon and the others had asked his leave to open the wine rations for the journey and Hugh had given it, seeing the whole company had been shaken by the brush with du Bois's men back at the beach. The men played dice on the wooden planks of the deck at midship, their conversation more boisterous with each tip of the flagon.

"May I speak with you?" Sorcha had approached so softly he had not heard her, his head swimming with memories as he tried to sort through his past.

Nodding, he moved over on the trunk to make room for her. The chest was nearly as big as a trestle table and contained the silver Sorcha's father had insisted on sending with her. The ruler's love for his daughter had been obvious to him, even if Sorcha didn't recognize it.

"Where is Onora?" He didn't see her on deck.

"The captain showed her a place belowdecks where she and Conn could rest." Sorcha tucked her skirts beneath her to prevent them from blowing in the wind off the water.

She'd plaited her hair to keep it confined in the breeze and he noticed her veils had been twined around the heavy plait to weight them down. She had spoken little after the incident on the beach, staying close to Onora. He'd learned the dead man had been the false clergyman who'd performed her wedding to du Bois, but she'd been too distracted by caring for her son and her sister to speak about what happened in any detail.

As the creaking craft eased through the slapping waves, Hugh took in a bracing breath of the salty air.

"My memories had been returning by slow, maddening degrees until the encounter in the clearing brought it all back. Something about hearing my name—just that one piece of the title that should be mine—made me remember it all. I was on my way to Connacht to warn you about du Bois when I was struck down by his servant." He launched into the basics before she could ask, wanting her to understand that his intentions had been noble despite his relationship to du Bois. "I knew he had been in Ireland to wreak havoc among the enemies to the Norman cause, but until shortly before my accident, I did not know that meant he had seduced and deceived the daughter of a royal household."

Hugh had been fighting wars of his own, protecting the Montaigne earldom, at the time Edward had been in Ireland. Edenrock Keep was a new holding for him and the former baron continued to attack Hugh's tenants whenever they left the town walls. By the time he'd vanquished that enemy for good, he'd heard rumblings of Edward's return to London and rumors of private meetings with King Henry about his reward for what he'd achieved in Ireland.

"He wooed me to backstab my father." Sorcha's hands clenched into fists, her gaze fixed on the sea as they cut through the waves. "I can see how much cheaper it would be to besiege a woman as opposed to a strong keep. Especially when the woman in question is a foolish girl."

The bitterness in her voice did not surprise him, but Hugh could not tell if it was all anger at what had happened or if the anger was tinged with regret. He knew that people did not always love wisely. His experience with Rosamunde had taught him as much.

The woman he'd recalled in his dream had indeed been promised to him. Between his conquering of a new keep and his betrothal to one of the richest women in the kingdom, Hugh had had a solid future mapped out as the new Montaigne lord. He would have been one of the king's most important knights, a position that would guarantee him security. But he'd been betrayed by both his cousin and his betrothed. Rosamunde had defied her father's choice in husband in the same way Sorcha had protested the men Tiernan suggested to his headstrong daughter. The difference was that Rosamunde had been obligated—legally promised to him. Not only that, but Rosamunde had spoken sweetly to his face and behaved as if she wanted him.

Hugh could not forgive such deception, as he would have never entered into the arrangement if he had suspected the woman did not want him.

He remembered Rosamunde clearly now that his memory had returned. Her carefully perfected beauty paled in comparison to Sorcha's windswept magnificence.

"A foolish girl could not have acted so bravely back there

on the beach." He reached for her hand, unable to resist that small connection with her after all that had happened today. It had been hard enough resisting her the night before when they lay so close to one another without touching.

His blood still ran hot and fast in the aftermath of the fight. He burned to hold her, taste her, claim her so fully no one dared try and harm her again while she was under his protection.

"Any mother would do as much for her child." Her voice shook and he feared her tears.

Comforting her would test his restraint uncomfortably, especially now that he knew without a doubt he was free to court where he pleased. To lay with Sorcha without reservation—or at least he would as soon as he was certain she saw no one but him.

"You are wrong." He had seen villagers and noblewomen alike treat their children with far less compassion than Sorcha showed Conn. "And even if that was true, how many other mothers would have known how to elude capture? Falling to the ground where the rider could not reach you was brilliant. Perhaps you don't know how close you were to being swept up onto that destrier, but I'll tell you, I did not think you would escape."

Sorcha finally pulled her gaze from the water, her eyes clear now. "I learned well how to elude my father's guards when they were forced to chase me around the courtyard at bedtime or when they needed to drag me back to the keep because women were not supposed to join them on their warmongering journeys."

"Your father told me about some of your adventures." He had not believed a woman could have such audacity or be so quick-witted. He believed it now.

A man would be proud to claim such a woman for his own. If only he could trust her. The doubt frustrated him when he wanted her so badly. He needed to start replacing her old memories of her first lover with moments so heated they would burn away all else.

"But tell me why you came to Connacht. You wanted to tell me what Edward had done?"

"Nay. I wanted to inform you that your life and your son's were at risk. I heard that du Bois was to be wed and that he wanted to make sure his legal heir would be the only claimant to his growing legacy."

He'd heard that Edward had debauched a princess while in Ireland—an act that stirred political trouble without ever swinging a blade. Of course, Hugh hadn't known that Edward had tricked the girl in question into a secret, false marriage. When her father had written to important families in England requesting information about the Norman who had visited his daughter, Sorcha's claims had been dismissed as the lies of a desperate woman.

All of which he was certain Sorcha understood. There was no need for him to reiterate the past she'd grown to resent.

Sorcha paled and he knew the rocking boat was not the cause. She stared at him in silence for a long moment while the men-at-arms shouted insults at one another and argued over their dice game.

"Onora told me the men in that riding party forced her to tell them where I was. They were after me and Conn. And you knew Edward wanted to kill us."

"I did until the fake friar poisoned me and then bludgeoned me." His head ached with the old wound just thinking about it. "I am fortunate he did not skewer me when he had the chance."

"Perhaps he did not possess as black a heart as his over-lord." Sorcha shook her head and frowned. "I cannot believe any man would target his own child."

Hugh could see the disillusionment in her eyes. Surely any feeling she had for du Bois had to have withered under the harsh light of truth. No woman could care for such a man. But would her new understanding make her all the more wary of the feelings she had once had for Hugh? It was too soon to tell.

"Du Bois was raised by a cruel stepfather." They had not met until both were already knighted, and Edward had coveted the family legacy of power and influence that had been Hugh's. Instead of political importance, however, Edward had inherited a mean streak. "He sided with the baron I deposed at Edenrock. And even though I had the king's blessing to take the keep, Edward was trying to intercede by suggesting to Henry that I used excessive violence."

Sorcha blanched. "You would not."

"Of course not. But he had his men make random attacks on my new villagers and flew my banner while he did so." He'd been on his way to London to argue his case to the king personally when Edward's man had waylaid him. Hugh had met Gregory to discuss the possibility for a peaceful resolution between the feuding cousins, but Hugh's efforts had been rewarded by treachery. "His cause was helped by the fact that we bear some family resemblance. Our mothers were sisters."

"Onora could have ended up with a son like Edward," Sorcha mused, her voice unsteady with the realization. "For that matter, Conn would have grown up with a cruel father if Edward had not left me. My own son could have turned into such a person."

He reached out to touch her. Comfort her.

"I do not think your father will thank me for harboring your sister for long." He thought it too risky to send her back to Connacht with Edward's men searching for them, but that didn't mean he could allow an Irish princess to reside with them indefinitely. The king would need the political affiliation that came with her marriage, especially since Sorcha's nuptials had cost him more than they benefited him.

Hugh was not sure if his marriage would be sanctioned by his king and ultimately blessed under his real name, but until he could make Edward pay for what he'd done to Sorcha, Hugh would not risk upsetting the Irish king. Fate had tied Hugh to the feisty ruler as surely as it had tied him to the man's daughter.

Sorcha bit her lip as a rogue wind caught one of her veils and freed it from the heavy plait of her auburn hair. The airy linen snapped in the breeze as the rolling water splashed up on the side of the vessel and dotted their faces with cool spray.

"Would you consider waiting to decide Onora's fate until after the winter?" She busied herself with tucking the veil back under her hair with the others. "She would be of great help to me in a new household."

"You assume I will have a household to return to."

Her hands fell away from her hair as she straightened.

"I thought you recalled your holding. You said your conquest of Edenrock was ordained by your king." Her forehead furrowed with confusion.

He heard her distrust of men in the question and he knew she had reason to doubt him. Because of that, he took his time to answer her question patiently.

"It was a new holding and my reign was marked by turbulence. Considering I'll have been gone for nigh on three moons and that Edward has coveted it from the start, I will be surprised if my men have retained control of the holding." Hugh suspected that taking control of Edenrock had been a key motive in Edward's attempt to kill him. And perhaps Edward had spread word of Hugh's death from the moment his vassal had said the deed was done.

"Then we must devise a plan to win back your lands." Sorcha's jaw flexed with the intractable will of a woman who did not like to lose.

A woman who had not only survived exile, but who had thrived like her profuse roses at her cottage in the wild. Hugh wanted to believe her thirst to win the upcoming battle was rooted in the connection they shared—a passion apparent to him even when he had no idea they'd been destined to meet. But he knew the fire in her eyes could well be all about revenge on the lover who had repaid her trust with the worst kind of betrayal.

"Very well. We will remain true to our unlawful wedding vows for at least as long as it takes to ensure Edward is stripped of his power and stands accused of his wrongs."

"Agreed." She nodded with cool satisfaction, assuring him she would not request freedom from the fictional Hugh Fitz Henry for at least a little longer.

Seeing the fierceness in her expression, Hugh guessed he made a powerful ally, whether or not she could wield a sword. And consequences be damned, he couldn't help the swell of pride in her fearlessness. She had faced down six riders today with nothing more than a dagger and her wits before noontime, yet she was ready to take on the world by nightfall.

"Shall we seal the deal?"

She reared back, her eyebrows lifting in surprise. "You require a blood oath?"

"Hardly." Another time, he might have laughed at a misunderstanding so far from what he had in mind. But right now, the heat in his veins burned away any other emotion. "I was thinking more along the lines of a kiss."

Chapter Eighteen

Like bellows to a flame, Hugh's suggestion fanned a roaring blaze out of little more than ashes for Sorcha.

She had been thinking about a strong partnership to defeat a common enemy. A battle plan to protect her son. Yet with a handful of words and one lengthy, assessing look, Hugh de Montaigne had set fire to her skin. She feared no amount of sea spray misting over her face could cool the sudden desire.

"You play a risky game for a man who has vowed not to touch me." She acknowledged that his declaration had hurt her heart far more than it tweaked her feminine pride.

He had used her silence about her husband's resemblance to him as evidence of her deceitfulness. Yet why should she have trusted him any more than he trusted in her? The only reason he'd confided about his loss of memory was because she had guessed something was amiss and he had needed her cooperation to solve the mystery of his past. Besides, as a woman with a child to protect, she'd had far more to lose than he if she had put her faith in the wrong hands.

"We need not touch save for the kiss." He negotiated the deal as smoothly as a foreign courtier bartering for a handsome bride price.

If he had been a guest at her father's dinner table, she would have smiled at his easy persistence and seductive logic. But they were as good as alone considering all the supervision three drunken men-at-arms would provide. One of whom was already so deep in his cups that he snored.

Perhaps that was just as well, Sorcha thought, a plan coming to mind. He wanted to kiss without touching? Any man who would be her husband—even for a short time— would do well to learn she did not take orders like a common servant.

"Very well." She forced herself to be still and allow him to come to her. She would not aid him in his quest.

Instead, she hoped to thwart him mightily.

For a moment, his expression registered surprise and perhaps a touch of suspicion. Soon enough, however, his amber eyes darkened to the deepest gold. He moved closer, nudging her heart to a faster pace. Her breathing quickened and she licked her lips at the last possible moment, anticipating the taste of him.

It was no chore to put her plan into action. As soon as his mouth brushed hers she arched into him, pressing her breasts flush against his broad chest. She wound her arms about his neck, anchoring him there. It was then, when she'd touched him beyond any doubt of an accidental caress, that she had planned to pull away.

She'd only wanted to make a point, after all.

But the firepower of the kiss worked both ways, sliding over her senses with the thrill of a lightning storm. A bolt of pure sizzle struck her deep inside, sending waves of warmth tingling through her limbs. She shivered with the power of it, her whole body responding to contact with Hugh.

She'd been drawn to him from the beginning, but the pull was even stronger since the return of his memories. There was an easy self-assurance in him now, an intensity that called to her on every level. Being around him felt familiar and new at the same time.

A soft hum of pleasure vibrated through her and she loosened her hold on his shoulders so she could simply absorb the feel of him. His muscular form embodied strength, his flesh twitching beneath his tunic with the effort it cost him to hold back. She did not know if she could have done so were she in his place.

If *she* was the one determined to make their marriage a union of cold self-denial.

With that chilling thought, she released him. Pulling away sharply, Sorcha knew the only way she could end that kiss was with quick, decisive separation. Her heart pounded with the loss of his shoulders under her fingers. His hard chest to her aching breasts. His hot, demanding mouth guiding hers to kiss him in a way that pleased him best.

What if she didn't know him as well as she thought? She trusted his honor not to abandon her, and she believed he would protect her physically. But could he deal the final blow to an already wounded heart? She would need time to trust him again. To know this new man.

By the time she raked her eyes open, he stared at her with the same wary respect one might give an enemy in the practice yard. It was a far cry from the yearning devotion she ached to see in a man's eyes just once in her life. But perhaps it was the best she could expect from this marriage made in haste and practicality.

"Next time I had better make it clear you should not touch me either." His statement lacked conviction or else she might have been offended.

She straightened the bodice of her surcoat, only too glad to reward his cold heart with a glimpse of her breasts as she did so.

"Since you cannot command me, that would be a difficult vow to enforce." She stood, seeing no good that could come of remaining beside him, trembling with unfulfilled needs.

She peered behind her as she stood, grateful to see the men-at-arms were all suitably drunk and oblivious to what went on in the bow amid the chests containing her dowry.

"I have a mind to enforce it quite easily, Princess." Remaining in his seat, he reached up to her hair and—before she knew what he was about—he tugged one of her veils free from the silver circlet she wore. "I shall keep this on my person for next time we meet privately." He waved the thin length of linen for emphasis before he tucked it into the waist of his braies. "And if I feel the need to kiss you, I'll tie your hands behind you."

Her face must have betrayed her dismay—along with the desire—for he grinned like the devil himself.

"You wouldn't dare." Her provocation did not come out quite as threatening as she would have liked, but the air seemed to have left her lungs.

His hands briefly circled her wrists, just long enough to make her jump.

"Not only would I dare, I am confident you would enjoy every moment."

Horrified at both the thought and the treacherous leap of her heartbeat that suggested the knave might very well be correct, Sorcha spun on her heel and walked away to the sound of his laughter in her ears.

Edenrock appeared as Hugh had expected.

The journey there had been slow but uneventful with late rains rendering some roads impassable. The wretched weather not only made the trip treacherous, but it had been almost impossible to steal a moment alone with Sorcha. Now, almost a fortnight after their arrival in England, he rode the perimeter of his old keep where the standard of the du Bois family flew. He'd heard reports of this en route to Edenrock. Edward had been quick to spread word of his death after Gregory had struck him with the blow to the head. And while the king had not yet granted him an audience to make the transition official, Hugh's men had believed du Bois's claim when Hugh never returned from London three moons prior. They'd admitted Edward freely, no doubt grateful to have an overlord who would maintain their pay.

"The thieving, murderous bastard." Sorcha's outburst was uncharacteristic as she rode her courser beside him, her surcoat artfully arranged for her to ride astride in a fashion that both amused him and earned his grudging respect. They would have never made it through the muddy terrain if the women had not been capable of handling their own mounts.

But Sorcha had been unnaturally quiet on the subject of du Bois on the trip. After her bold embrace on the ship to England, she had retreated. Hugh had suspected she'd taken his teasing too seriously and sought to avoid him because of that. He refused to regret giving her fair warning, however, since he meant to tempt her beyond reason the next time they found time to be alone that was not consumed by plotting Edward's downfall.

"You realize I will have to act quickly." He had come to admire Sorcha's political knowledge during their long talks while riding, a faculty he'd recognized in her shortly after meeting her. Her years at her father's elbow had given her a shrewd understanding of men's ambitions and how to wield power assiduously. The lure of her intelligence appealed to him as much as the draw of her sensual nature and bold embrace of life. "Henry could approve du Bois's seat as ruler here at any time."

Sorcha's courser slowed and he had to tug on his own mount's bridle to remain close to her. He'd been grateful to get her all to himself for a little while, if only to speak of a plan for recovering Edenrock. She'd barely left her son's side this last fortnight, trusting no one but Hugh or her sister to watch over the child. Onora was with the boy now at their encampment in the woods while all three of the men-at-arms stood guard during Hugh and Sorcha's absence.

"Perhaps the king will give it to him as a wedding gift." She looked up into the walled city surrounding Edenrock. They had reached a low-lying section of lands where the wood and stone walls were built just above a deep ravine to deter invaders, yet the pitch of the hillside allowed them to see into the village all the way to the keep from their position on the other side of the ravine.

As Hugh followed her gaze, he spied tents being erected and huge slabs of meat being smoked over low-burning pits. Men and women hurried through the village and around the courtyard in a swarm of activity. Wood for bonfires was being assembled in giant piles. Tables and benches were being carried from the hall and from the wealthier homes closest to the keep. A steady stream of people poured into the courtyard from the direction of the city gate.

Hugh knew at once she was right. No man went to this much trouble for his nuptials unless a king would be in attendance. Unless the event might result in lands and a title to go with them.

"We haven't much time." He couldn't possibly wage a successful siege before this event. The wedding celebration had to be in the next few days, judging by the level of preparation.

"You must see the king first. Before Edward has a chance." Sorcha's face had grown lean from long days on the road without proper meals or adequate rest.

He had watched her sleep restlessly many nights, no matter that he took time to build small shelters to keep out the rain.

Hugh was struck by the thought that he had not cared for her properly. He'd not trusted her father to keep her safe, yet she had known more danger and heartache since meeting him than ever before.

"But possession of the lands is nine-tenths of the law." He knew Henry well enough to recall the king would not approve Edward's claim if he wasn't already sitting in a secure keep. Then again, he wouldn't approve Hugh's claim without the same.

The king had enough battles of his own without fighting those of his nobles.

"So you must be at the helm before the king arrives." She frowned. "How?"

"Stealth." He had never been one to fight battles with underhanded techniques, but how could a man wage combat honorably against a foe that excelled in dark and ignoble acts?

Any man who would harm a child—his own child, no less—had already sunk to unspeakable depravity.

"We sneak in?"

He shook his head. "No. Or rather, *I* will choose that path, but you must realize you could have no hand in such a dangerous scheme."

"I do have Conn to think about," she admitted, though she did not appear quite as resigned to a passive role as he would have liked.

"Exactly. But sneaking into Edenrock won't be so difficult since I have an advantage now."

"How so?"

"Recall there were no survivors in Edward's riding party back on the beach in Ireland. Du Bois does not know what became of his men or us during that attack at the harbor, so my presence here will take him by surprise."

"None of his men know we are alive." Sorcha nodded, her jaw clenching with grim determination. "We must act quickly."

"We'll start by sending in an advance party tonight." If Hugh could find out the time line for the wedding and the king's arrival, he would begin making his plans to take over the keep. "I'll send someone into Edenrock as a peddler or a jongleur for the wedding. There is so much activity through the gate, no one will notice an extra minstrel or cheese maker."

"Who should we trust to play such a role?" Sorcha's gaze went back to the activity inside the city walls.

The smoke from the roasting meat was so thick Hugh could almost taste the boar and venison.

Nay, he tasted imminent victory. The wedding would be a godsend to accomplish his goals and recover the keep that should belong to him. To the woman who had entrusted herself to his care before she even knew his real name.

"We shall send Eamon." The Irishman would be ideal. He was young and canny enough to play such a role. "No one at Edenrock will recognize him."

Chapter Nineteen

To refuse Hugh's assignment would have roused suspicion.

Eamon strode through the gates of Edenrock with no problem, declaring himself a storyteller to entertain the wedding guests as Gregory had suggested during their meeting in the clearing. Gregory had been displeased with Eamon's lack of cooperation so far, but Eamon thought he'd successfully convinced the man he needed more time. He'd already learned the wedding ceremony was two days hence, though the king planned to arrive the following day. Many of the meats and preparations were to welcome the sovereign's arrival.

Now, striding through the village to bide his time while he came up with a plan, Eamon wondered what to do next. Did he gamble that he could persuade Onora into his bed and keep his alliance with Hugh and Sorcha? Or did he run to Edward to reveal everything he knew in exchange for a lucrative reward?

He could not truly believe Hugh's cousin meant to hurt his own brat the way Sorcha believed. Eamon had come to see the fire at the cottage as more of a warning to him that he needed to do his job if he wanted to maintain his standing with Conn's father. After all, no one had been hurt.

And by the saints, he hadn't been making any progress with Onora after leaving Connacht. Eamon paused in the door of a baker's hut to ask where the town's tavern was located. It would be the best place to gather information no matter what he decided to do next.

Taking the route the baker suggested, he wove around the village well and received giggles and glances from a handful of maids filling their jugs. The feminine attention was far more than he'd received from Onora of late. The Irish princess had grown more cautious since leaving her father's keep, maintaining her distance from him. Could she have sensed his interest and felt threatened somehow? Or was she simply a tease?

"Ale, please," he told the tavern wench, a plump mistress with strong arms and an inviting smile.

She, too, kept her eye on him as she filled his cup, swaying her hips as she crossed the small drinking hall to serve him.

"Here ye are," she announced with a flourish, leaning down to set the cup on the rough-hewn table. Her movements placed her ample breasts within tasting distance were he so inclined, an invitation he did not miss.

Would he toss aside his opportunities to swive at will to seduce a cold princess? As much as Eamon would have liked to know the power and influence that came with being son-in-law to an Irish king, these English girls were pleasing to his eye. And with the kind of coin he could earn from du Bois by revealing Hugh de Montaigne's presence, Eamon could support himself better than he'd ever done as a groom or even a man-at-arms.

Waiting to quench his thirst, he tumbled the barmaid into his lap. The tavern was empty save for a few old men who were probably too nearsighted to see what went on under his table anyhow. Eamon would sate another hunger first, then proceed into Edenrock to renew his acquaintance with Edward du Bois.

"Have you agreed upon a way to breach the keep quietly?" Sorcha asked Hugh late that night after he had finished making plans with his men.

She hated being left out of much of the discussion, but she understood a foreign woman in the midst of men who did not know her might make the small force uneasy when Hugh had to prepare for the next day. In addition to the men-at-arms who'd accompanied them from Connacht, Hugh had managed to reach a handful of knights who had sworn allegiance to him once. He'd stumbled onto one in the forest on the man's return to Edenrock for the wedding, and had quickly confided the tale of du Bois's treachery. That knight had gone on to secretly contact five others who either owed Hugh tribute or had suffered at du Bois's hands. The company had broken up after talking late into the night.

Now Sorcha cornered Hugh outside the tent she shared with Conn and her sister. No torchlight ringed the camp, a measure they'd taken to help keep their presence a secret. The only light came from the filtered glow of the moon through the trees and the dying red smolder of ashes in the fire pit. There were no stars to sleep under tonight between the dense trees and the low-lying clouds that made her feel trapped.

Anxious.

"We think so, but we will need Eamon's help when he

returns. He probably couldn't discover all we needed to know before the gates closed at dusk." Hugh kept his voice down, more mindful of potential spies in the wood than out of concern for her sleeping family members. "He will arrive back at first light."

She nodded and, for just a moment, took comfort in his warrior strength so close to her. She had avoided much physical contact with him ever since the incident on the ship. Not out of fear. His teasing suggestion had surprised her, but over time, it had stirred a deeper hunger. She knew Hugh would never harm her. No matter that her trust in men did not come easily after her poorly placed faith in Edward, Sorcha at least trusted *herself* enough to know she was right about Hugh's honor. Her judgment was far more keen than it had been two years ago. Being a mother had given her a wary sense of caution to balance out her passions.

Instead, she had avoided being alone with Hugh because she feared he could hurt her heart, and that he might do so unwittingly. She had come to care about him that day of the cottage fire. And while she had still been reeling with the knowledge that she could still harbor deep affection for a man, Hugh had already been accusing her of being secretive. Deceptive.

It was a view he might still hold about her and it was a view that stung. What would it be like to care for him all the more, only to have him set her aside because he would never trust her?

"What will be my role tomorrow?" She had Onora's help with Conn. That meant she was free to aid Hugh and his men.

"Let us speak privately." He waved her toward his tent beside hers.

The other men-at-arms were surely still awake, though

their tents were farther away. Sorcha did not blame him for wishing to keep his plans secret, but a shiver of awareness danced over her skin as he took her by the arm to escort her into his tent.

"Wait." He halted her as soon as she ducked inside the tall, narrow shelter. His arm blocked her passage, the thick rope of hard muscle brushing just beneath her breasts.

"What is it?" Her breath hitched, her heart jumping at his nearness.

"The fur extends almost to the door," he informed her, explaining the layout in the dark. "If you remove your slippers, we can sit there to speak."

Suddenly, their private discussion took on a whole wealth of new possibilities. She took his arm to steady herself while she slid off her shoes and then tentatively stepped forward.

Feet landing on soft pelt, Sorcha sighed at this small decadence after their trek through the rain and mud in his cloudy and cool homeland.

"I did not know a hardened warrior would spoil himself with such luxury," she chided, grateful he could not see the way her whole body practically melted at the soft, inviting warmth beneath her toes.

"I bought it in Connacht when I thought I might have a wedding night sooner or later." Through the dark, he reached for her hands and encircled her wrists, drawing her down.

The feel of his hands creating gentle manacles around her limbs sent a fierce shiver of longing through her. Memories of his sensual threat to tie her hands behind her spurred a tingle of anticipation in every pore of her skin.

"Have a seat," he urged, releasing her when she settled beside him in the dark, cocooned in the warmth of the hide tent and thick pelt. "Tell me what role you think you should take in the conquest of a keep."

With an effort, she steered her thoughts away from the warmth and strength of the man beside her to make sure he understood that she was utterly serious.

"It would be different if you were taking Edenrock by sword. But you said yourself, you must plan a conquest by stealth. I am offering my help."

"Tomorrow, I want you to remain here, close to the tents and one of my guards at all times." Hugh's warning cooled some of the warm tenderness flowing through her veins for him.

"All my hopes for the future—for my son—ride on your shoulders tomorrow." She knew if Hugh was not successful in recovering his lands, she and Conn would be running from the threat of Edward du Bois forever. "If I can help in any way—"

"I cannot fight this battle if I fear for you and Conn." His hand cupped her face, his voice steely and soft at the same time. "I swore to your father I would keep you safe."

A stab of disappointment filled her as she realized she had been hoping for more—a sense that he wanted to protect her for her own sake. Because he had grown to care about her the same way she had come to care for him.

He had taken her cause when she was an exile, pulling her out of her banishment and back into the world. Renewing some of her faith in herself. And even if he had done none of those things, the tender way he treated her son alone would have stolen her heart.

"I will try to remain hidden here, but winning the day means my son is free from du Bois forever. If I think I can help you and still keep him safe, I will do so."

"A warrior at heart," he whispered, his fingers tunneling under her veils to twine in the hair at her nape.

Fire skipped from his touch to set her senses ablaze.

"I cannot allow anything to happen to you." She had many reasons, but she could not share them with a man who only claimed to protect her because of a promise to her father. Sorcha had already loved once without having those tender emotions returned. She would be careful not to fall into such a treacherous state with this man, as well.

And yet, if tomorrow did not bring success to their campaign, would she not mourn the loss of this chance to be with him? To deny them both something that brought such pleasure when they might not have another opportunity…

Perhaps she only justified what she wanted so desperately, but right now, she needed to take whatever she could from this time with Hugh.

"You think you cannot stay put? Perhaps I should make good on an old threat then." He leaned close to brush a kiss along her jaw while his fingers massaged the back of her neck.

Dazed with the feel of his hands on her after all this time, she was slow to make sense of his words.

Until he tugged free one of the veils from her circlet.

She stilled beneath his kisses, her heartbeat hammering madly in her breast.

"You would not dare." She trembled lightly as the veil trailed down her neck, slithering over her bodice to pool in her lap.

"I warned you I would tie your hands," he reminded her, retrieving the delicate linen from her thighs with a slow, deliberate draw of his fingertip across her legs. "It might spur me on in battle tomorrow if I think of you here, bound completely to my bed."

* * *

Hugh seized upon Sorcha's quick intake of breath, pressing his mouth to hers. He hadn't intended to touch her until he was certain Edward had been swiped from her memory for good. Now he knew she hated the man, but he didn't have any assurance she was ready to care about anyone else in his place.

If tomorrow ended badly, however, he would never have another chance to touch her. To feel the tide of her incredible passion sweeping through him, dictating everything else in the world but them.

Sorcha had been the first woman he'd had when he awoke with no memories. Now she could be the last. And he wouldn't trade that chance for anything.

Her hands landed on his chest in a soft slide of fingertips that quickly turned into a scratch of light nails as she gripped his tunic and tugged him closer. He teased the fabric of her veil up her back and over her shoulder to drift down her arm.

He had the feeling she had thought about being bound and at his mercy nearly as often as he had over the last weeks. Sometimes when they were riding through the forest on their slow journey here, he would turn to see her looking at him and her cheeks would burn.

Pulling away from his kiss, she held him at bay, breathing hard.

"Your suggestions are wicked," she accused, her sweetly quivering form assuring him she did not find his wickedness unappealing.

"You should not dismiss them so easily until you've tried them." He tugged one of the laces that tightened her surcoat and freed the heavy fabric.

Shedding her of her garments now would prevent him

from having to do so after he'd cinched her wrists together for the sensual feast he planned to give himself before morning. He had been operating on pure instinct the last time he'd bedded her, but now he had the benefit of experience working for him and he planned to make sure Sorcha never forgot this. For all intents and purposes, this would be their wedding night.

"You've seen me wield a knife," she returned, her fingers at work on the ties of his tunic, her hands trembling with a need that inflamed his own. "So you must know how dire my retribution will be on the next man who treats my affections lightly."

Her words—however threatening—ignited new hope in his chest. She spoke of affection? The idea that she wanted him for reasons that went beyond passion made him all the more eager to claim her as his wife, if only for tonight.

"Never," he swore, releasing her veil to fall silently into the fur while he peeled her surcoat down and off.

His eyes had become more accustomed to the darkness and the moonlight filtering through seams in the hide tent helped him to see her pale, womanly form clad in only a thin white kirtle. Her breasts pushed at the fabric, stretching the loose material almost taut so that the swell of full breasts was visible beneath. Hunger surged through him, prompting him to take a nip at her through the fabric until the linen clung moistly to her beaded nipples.

She repaid him by gripping his thighs with her splayed hands, stroking up the muscle and then back down, never reaching the place where he most craved her caress.

Impatient for more, he sought the hem of her kirtle and tugged it up her legs. When he reached her hips, he palmed her bottom just enough to lift her slightly and free the material. As tempting as it would have been for his hands to remain right there, to drag her hips against his and take what he wanted, he released her to drive her passions higher. Hotter.

Pulling the kirtle the rest of the way off, he tossed it aside in the tent, rendering her completely naked except for the circlet adorning her head with two remaining veils. He pushed her down to lie in the fur, her body temptingly displayed for his pleasure.

"I used to have the narrow frame that my sister has." Her soft assertion, tinged with a hint of regret, surprised him from such a bold and otherwise confident woman.

"What man would not prefer the lush curves of fruitful womanhood to the untried body of a girl?" He bent to kiss the indentation of her slim waist above one round hip. "You are all the more beautiful for the life you give."

"Your touch makes me believe you." She twitched restlessly beneath him, her hands scratching lightly over his shoulders while her legs rubbed against his.

He rose to stand, shedding his tunic and his braies, unsure how long he would be able to deny her when the scent of her desire made him drunk with need. Yet he knew he had a little while to wait, since he planned to fulfill the fantasy they'd shared these past weeks.

Stretching out over her, he covered her. Her skin was creamy smooth and sweetly scented by her soap. Roses. He would forever associate the flower with her from the ramble of blooms that used to adorn her cottage. He twined his fingers with hers and then drew her arms high above her head.

"What are you doing?" Her voice was thin and breathless as her breasts swelled against his chest.

Carefully, he wound the linen of her veil around first one wrist and then the other.

"What does it feel like I'm doing?" He cinched a knot between her hands, pulling the fabric taut but hardly inescapable.

"Wicked deeds," she whispered back, twining her soft thigh between his legs. "You must teach them to me so I may take revenge one day."

Arching her back against the fur, she pressed her hips to his, sealing his shaft against her belly. The contact lit a fierceness in him he would not be able to subdue.

"You learn too much all on your own." He cupped her hips and savored the softness of her flesh there before ducking to kiss her breasts thrust high because of her raised arms.

Her sighs were sweet music as he learned the taste of her all over again. It had been too long since he'd last lain with her, and his body urged him faster.

"I am helpless," she complained, her breath hitching on the words as he licked a path down her abdomen to the curls between her legs.

"All the more reason to kiss you here." He positioned his mouth above the plump, hot center of her and gave her the most intimate of attentions. "Once I free you, I fear you will only incite me past the point of no return."

He spread her legs wide, taking his fill of her while she tried to stifle the urgent noises she made. In the end, he had to still her hips with one hand and cover her mouth with the other as she came for him in a spasm that convulsed her whole body. She whimpered against his palm as she found her release, the waves of pleasure rolling through her and into him for long moments. When at last she stilled, he released her, leveraging himself over her to untie her hands.

He was unprepared for her full-on attack. She rolled him to his back with one shove to his shoulders, using his surprise against him.

She did not hold him down for long though. Rising up on her haunches she sat astride him, peering down at him while a column of moonlight cut across her face, illuminating her delicate features.

"You are my prisoner now." She arched a sandy eyebrow at him as she trailed exploring fingers up the length of his shaft. "Subject to my will."

At another time, he might have grinned at this bit of outrageous audacity. Right now, he wondered if she was right.

"Sorcha." He placed his hand over hers, guiding her fingers to grip her tighter.

Of course, giving this woman additional power over him proved a dangerous thing. A handful of strokes later, he was hanging by a thread, his jaw clenched tight with the need to be inside her.

He rose to sit, keeping her on top of him, balanced on his lap. She made a soft cry, but did not protest as he lifted her hips, positioning her above him. He peered up at her, needing to see her as he came inside her at last.

If this was to be their only night together as man and wife, he would make sure she did not forget it. She would never think of any other man but him.

"Hugh." Perhaps she picked the thought out of his mind as she steadied herself on his shoulders, her eyes never leaving his.

When he entered her, he watched her every moment of the way. Her legs locked behind his back, holding him close. Her breasts swayed with the movement as they rocked together in a timeless rhythm.

The heat they built bound them together like no ties ever could have. At the last minute he pulled her to him and kissed her, needing to taste her as he spilled his seed inside her. There would be no withdrawal now that they had spoken their vows.

He did not risk his life tomorrow just for himself. He did it for her. For their family. For a future they might forge together.

Holding tight to his passionate wife, Hugh lost himself inside her, the desire burning away everything else between them until there was only this elemental connection.

When the night cooled along with their bodies, he laid her by his side to pass the night. No matter what the morrow brought, they had—at least for one night—come together with no secrets and no memories of the past. If Hugh fell in battle, it would be Sorcha's name on his lips.

But long before sleep claimed him, he vowed to do anything in his power to win her for all time.

"Are you surprised Eamon hasn't returned?" Sorcha asked as Hugh held her hours later.

They had slept little, the night passing in a blur of ecstasy. She'd never been so exhausted in such an utterly blissful fashion, though Hugh didn't seem tired in the least. Her head lay on his chest and she took comfort from the rhythmic beat of his heart beneath her ear.

The only thing that kept it from being the most beautiful night of her life was her fear for the coming dawn. Nay. Even with the fears, it had still been the most beautiful night of her life.

She feared she had already lost her heart to Hugh, but she could never regret the alternate tenderness and fierceness of what they'd shared. The night far overshadowed anything she'd ever experienced.

"I know they've been closing the gate at night in the village," Hugh answered, his lips coming to rest on the top of her head as he stroked her shoulder. "I assume he will not be able to leave until the drawbridge lowers again at first light."

"I hope you are right." She did not know Eamon well despite all his years as her groom. But her father trusted the man enough to make him a man-at-arms. Surely that meant he would fulfill this duty well. "But what if he does not return?"

"Do you have any reason to doubt him?" Sliding out from under her, he propped his head on one hand while he watched her in the shafts of moonlight.

"I may be worrying overmuch since I do not trust easily anymore." She sighed anxiously. "I cannot point to any one thing that makes me uneasy. But I do recall he did not inform me of my sister's presence in the woods that day near the harbor before we sailed for England."

"And he should never have left her unguarded for the sake of keeping her presence a secret," Hugh agreed. "I credited his action to a youthful mistake, but did not think it would be one he'll make again. He seemed genuinely distressed at the idea of anything happening to Onora."

Sorcha's heart eased a little, remembering Eamon's overtures toward Onora in the days that followed her abduction. She relaxed into Hugh's touches that still sent dizzying sparks through her even after all the times they'd come together this night.

"You do not think his attentions seemed a bit—inappropriate?" She couldn't quite pin down what had bothered her, but there had been something in his manner that made Sorcha fear he liked Onora a little too well.

Hugh set aside a blanket that he had pulled over them sometime in the night. Tucking the one end under her arm, he rose from their bed.

"I have not observed him do anything more than sit close to Onora and perhaps gaze at her longingly, but if you sensed something amiss, I will check on his whereabouts immediately."

"Nay." She reached to brush his calf as he tugged a tunic over his head, wondering if she should not have spoken. She did not want to become foolishly apprehensive, seeing danger around every corner. "I would not have thought twice about Eamon's task inside the walls of Edenrock if he had returned last night. I thought he would have been back by then to tell you of his findings."

"As did I." Hugh pulled his braies into place and tied them snug around his hips. "Your concern reflects my own. Nay, I only had vague notions that Eamon was not as competent as he should be, but I told myself he had not been at his task for long. Knowing his behavior with Onora only underscores my own thoughts."

"Will I see you before you head to Edenrock with your men?" Sorcha still did not know how the keep would be taken. They had not passed the night talking strategy, but then again, Hugh had needed Eamon's help to finalize his plans.

"I do not know." Kneeling beside her, he reached for her. Kissed her hard. "If it is close to first light there might not be time. Promise me you will not go anywhere near Edward du Bois no matter what happens."

Sorcha knew the only thing that could make her do so was if Conn's life was endangered. Or if Hugh needed her. She squeezed him tighter and prayed for his safety.

"You know I cannot make that promise." Placing a kiss upon his cheek, she released him.

Only to see the dangerous glint in his golden eyes.

"Would you still be the rash and reckless princess?" He rose to stand, his shoulders appearing all the more massive from her view. "Can you not yet see the danger you could bring to others by acting upon your own impulses?"

His words cut her to the quick, especially falling so close on the heels of what they'd shared. What she thought they'd shared.

She shook her head, not trusting her voice to speak.

"I only want to keep you safe." He buckled his sword belt about his hips and then ducked to kiss her once more, but it was a chaste kiss. A goodbye. "That's all I've ever wanted."

He departed the tent, leaving her alone with the realization that keeping her safe had motivated every move he'd made from his initial arrival in Ireland, to his marriage to her. A marriage he had not bothered consummating until now.

Perhaps that had been part of the plan as well. Claim her as his own only so that he could sway her to his will with sensual sorcery. Heart in her throat, Sorcha rose to dress for the day that would decide her future and her son's.

Chapter Twenty

Eamon had not recalled that Edward du Bois possessed the soulless eyes of some creature returned from the grave.

He stood in front of du Bois's seat in Edenrock's great hall with the tavern wench—Nelda—behind him. She had been hot to enter the keep, but he noticed she shrank back now that du Bois's attention had turned to them. Maybe he shouldn't have brought her here. Nelda was no Onora. She did not make him appear successful or important.

And du Bois was no ordinary man. He had grown thicker through the shoulders and chest since Eamon had last seen him, as if the man took additional broadsword practice for sport.

His dark, dusty robes looked as if he had just been in battle and hadn't bothered to brush himself off. Eamon fervently hoped the dark red stain on his tunic was wine.

"So Sorcha lives?" the soulless knight asked, entertaining himself and a few other men by throwing knives—end over end—into a large board of soft wood. Someone had outlined a star shape in ashes on the wood, perhaps guiding where each man made his target.

The small triangle where the overlord threw was chock-full of slit marks. Du Bois, it appeared, was a very good shot.

"Aye. I was prepared to bring her and her son to you in Connacht, my lord," he lied, knowing that while he could have easily transported a baby without much notice through the Irish forests, he would have never tried to take the princess.

Lady Sorcha was no mild maid who frightened easily. Eamon had realized, even before he saw her wield a blade that day at the harbor beach, that she would not hesitate to lop off a man's hand if he touched her against her will.

"But you did not." Du Bois waited while his men cleared the board for a new game.

No minstrels played here as in Tiernan Con Connacht's great hall. This place was full of men throwing dice and hounds gnawing bones or—in some corners—fighting one another while the men placed bets on the winner. Eamon could not wait to depart. He thought of Onora's gentle beauty and sharp wit. She would have never set foot in such a hall as this.

"The lady's cottage was torched before I could bring them to you. By the time I caught up to Gregory to arrange an exchange, he was killed in a skirmish with Sorcha's new husband."

Some of the men around du Bois grew quiet and he sensed a new stillness in the hall.

"My man is dead while the Irish whore goes on to make new conquests?" A tick pulsed beneath du Bois's right eye.

The sweat flooding Eamon's brow assured Eamon the only thing scarier than a soulless knight was one who was both soulless and angry. Hoping to end their talk as quickly as possible, he came straight to the point.

"I can bring Sorcha and her son to you now, under the same terms we agreed upon for my silence about your death." He had hoped for far more coin than he'd received then, but he valued his neck more than gold in the end. Upon further reflection, he did not trust the soundness of du Bois's mind.

"You did not keep your silence about that though, did you?" Du Bois accepted a new dagger from one of the men beside him. "You have revealed to all of my guests that I am not dead."

A few of his cronies chortled at this while Eamon struggled to follow the logic.

"I did exactly what you asked—"

At a nod from du Bois, Eamon was surrounded by two knights who outweighed him by ten stone apiece. He did not even have time to reach for his sword. They grabbed him roughly by the arms, jerking him forward as he fought. They dragged him close to their leader while Nelda screamed.

"I have no need of you, witless worm. I already knew my cousin went to Connacht to find the whore. And thanks to you, I now know he has returned and most likely lurks outside my gate." His dark gaze moved from Eamon to one of the knights who held him. "Take him to the dungeon and consider what piece of him you'd like to send back to my cousin."

Nelda screamed again and she would have fled except she was trapped by the bodies of several men-at-arms who had lost all interest in their dice game. They crowded her, surrounding her like dogs circling a sheep. Eamon knew what would become of her.

And him.

Oh God, if he could only take back what he'd done.

Somewhere in the hall, another woman cried out, earning more laughter from the men. And then, just as a hulking knight reared back a fist in front of him, Eamon realized the high, womanish cries were his own.

His last thought was a fervent prayer Onora would not suffer for his sins.

Hugh's hand itched to reach for his sword.

He lay in the back of a peddler's wagon with two other knights, their backs pressed to rough and rotting floorboards while they balanced piles of wood on their chests. They decided against loading the wagon with food products for fear a cook's helper might be called to the gate to look through the delivery. But loads of wood they claimed were already paid for by the overlord himself seemed like a sure bet for quick admission into the castle's walls.

Now, as Hugh took shallow breaths under the weight of small logs and sticks, he wished mightily he could have ridden through the keep's front gates with a mass of men behind him, brandishing his weapon while astride his biggest warhorse. Unfortunately, success in battle was not necessarily achieved by indulging a man's pride. Today's outcome was too important to risk.

Sorcha and her son were too important.

He feared he had spoken harshly to her earlier this morning in his haste to find out what happened to Eamon and his desire to keep her from harm. Thoughts of her were never far from his mind, even with such a crucial strategic task in front of him. He wanted to win the day for her. For their future. By the saints, he wanted to claim her as his wife in front of the world.

Beneath his right shoulder blade, Hugh felt the nearest

wheel of the cart slow to a halt. They must have reached the gatekeeper. With any luck, the wheels would move forward again very quickly. The longer they were stopped at the gate, the better the chance they would be discovered.

Outside the blackness of the wood cart covered with a stretch of tattered hide, Hugh heard their man-at-arms, Peter. The man had been chosen to drive the cart because he had none of the polish of a knight. There was a coarseness about him, from his accent to his unevenly shaven jaw, that marked him for a simple villager. Even his size helped disguise his battle prowess. He was not huge, but wiry with a steely strength easily hidden under a dirty robe and hunched shoulders.

"Let me see yer load," hollered the gatekeeper from up above the cart. The sentry in charge had a post atop the castle walls near the gate, though guards on the ground did his bidding and checked the incoming visitors.

There was a pause after the request, while Hugh's heart pounded so viciously hard he feared the force of it would raise and lower the wood piled over him and give them all away. Then a scraping noise above him suggested the cover being pulled away. No shafts of sunlight leaked through, however, since the knights had laid leather coverings over their bodies beneath the wood, as well. The disguise was thorough, but rendered them all the more helpless in an ambush since they would not see until too late if they were found out.

Hugh listened for the breathing of the knights beside him who had sworn him their allegiance. They were separated by small timber pieces, but still rested close enough to hear. All was silent.

If only they could pass the walls, they would be able to join with three other knights loyal to Hugh who had entered the city that morn after sharing wine with him around the fire last night. Those men inside would spread the word to Hugh's men. But they needed Hugh to send a signal to them, to rouse their warrior hearts for battle, else they would not risk battle with du Bois. By all accounts, his cousin had only grown crueler.

"Wave them through!" the guard from high above shouted, sending a cooling surge of relief over Hugh's fevered body.

They were in. The battle would begin soon.

But the cart wheels were hardly under way again when they slowed to a stop once more.

"Halt!" another voice called out.

A man.

And a familiar one at that.

"I wish to inspect this load myself." The sneering, arrogant tone belonged to someone Hugh hated to call family. Someone who could end all his hopes for a future with Sorcha right here.

Outside the cart, a heavy horse approached them, bringing a rider close. Hugh knew he did not have long to plan.

Edward du Bois was about to expose him.

Back at the camp, Sorcha had been awake since before dawn.

She could not rest after Hugh left, hating that he was frustrated with her when they needed to work together today. She did not know how she'd come to understand that, but she did.

Perhaps it was because they could have anticipated Eamon as a weak envoy if they had discussed it earlier. She had reservations about the man-at-arms and so did Hugh. But because they had not shared them—they might both pay a hefty price for their inability to work together.

So she was taking down their tents at first light, trying not to pass along her anxious, skittery mood to Onora and Conn. Her sister and son sat on a blanket near a brook that fed Edenrock while Sorcha rolled the tents against the man-at-arms' protests. She could not sit idly by. And whether Hugh won or lost, she would not be lingering outside Edenrock's walls tonight.

"By the Blessed Virgin." Onora's oath was an expression of soft wonder and Sorcha turned to see what had surprised her.

Onora's gaze was fixed on the wall at the top of the deep ravine where Sorcha and Hugh had ridden the day before. From here, they could see a bit of the village inside the walls. It was not activity within the town that claimed her sister's attention, however.

It was the man climbing over the wall.

Even in the half light of the earliest part of the day, Sorcha recognized the dark houpeland and the sandy curls. But as he slid down the wall, stumbling and falling into the ravine, she realized something was drastically amiss with her former groom. His body moved awkwardly, head slumped to one side, his hair matted to one temple. He limped forward and collapsed.

"Eamon!" Onora was already on her feet, running toward him through the low undergrowth of the forest.

Sorcha scooped up Conn and followed, her pace slower as her son bounced on one hip. She told herself to be safe and, by the saints, she did think to watch the walls for signs of someone following him.

But no man as broken, dirty and bloodstained as this one could pose a threat to her son. Especially not when she carried a dagger at her side for protection. If there was any chance Eamon knew something that could help Hugh, she would seek it out.

By the time she reached his side, Onora was already leaning over his huddled form. With another wary glance at the town's walls, Sorcha urged them both under the cover of a thick bush nearby so they would not be seen so easily. Guards passed this way now and then, and although they were unthreatened by beggars in the wood, they could be looking for someone who had made such an unconventional exit from their city.

"What happened to you?" Sorcha asked, raising her voice above Onora's soothing words as she scraped Eamon's bloodstained hair away from a wound on his forehead.

Her sister cried out when swiping away the hair only encouraged the gash to bleed more. His nose was bent to one side. His eyes were both blackened and his lip had been split in two places. Sorcha turned Conn's head in toward her shoulder so he would not see the frightening mess of Eamon's ruined visage.

"It is my fault," he croaked through his swollen lips. "They know you're here because of me."

Onora's eyes met Sorcha's over his head.

"Are you certain they are aware of us?" Onora asked, tearing off a chunk of her sleeve and dipping it in the cold, clear water of the nearby brook before wiping it across Eamon's forehead with infinite tenderness.

Sorcha wondered if there had been more between the two of them than she had first realized. She had not sensed that her sister returned Eamon's feelings for her, but had she been so distracted by her own trials that she'd missed it?

"I told them." Eamon opened his eyes. "And I knew Edward was not dead. He paid me well to—"

He broke off, his chest rising and falling with an effort.

Sorcha reeled at the level of betrayal. And from another person she'd trusted—at least to a degree. Even her father had been fooled.

She prayed her sister had not been deceived to the extent she herself had been by the first man she fancied. Although how could she ever blame Onora if she had been taken in by someone who showed her tenderness?

"Eamon…" Sorcha leaned closer, panic rising thick in her chest at the idea of Hugh and his knights riding into a trap. He had never returned to tell her of his plans. How would she warn him? "You did the right thing—the brave thing— returning to us."

At least Sorcha prayed it was a brave thing and that he had not led du Bois's knights to them on purpose. But judging by the condition of Eamon's beaten face, she guessed he had left at great risk to himself.

"I am sorry." Eamon breathed the words softly, his cut lips scarcely moving. "I only wanted to warn Hugh so he could protect you." His eyes opened briefly, flickering over to Onora. "Both."

Accepting that it might already be too late, Sorcha did not need to weigh the risks of disobeying her husband. She was no longer the headstrong girl who followed her heart's command with no thought to how it might hurt others. She was a headstrong woman who thought carefully about her actions and then found the best way to follow what her heart commanded. And she loved Hugh too much to allow him to walk into an ambush.

This was a man worthy of every risk.

That was why she could not promise Hugh that she would remain in the forest today. Her son would never be safe until Edward du Bois was defeated. That gave her only one choice, even if it tore Hugh away from her forever.

She must warn him.

"You will be too late," Onora warned her, picking her thoughts out of Sorcha's mind with the uncanny ability the best of sisters possessed.

Tears stung Sorcha's eyes as frustration and fear both told her that Onora might be right. And then inspiration struck.

"But not too late to intercept a king." Standing, she handed Onora her knife. "You must protect my son at all costs and I swear to you, I will intervene with Father to find you the best, most honorable husband in all of England."

Onora shook her head. "You do not—"

"Will you care for him?" She needed the fastest horse she could find. Along with a miracle.

"Of course." Onora gripped the knife with the ease of a woman who did not need to flaunt her skill. "You already saved me from the most hellish marriage I can envision. I owe you everything."

Sorcha kissed her son, embraced her sister and sprinted through the wood to the freshest courser among Hugh's mounts. She was not a banished princess any longer. And nothing would stop her from taking on the king.

Hugh had not required a horse.

He broke out of the woodpile like a monster arising from the grave, his sword drawn and his battle cry on his lips. Mayhem reigned all around as women and children scattered and the gate guards shouted orders to raise the drawbridge.

An impossible feat with their overlord standing in the middle of it.

Hugh stared at his enemy from his perch on the wood cart as Peter fought to control the nag who pulled it. From his higher position, Hugh leaped on his hell-hated cousin, knocking Edward to the ground.

"For the lord de Montaigne!" one of the knights shouted nearby, extending the rallying cry through the courtyard and onto the guards at the castle walls.

It was part of the plan as they'd discussed, but Hugh hadn't counted on how it would fill him with pride. Strength. Vengeance.

After days and months not knowing his identity, hearing his true name resonate through the crowd and vibrate off the stone was like an elixir from the gods of old.

Du Bois's sword skills were diminished by the lack of support all around him. He fought like the damned, his blade flying with a fierceness Hugh had never encountered in any opponent.

"Your wife was my whore," he shouted as one of his blows connected with Hugh's knee.

Only his staunch will to defend Sorcha could have kept him upright after such a hit. He swayed but did not fall.

Around him, he became aware of the crowd quieting. They did not dare think Hugh would be defeated, did they?

Never taking his eyes off his opponent, Hugh raised his sword.

"My wife is avenged." The blow he wielded hit du Bois in the temple, landing in the very spot that had felled Hugh three moons ago. Edward du Bois crumpled to his knees on the drawbridge.

Hugh's victory was clear.

The crowds did not cheer, a fact which surprised him after the support they'd given him so recently. Instead, they all peered out of the gates to the road beyond. Straightening, he turned to follow their gaze.

And spied King Henry's procession riding up to the gate, banners flying while the sovereign broke away from his men to lead the way. Their arrival was not nearly as much of a surprise as was Sorcha's position at the king's side.

Chapter Twenty-One

Hugh's gut roiled with the knowledge that he had cut down one of the nation's most powerful knights in front of their shared overlord. By God, he could be taken in chains for trial for this. For that matter, he had killed the father of Sorcha's son—a man she'd once loved. He knew it had to be done to keep her safe, but would she look at him with different eyes for having been the one to deliver that devastating blow?

He watched his wife leap from her courser before the animal had come to a full stop. She ran to him, her feet flying almost as fast as the horse's had been.

He did not know if she ran from the king or if she had interceded on Hugh's behalf somehow, but he noticed she did not look to the ruler for permission as she flung herself into Hugh's arms.

All the rest of Edenrock's villagers—Hugh's people now, he reminded himself—fell to their knees before their monarch.

At thirty-six years, Henry II was a vital ruler in his prime. With his groomed beard and brisk manner, he possessed a noble bearing that had naught to do with his crown and owed much to his self-assurance and quick mind. As he reined in his armored mount, he peered around the assembled company with assessing gray eyes that missed nothing. Least of all the dead man at Hugh's feet.

Hugh offered as much of a bow as he could manage with Sorcha wrapped tightly about him. He nudged her slightly away from Edward's body, wishing to protect her from the hardship of seeing him up close.

"Do not be angry with me," she whispered in his ear, her words urgent. "I learned Eamon betrayed you so I intercepted the king on his way to the wedding."

She released him, her sweetly scented arms falling away from his neck before she offered a deep curtsy to the king.

Her respects to the monarch were late in coming, but to Hugh's surprise, the quick-tempered sovereign merely appeared amused. The King of England, Duke of Normandy and Aquitaine and Count of Angevin had been thoroughly charmed by an Irish princess.

"I have come for a wedding," the king announced, his voice projecting for all the silent villagers to hear as he motioned to two of his men to clear away Edward's body.

Even the handful of knights who had been loyal to du Bois did not dare to speak. Two of them had been lost to the swords of Hugh's fellow knights and those who remained standing seemed content to hold their peace.

Hugh noticed his banner flew over the keep's walls, no doubt carried there by Peter, the loyal man-at-arms who had been given the task in their plans that morn. As Hugh considered how to welcome the king, he realized there was only one way to keep Sorcha safe. Only one way to keep her by his side forever.

He only hoped Sorcha would agree.

"Edenrock awaits you, sire," Hugh said, careful not to contradict the king. "My wife and I were married quietly in Ireland but we wish to have our vows recognized in front of my people."

The king waved the whole courtyard of people to their feet, his short mantle swaying with his brisk movement. Then he turned his attention to Sorcha.

"Lady Sorcha, are you well pleased with your Norman lord?" he asked, taking careful stock of Hugh's fiery Irish wife.

The king was giving her a way out. Henry knew all too well who was supposed to wed here today. But if he could wed a new lord and keep the peace, he would do so without comment. Unless, of course, Sorcha spoke up now.

"I am truly blessed, sire." She bent her knee low, her eyes never leaving his.

Hope fired in Hugh's chest. She had acquiesced to the scheme. But did she do so only to keep the king's peace and help Hugh secure Edenrock? Or did she wish to be joined with him as much as he wanted her?

"Then join me, good people of Edenrock," he lifted his voice to ring through the crowd, "in a celebration this eve that will allow me to join your lord and lady myself."

Hugh guessed his words were a challenge to any who would call it false. As Hugh had suspected, Henry would not wish to support any uprising against a keep as important as Edenrock. But he'd given the keep once to Hugh, and surely he must not see anything to indicate Hugh was not in charge at the moment. Still, Hugh held his breath, half expecting one of du Bois's former followers to denounce him.

After a tense silence, a cheer rose up from the castle

walls. The cry was taken over by the villagers below. Sorcha raised her hand and waved to the people as if she had been born to be their lady.

And, just then, Hugh wondered if she had been. Not for all the world would he have wanted this day to unfold any other way. He could not wait to take away the anxiousness in Sorcha's fair green eyes to tell her as much.

"You are to wed before we sup."

Onora's eyes were wide as she closed the door behind her in Sorcha's new chamber a few hours later, her surcoat stained and her hair slipping free of its circlet as she cradled Conn in her arms.

Sorcha had been parted from Hugh within moments of the king's pronouncement that he would renew their vows and bless their union. Because Henry had business to attend elsewhere, he wished to leave in the morning. In the meantime, he had stolen Sorcha's groom to give him a tour of Edenrock. Part of her still feared he would discover what had happened with Hugh's speedy takeover and charge them both with disturbing the king's peace, but the maids and ladies she'd met in her own harried introduction to the massive keep had all welcomed her with such effusive praise that she had to think Edward du Bois had been as awful to these people as he had been to her.

She hoped one day she would forgive herself for seeing only what she wanted to see in him. An escape from her father's rule and ancient suitors. A chance to make her own decisions. But then, looking into her son's gorgeous amber eyes—so close in color to his father's cousin—reminded her that she had salvaged the best part of the deceased lord.

She had not mourned his passing, but as she hugged her

son tightly, she hoped he would not ever feel the lack for a father. If only Hugh were ready to accept her and her babe despite her flaws.

"I know," Sorcha responded, finally remembering her sister's words about the imminent wedding. She called for one of the maids bustling around a large, airy solar with the tapestries drawn aside to let in air through multiple windows. "I am so happy that Hugh seems to have remained in the king's favor despite his long absence from this place. And it is lovely that he will surely be given an earldom for his trouble, but—"

She broke off, handing Conn to one of the many maids who had hastened to respond to the call for wedding preparations in the lady's chamber. From the chorus of coos and exclamations that went up from the collected girls at the sight of Conn, Sorcha knew he would be in good hands.

"If you could just wash him up," she asked the closest maid, "and perhaps find him something to eat before the sup so he is restful?"

As the women hastened to do as she asked, calling for a basin to wash Conn, Sorcha excused the ladies who had been kind enough to help her prepare for the meal. They had found her a surcoat that had belonged to the former lady of the keep. Not Edward's betrothed, who was rumored to have sneaked out the gates as soon as she heard what had happened, but the lady who had ruled here before Hugh had conquered the holding. The surcoat was the deepest shade of blue Sorcha had ever worn, the kirtle a magnificently soft hue of a robin's egg in spring.

"But what?" Onora prodded, picking up a wet cloth on the side of a wooden tub Sorcha had recently used. "You have won the day! The king himself wants to be sure all of your people know you have his blessing to rule."

"Aye." Sorcha nodded, unable to keep the heaviness in her heart out of her voice. "But I am not certain of Hugh's position right now. I—I want him to wed me because he wants to and not because his noble, honorable, too-good heart tells him he should."

Onora ran the wet cloth over her face with one hand while she untied the laces on her surcoat with the other. Sorcha toyed with a few flowers one of the maids had brought into the huge chamber in a basket, knowing she should be weaving them into a chain for her hair or for around her throat.

"You cannot be serious." Onora slapped the cloth back into the tub, wetting it and wringing it out again. "It is entirely obvious to everyone who sees the two of you that you belong together. I heard the king of England himself wasted no time in pronouncing your wedding."

"For the safety of his keep," Sorcha agreed, wishing she could take more pleasure in the preparations everyone else was obviously thrilled about. The excitement in the air to welcome Hugh home was as tangible as the scents of roasted capon and pigeon drifting up from the courtyard.

Hugh was the conquering hero everyone wanted to welcome. And while she could not have been happier for him, she feared his reaction to what she'd done by running to the king to request that he stand by Hugh's bid for Edenrock. She'd told him how Edward used Hugh's banner to commit crimes and turn public sentiment against him. She had not spared a detail about the depths of Edward's cruelty, including his bid to kill her son.

The king had not been surprised to hear any of it. He'd been so quiet and matter-of-fact about her plea, she had feared right up until the last minute what tact he would take when he arrived at Edenrock. She would be grateful to King

Henry for the rest of her days for his help in welcoming Hugh back to his rightful place as lord here.

"Nay." Onora eased out of her surcoat and went to a wardrobe chest filled with stored garments. "I have never seen a man look at a woman thus. It is how I imagine our father looked at our mother. It is how I knew that what Eamon felt for me was not love."

Sorcha stilled, remembering the way she'd left Onora in the forest with her former groom.

"I'm so sorry." Dropping the flowers she'd been toying with, she joined her sister on the floor near the chest. "I can't believe I forgot to ask about Eamon."

"He lives," Onora informed her. Her fingers played over a length of red silk. "And he is asking for someone named Nelda. I felt a moment's jealousy until he told me he feared she'd been brutalized by du Bois's guards."

"I will have Hugh find her at once." Sorcha squeezed her sister's shoulder. "You did not lose your heart or your virginity to Eamon, did you?"

Onora's cheeks pinkened. "I used all my boldness in following you across two countries, sister. Besides, I might have defied Father by forsaking the betrothal he arranged, but I understood well his warning that he wanted me to remain chaste. I will make a marriage to his liking yet, although perhaps it will be with your help now that you are an English countess as well as an Irish princess."

Sorcha embraced her sister. "We will make it all right with Father, I promise. You do not need to wed until it suits you."

She was touched to think Onora saw something in the way Hugh looked at her. Perhaps the tenderness they had shared the night before would not be chased off by her disobedience in running to the king.

Hugh could have carried the day without her help. She saw that now. But she could not sit idly by and hope that the conquest worked out to her longing. She simply could never be that kind of woman.

A hard knock at the door startled her back from Onora.

"Sorcha, I must see you at once." Hugh's voice penetrated the oak barrier, his tone tolerating no refusals.

"Here." Sorcha pulled a saffron-colored gown from the trunk for her sister and plunked it over her head. "This will match your kirtle well enough. It looks lovely with your eyes."

"Sorcha?" Hugh knocked once more.

Oh, how she prayed they were not back to being mistrustful strangers after all they'd been through. After the sweet surrender of the night in his tent.

"Coming," she called out, hastening toward the door. When she pulled it open, all her hopes and dreams stood on the other side.

"I wish to speak to my wife alone." Hugh had never seen so many females gathered in one chamber before. Maids and ladies, well-wishers from the village and a few random servants crowded the solar he hadn't even set foot in when he'd resided here briefly before his fateful journey to Connacht.

Women scattered like fall leaves, taking basins and clothes, flagons and a small chest with them. Onora was the last to depart, following a beaming maid who held Sorcha's son. Conn gave him a gummy smile that showed two fresh teeth and Hugh could not resist ruffling the lad's silky curls. Onora arched up and kissed him on the cheek on her way out, congratulating him for his success on the day.

He touched the place where her lips had brushed, grateful

for her good wishes and hoping her mood was a sign of the warm welcome he hoped to receive from his bride.

"Hugh, you must find a woman." Sorcha approached him without prelude, dispensing no niceties even though she was garbed as regally and finely as he'd ever seen her.

Her expression remained serious, her green eyes worried and her jaw tense.

"What is it?" He had not forgotten his terse words before he left her bed this morn and hoped it was not too late to smooth them over.

"Eamon spoke of a woman he thinks was brutalized last night by du Bois's men." She crossed her arms and brushed her shoulders as if to ward off a chill. "Onora says she is called Nelda, the tavern keeper's daughter."

Relief slid over him as he closed the door behind the departed women and moved near Sorcha.

"You may rest easy. Peter found the girl straightaway after he raised my banner. She was on the castle wall hoping to climb down to follow Eamon."

"She was not—" Sorcha shook her head helplessly. "Is she all right?"

"Peter did not say she was overly beaten." He pulled Sorcha to him, sorry for the hardship he'd put on all his people. "We will send a wisewoman to her hut to see if she needs care."

Sorcha nodded against his chest.

"Eamon betrayed us. He knew all along Edward lived."

He hated the hurt in her voice. He was so accustomed to seeing her be fearless that those moments of vulnerability undid him. Wrapping an arm about her shoulders, he guided her over to a wide, polished bench beside a loom bearing a half-finished tapestry.

"Did I not tell you how my cousin deceived everyone around him from the time he was a small child?" Hugh did not like to recall the way Edward had maneuvered people around him, hurting those who attempted to care for him. "He used charm and intelligence to lure his friends into thinking he was a good person, but he was entertained by hurting them sooner or later. He poisoned my dog when I was ten and I never could forgive him. But I also could not convince my father or anyone else that he would do such a thing."

Sorcha lifted her head, the fire back in her green gaze.

"He hurt an innocent animal?"

"I swear he did. And I do not tell you that to make you feel bad for trusting him, but only to assure you that he excelled in charming people before he hurt them. That's why he had many knights who swore oaths to him and they are all relieved to see the end of him." Hugh had as good as vanquished a demon. He'd never anticipated how warmly he would be received upon his return. "None of us has impeccable judgment about who to trust."

She nodded, her head dipping and her hands shaking just a little in a display of worry he had not expected from the bold wife who had faced down a king for him.

"Hugh, I do not want to go through with our vows if we cannot commit our hearts to each other this time."

Her words came from nowhere, the blow more effectively delivered than the chop to his knees earlier.

"You do not wish a lawful union?" He would undress her here and now and remind her why she could belong only to him forever. By God, he would—

"Nay! It is not that." She clenched her hands into tight fists. "I want to wed. I want to be lady of this keep and rule at the side of a man who will not relegate me to a corner to weave."

She gestured weakly to the loom and it occurred to him he had never seen her engaged in such a pursuit.

"You are upset that I told you to stay out of danger today." He knew she was distressed this morning. And while he regretted hurting her, he thought it boded well for their marriage that he had understood her feelings so readily. "I did that because I was scared for you. Because I remembered what it was like to see you chased down by du Bois's men on that beach and know I could not possibly reach you in time."

"But you did." Sorcha pressed a hand to his chest, her fingers tracing the gold embroidery of his finest mantle. "Between your arrows, your men's arrows and my own wits, we managed it."

"It was not an experience I cared to repeat."

"But don't you see that I wanted you to live through the day as much as you hoped that I would?" Her hand moved up from his mantle to his jaw and she stroked a cool touch along his skin. "Perhaps we could trust each other a bit more."

Hugh should not have been surprised that she would ask for this. Edward had hurt her so badly and maybe he had too, by accusing her of deceit when she had not told him about his resemblance to Conn's father.

"I will trust you. I do trust you." He knew she was not the same woman who had given herself to his charming, false cousin. She was still strong and bold, but her reckless ways were tempered by her maternal heart and intelligence that had only grown keener.

He wrapped her in his arms, so grateful to have this kind

of woman in his life. Rosamunde had taught him how rare
someone like Sorcha could be.

"Are you certain?" Sorcha asked, head tipped up to meet
his gaze. "I will not wed you again just because you are unnaturally handsome or because you make me feel extraordinary when we lay together."

His heart beat faster, his hope for the future soaring even
higher as he held her. Out in the corridor, he could hear the
galley filling with guests heading outdoors for the vows.
The meal. The celebration that would last long into the night.

A celebration that would not compare to the night he
would share with his wife.

"Sorcha, I trust you so much that I give you my heart. My
love." He brushed his lips over hers, letting her feel the
words on his mouth as he spoke them. He was fairly certain
she returned the sentiment even though they hadn't said as
much the night before.

A woman like Sorcha wore her feelings for all to see.

"Hugh, I—" Her voice broke.

Her arms wound around his neck and he experienced a
moment of fear that he'd been wrong about her feelings.

"I love you desperately," she whispered against his neck
and he thought perhaps the hot moisture he felt there was a
tear. But then it was replaced by hot, wet kisses.

"Wait." He unwound her arms, mindful of a bell chiming
below stairs. "We are wanted for our wedding, I think."

"Yes!" She leaned close and kissed him on the mouth.

This time he could not pull away.

Her breasts pressed sweetly against his chest, her whole
body thrust into her passion. He could spend a lifetime
counting how fortunate he was to have been given such a
treasure and still not find the limit of his blessings.

His skin heated as his fingers roamed her back, her shoulders. Up her neck. He sifted through the silky mane of burnished hair and tugged lightly on her veils, teasing her.

"You will learn not to kiss your wife lightly, husband," she threatened. "What will you say if I keep all your people and the king himself waiting for you now?"

"They wait for *us,* Princess." He bracketed her hips in his hands, calculating the hours until he could have her all to himself. "And I think we will fool no one when we arrive at the table with red cheeks and breathing hard."

"And I'm trying so hard not to be rash anymore," she murmured sadly. "Perhaps we should answer the bell."

"Only if you are certain now about the vows we exchange." He wanted this wedding to start a lifetime of happiness for both of them. For their people who had suffered too much at Edward's hands.

"There will be no going back on this marriage." Her words were part promise, part warning.

And that felt just right to him.

"I will never leave you, Sorcha." He drew her closer to the door, knowing they needed to depart and still loath to share this incredible woman who would sleep beside him every night of his life. "I hope you will allow me to claim Conn for my son. I already love the boy as much as if he was my own child."

She blinked fast and this time he saw the tears she had hidden from him before. But they were the most beautiful happy tears he'd ever seen.

He swiped one away with his thumb.

"I would have no other man for his father." Her voice wobbled, but her smile never wavered.

"Come," he urged her, opening the door to a future they had earned together. "Let us begin anew."

Epilogue

Sorcha's third wedding outshone the first two, her happiness radiating from her like a light from within.

Music swelled in the courtyard as the dancing began after a meal more lavish than any she'd ever enjoyed. Bells and flutes trilled their song into the warm breeze as the musicians found their rhythm, and Sorcha contemplated the way her joy overflowed. Perhaps her guests could not see it, but she felt it from the moment the king had declared her union sacred.

Nay. The glow within began when Hugh had sealed his promise upon her lips with a kiss witnessed by hundreds of villagers, a full contingent of knights and a royal retinue. The kiss had been one of love and not duty, the kind of magical moment she had dreamed about since she'd been a lonely little girl and her father had filled her head with romantic visions of the abiding love he'd shared with the most beautiful woman in the world—Sorcha's own mother.

Sorcha's heart had searched for that kind of love all her life, and at last she had found it with Hugh de Montaigne. He caught her eye from his place near the minstrels now, his handsome face lit with pleasure and more than a little hunger for her.

She could not wait for their wedding night. They would make love, safe in their new home. Secure in their new trust for one another and the promise of forever.

"Sister," Onora whispered at her elbow suddenly, tugging Sorcha away from a table full of flower chaplets one of the villager girls had made for the day's event. "I need your assistance."

Sorcha tore her eyes away from her husband to focus on Onora, knowing the glow of happiness in her heart was not going anywhere. She could spare her guests—and especially her beloved sibling—a little of her time.

"Aye?" Sorcha hugged Onora, grateful she could be here today after they had been separated for so long. "How can I help?"

Onora grinned, her blue eyes dancing merrily as her dark hair glimmered under the strong sunlight.

"You can introduce me to yonder knight." She pointed toward a tall, exceedingly handsome gentleman dressed in the rich fabrics of someone with noble standing.

The man spoke to a friend close to his own age, but he glanced up once as if seeking someone—only to find Onora in the crowd.

The look they exchanged told Sorcha all she needed to know, and it gladdened her heart all the more.

"I do not know him, but I will speak to Hugh about him at once." Thrilled to have an excuse to steal away Hugh from the crowd if only for a few moments, Sorcha brushed a kiss along her sister's cheek. "I will be back in but a moment."

Hastening toward the minstrels where she'd last spotted

Hugh, Sorcha was stopped twice by well-wishers who wanted to welcome their lady to Edenrock. She promised to visit them both in the coming weeks, for she had vowed to herself that she would be an industrious lady who was no stranger to the men and women who served the keep.

For now, however, she kept her eye on the prize—her strong and noble protector. The man who wanted to call Conn his own.

"My lady." He bowed politely to her as she approached, although his eyes told her he'd rather wrap her in his arms.

"My lord." She dipped her knee in equally polite greeting. "May I speak with you a moment?"

He wasted no time in spiriting her away from the crowd. They ducked behind the raised platform where the minstrels performed a merry tune. Hugh tugged her past a fire pit where a few old men took refuge to play dice. They raised their drinking cups to the new lord as the pair dashed alongside a storage shed for wood that served the hall hearth.

Pressing her up against the unforgiving plank wall, Hugh kissed her. Sorcha's senses ignited, her arms winding about his neck as she gave herself to him.

Strong hands clamped her hips, drawing her close. His lips lingered over hers as if they had all the time in the world.

She would have liked nothing better than to lose herself in the moment, but she mustered all her restraint to break free. It took a long moment to catch her breath, but when the capacity for speech returned, she shook a chiding finger at him.

"What happened to the man who would not keep his wedding guests waiting?" She recalled those moments before their nuptials when he refused to delay their vows for the sake of kisses.

"It was the king I would not keep waiting. And now that he has seen us wed, I doubt we interest him overmuch." He brushed his jaw along her cheek, his thigh pressing hers. "We have earned a few moments alone."

Her heart picked up speed.

"I fear if we indulge more than a few moments, we will be in no condition to return to the feast." The chaplet of flowers perched on her head was already sliding sideways. "And I have a favor to ask of you before we—retire."

Hugh straightened.

"Name it."

Oh, but she would enjoy this marriage if that was his response to her requests. Not that she anticipated many wishes that hadn't already been met simply by becoming his wife. His love.

"I would like you to tell me if a certain gentleman would suit my sister, and if so, perhaps you would introduce them?" Sorcha tugged him back toward the fire pit where the drinking old men hardly noticed them. Or perhaps they were too discreet to pay them any mind. "He's over there."

She pointed out the well-dressed gentleman.

"Ah." Hugh grinned. "Your father would approve, you can be sure."

"Really?" Sorcha had thought of her sire more than once today, hoping he would forgive her fully when he heard that she'd been wed by King Henry himself.

"Young Niall has lands to the north and his mother is as Irish as yours, for one thing. He will not support any Norman invasion of Connacht."

"No?" Sorcha realized his answer did not address her biggest concern. "But is he—kind?"

Hugh peered back at her, his eyes glowing with good

humor. In fact, she thought she spied the same radiance she felt inside this day.

"If he is worthy of his noble birth, he was probably born with a sword in hand and has killed men in battle. But if you're asking about his disposition toward women, I can only say I have not heard anyone speak ill of him."

"I cannot wait to tell Onora." She squeezed Hugh's arm. "How about if you introduce them and then we can take our leave for the night?"

Hugh peered up at the sky meaningfully. "Before night-fall?"

Lifting up on her toes, she kissed him full on the mouth, not caring if the old men could still see. She put all of her desires into that kiss, determined to have Hugh to herself soon.

"Aye." He broke off the kiss, his word raspy with want. "Before nightfall. But you should know that a message came for you a short while ago."

"For me?" Confused, Sorcha wondered who would know to send her tidings on her wedding day when it had been so hastily arranged.

"Here." He thrust a scroll into her palm. "One of the minstrels is from Connacht. He arrived a fortnight after we did."

Recognizing the unbroken seal upon the stiff parchment, Sorcha's gaze sought Hugh's.

"It's from Father."

Hugh nodded. "I considered waiting to give it to you until after the wedding in case he demands we send Onora back. But as I will not bend to his wishes where she is concerned, I hope whatever he says cannot distress you."

She appreciated his thoughtful concern and hastened to break the seal on the letter. As she unrolled the parchment, she angled it between them so they could both read.

My daughter,

It is with a grateful heart that I write to thank you for protecting your sister against a threat I did not perceive. After witnessing her betrothed upon the battlefield, I saw a man with a taste for bloodlust that turned many a stalwart warrior's stomach. I would have regretted submitting any daughter of mine to such a match.

To be sure, I did not think any of the suitors I suggested for you were such men. But I forgive you for acting on your own view. I did not raise you to sit idly in the hall when the fate of the realm was discussed, so I should not have been surprised that you did not sit idly by when I decided your fate for you.

You have my blessing. Onora has my blessing. I pray God blesses you both with happiness and many children. Perhaps you will find it in your heart to send one or two of them back to the land of their grandfather one day, as I have kingdom to bestow. No Norman bastard—begging your husband's pardon—will take it from me any time soon.

Father

"Oh!" With a cry, Sorcha clutched the note to her heart. Overwhelmed, she ducked her head against Hugh's surcoat and realized that tears were streaming fast from her eyes.

"But it is good news, is it not?" Hugh wrenched her away from him and tipped her chin up to study her face. "All is forgiven. And you don't need to send him any of our babes if you do not wish it."

A laugh slipped free as her emotions spilled over.

"It is only good news. And we have many years to decide

if we can part with any child for a summer or two." She could not imagine fostering her sons or daughters, but oh sweet merciful heaven, she liked the idea that her father cared enough to want his family around him.

The days of exile were well and truly behind her.

"I do owe your father a great deal," Hugh admitted, stroking a fingertip over the tender fullness of her lower lip.

"He did not even mention helping us with a dowry for Onora. And you'll recall the wily old king robbed you of your rightful treasure after you watched over me," she reminded him, tucking the letter from her father under her girdle so she could share it with Onora.

"Be that as it may," he said as he guided her back into the festivities where dancers spun and dipped their way through the steps of a round, "he gave me the only treasure worth having."

Her heart full of love and thankfulness, Sorcha pulled her warrior husband into the dance, her feet as light as her cares. She would be sure Onora had her introduction and that she greeted all the lovely people who had welcomed her into her new home. But for just a few moments more, she planned to revel in the pleasure of knowing that for this moment, everything in her world was just exactly right.

* * * * *

"I'm the illegitimate daughter of notoriously scandalous parents, Mr. Milford. Candidates for my hand are unlikely to be lining up at the gates."

"Don't be so quick to discount your charms, my dear. Or the charm of your substantial dowry. Or even your brothers' influence. There are as many reasons to marry as there are marriages."

Annalise snorted. "Oh, yes. Perhaps I shall marry for dynastic reasons, or perhaps for property or influence. After all, a loveless, practical marriage worked out so well for my mother."

"Well, you've routed me on that one. I can think of no suitable rejoinder." Ned rose to his feet and extended his hand. "And since that is the case, let me be the first to wish you a long and happy spinsterhood."

Her mouth gaped open. And then she laughed.

And he froze.

This was the first time, Ned realized. The first time he'd seen her eyes light up and her mouth curl. The first time he'd witnessed her features melded together in glorious accord to produce exquisite beauty.

Unbelievable what a change came over her face. Unheard of what effect her throaty, rasping laughter had on his body.

It pounded a beat upon his ear, quickly taken up by his pulse. It echoed through him, finally residing in his stirring nether regions.

So easily she did it, awakened these sensations within him—without any apparent effort at all. And she had called him potentially dangerous? Clearly the intelligent thing for him to do would be to steer clear, to leave her to the tender ministrations of Lord Peter Blackthorne.

"You were right." She smiled up at him as she took his hand and climbed to her feet. "I do feel better."

Ah, well. When had he ever chosen the intelligent path?

He did not relinquish her hand. He used it to pull her in, close enough that he could feel the warmth of her. "At the risk of repeating Lord Peter's mistake and anticipating too much—may I ask if you'll be my partner in battledore tomorrow?"

Her smile dimmed. Her breath came a little faster. His own had gone shallow, as if he'd just run a race—and lost. He ran his gaze over the appealing lift of her brow and the curious angle of her chin. His index finger twitched.

"I should like that," she said.

His finger trembled again and he lifted it, traced the pink and tender shell of her ear, the unique sweep of her jaw. Her pulse leaped beneath her skin, triggering his own. Slowly he tilted her chin up, waiting for her to object, to step back, to slap his hand away.

She did none of those eminently sensible things. Which left him free to do the entirely impractical thing.

Baby soft, the skin of her lips. Her whole body trembled when he touched her there.

He leaned in. Her eyes closed, even as she stood straight against him, strung as tight as a bow. He pressed his mouth to hers. It was a soft kiss, sweet and chaste. And yet he was hot and hard and as ready as he'd ever been in his life.

She drew back a little. Sighed. Their breath mingled a moment before she slowly backed away.

"Oh," she breathed. Her dark eyes were full of wonder and something that looked like fear. He took a step toward her, but she only shook her head. His outstretched hand fell to his side as she turned to disappear into the wood. This was the first time, Ned realized. The first time, since he'd come to the house party at Welbourne Manor, that he'd seen her eyes light up.

* * * * *

Follow Ned and Annalise's story in May 2009 in
THE DIAMONDS OF WELBOURNE MANOR
available May 2009 from Harlequin® Historical.

Available in the series romance section,
or in the historical romance section, wherever
books are sold.

We'll be spotlighting a different series
every month throughout 2009
to celebrate our 60th anniversary.

Look for Harlequin® Historical in May!

REQUEST YOUR
FREE BOOKS!

Harlequin® Historical
Historical Romantic Adventure!

2 FREE NOVELS PLUS 2 FREE GIFTS!

YES! Please send me 2 FREE Harlequin® Historical novels and my 2 FREE gifts (gifts are worth about $10). After receiving them, if I don't wish to receive any more books, I can return the shipping statement marked "cancel". If I don't cancel, I will receive 6 brand-new novels every month and be billed just $4.94 per book in the U.S. or $5.49 per book in Canada. That's a savings of 20% off the cover price! It's quite a bargain! Shipping and handling is just 25¢ per book*. I understand that accepting the 2 free books and gifts places me under no obligation to buy anything. I can always return a shipment and cancel at any time. Even if I never buy another book, the two free books and gifts are mine to keep forever.

246 HDN ERUM   349 HDN ERUA

Name	(PLEASE PRINT)

Address	Apt. #

City	State/Prov.	Zip/Postal Code

Signature (if under 18, a parent or guardian must sign)

Mail to the **Harlequin Reader Service:**
IN U.S.A.: P.O. Box 1867, Buffalo, NY 14240-1867
IN CANADA: P.O. Box 609, Fort Erie, Ontario L2A 5X3

Not valid to current subscribers of Harlequin Historical books.

Want to try two free books from another line?
Call 1-800-873-8635 or visit www.morefreebooks.com.

* Terms and prices subject to change without notice. Prices do not include applicable taxes. Sales tax applicable in N.Y. Canadian residents will be charged applicable provincial taxes and GST. Offer not valid in Quebec. This offer is limited to one order per household. All orders subject to approval. Credit or debit balances in a customer's account(s) may be offset by any other outstanding balance owed by or to the customer. Please allow 4 to 6 weeks for delivery. Offer available while quantities last.

Your Privacy: Harlequin Books is committed to protecting your privacy. Our Privacy Policy is available online at www.eHarlequin.com or upon request from the Reader Service. From time to time we make our lists of customers available to reputable third parties who may have a product or service of interest to you. If you would prefer we not share your name and address, please check here. ☐

HH09

The Inside Romance newsletter has a NEW look for the new year!

Same great content, brand-new look!

The Inside Romance newsletter is a FREE quarterly newsletter highlighting our upcoming series releases and promotions!

Click on the Inside Romance link on the front page of
www.eHarlequin.com or e-mail us at
insideromance@harlequin.ca to sign up
to receive your FREE newsletter today!

You can also subscribe by writing to us at: HARLEQUIN BOOKS
Attention: Customer Service Department
P.O. Box 9057, Buffalo, NY 14269-9057

Please allow 4-6 weeks for delivery of the first issue by mail.

Silhouette *Desire*

MAN of the MONTH

LEANNE BANKS

BILLIONAIRE EXTRAORDINAIRE

Billionaire Damien Medici is determined to get revenge on his enemy, but his buttoned-up new assistant Emma Weatherfield has been assigned to spy on him and might thwart his plans. As tensions in and out of the boardroom heat up, he convinces her to give him the information he needs—by getting her to unbutton a few things....

Available May
wherever books are sold.

Harlequin® Historical
Historical Romantic Adventure!

If you enjoyed reading
Joanne Rock in the
Harlequin® Blaze™ series,
look for her new book
from Harlequin® Historical!

THE KNIGHT'S RETURN
Joanne Rock

Missing more than his memory,
Hugh de Montagne sets out to find his
true identity. When he lands in a small
Irish kingdom and finds a new liege in the
Irish king, his hands are full with his new
assignment: guarding the king's beautiful,
exiled daughter. Sorcha has had her heart
broken by a knight in the past. Will she be
able to open her heart to love again?

Available April
wherever books are sold.

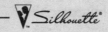

SPECIAL EDITION

FROM *NEW YORK TIMES*
BESTSELLING AUTHOR

KATHLEEN EAGLE

*In Care of
Sam Beaudry*

Maggie Whiteside's nine-year-old
"bad boy" had always given Sheriff
Sam Beaudry the perfect excuse to flirt
with the pretty single mom...until a child
with an incredible secret showed up in
town, bringing Sam and Maggie closer
than they ever dreamed possible!

*Available in May
wherever books are sold.*